PENGUIN BOOKS

EMPIRE OF GODS AND BEASTS

Joyce Chua is the author of *Land of Sand and Song* (2021), *Kingdom of Blood and Gold* (2022)—both part of the *Children of the Desert* triology—*Until Morning*, and *No Room in Neverland* (2023). Her debut novel *Lambs for Dinner* (2013) was one of the five winning entries of a nationwide competition jointly organized by *The Straits Times* and National Arts Council. She graduated from the National University of Singapore with a degree in English and is now a personal finance editor by day and author by night. Her articles have appeared in *Harper's Bazaar*, *Her World*, *The Straits Times*, and more. She can be found on Instagram, TikTok and Threads at @joycechuawrites.

Advance Praise for *Empire of Gods and Beasts*

'This has everything I love about a good wuxia drama. A must-read.'
—Audrey Chin, author of *The Ash House*

'Enchanting, engaging and beautifully written.'
—Eva Wong Nava, author of *The House of Little Sisters*

'Utterly captivating and engrossing.'
—Leslie W., author of *The Night of Legends*

'Filled with magic, mayhem, battles, and romance, Chua has crafted a wildly entertaining tale for the ages in *Children of the Desert* trilogy. Her compelling characters take us through the intricately built fantasy setting, from the deep desert to shadow cities, as they explore the powerful magic and myths of the world. An atmospheric, imaginative series perfect for genre fans of all ages.'
—Tanvi Berwah, author of *Monsters Born and Made*

Empire of Gods and Beasts

Joyce Chua

PENGUIN BOOKS

An imprint of Penguin Random House

PENGUIN BOOKS

USA | Canada | UK | Ireland | Australia
New Zealand | India | South Africa | China | Southeast Asia

Penguin Books is part of the Penguin Random House group of companies
whose addresses can be found at global.penguinrandomhouse.com

Published by Penguin Random House SEA Pte Ltd
9, Changi South Street 3, Level 08-01,
Singapore 486361

Penguin
Random House
SEA

First published in Penguin Books by Penguin Random House SEA 2024
Copyright © Joyce Chua 2024

ISBN 9789815144536

Typeset in Garamond by MAP Systems, Bengaluru, India

www.penguin.sg

Contents

Empire of the Gods

The gods of the past return as men to haunt us, for never has the new world been as chaotic as it is now.

Once ruled by the Damohai—the Children of the Desert, descendants of immortals, demigods who guarded the Khuzar Desert—the Hesui Kingdom was known as paradise on earth, until mortal invaders came with their special concoctions and weapons, debilitating the Damohai and weakening their control over the kingdom.

With the dissolution of the Hesui Kingdom, people's belief in gods and monsters eroded over time. New kingdoms—charted by irreverent kings—chipped away at ancient borders, replaced magic with weapons. The age of men has come, *they declared as they waged their wars against one another.*

But a handful of tribes in the Khuzar Desert remain, holding fast to the practices, rituals, and beliefs of the ancient. These old practitioners continue to safeguard the desert until their half-immortal, half-human saviours come to reclaim their role as guardians of the desert.

Many sceptics believe that the Damohai are but a myth, that they no longer have a place in this new world now in the hands of mortals. Others, however, believe that the descendants of the gods are simply waiting for a new leader to emerge from the depths of the Khuzar desert, or perhaps the far-flung edges of its ancient kingdom, to reunite them.

No one knows where the Damohai are, or whether any of them still exist. But should they still remain on earth, time is running out for them. As surrounding nations encroach further upon the Khuzar Desert, they press ever closer to the Immortal Spring, the last connection between the earthly and heavenly realms that has been locked ever since the war between the two realms.

Hidden deep within the desert, the last gateway to heaven can only be unlocked by the surviving Elemental, one of the five chosen among the Damohai imbued with unprecedented magical abilities, who will restore the balance and flow of magic between the realms. Yet, as those well-versed in the affairs of men know, all that will not stop mortals from exploiting the spring should they find it and even manage to awaken it.

So until the day the Elemental emerges, the Immortal Spring—and the sacred Khuzar Desert—will remain under siege, and the fates of the warring kingdoms hang in the balance.

—Excerpt from *Land of Sand and Song: Tales from the Khuzar Desert* by Lu Ji Fang

One

Desert Rose

Night in the Yeli Mountain brought about a different sort of darkness.

There were centuries of secrets contained here, ancient and unknowable, yet the mountains had seen everything from wars to famine to revolutions to purges. It bore the scars of a kingdom and its people. It had stories to tell, and Desert Rose thought if she listened closely enough, she could almost hear them, carried forth by the frigid northern winds.

At the foot of the mountain now, she stared up at them looming before her, their jagged peaks piercing the inky sky. The gods lay just beyond what her eyes could see, her tribe matriarch, Anar Zel, used to tell her. They saw and heard everything, even the smallest voice from the heart. It was her way of telling Desert Rose to keep the faith, to trust that she was never alone or forsaken in this world. It was easy, after all, for her to think that way, being an orphan child that the Dugur tribe chieftain had picked up in the desert and adopted. Anar Zel had always told her to trust that the gods were looking out for them, for her and the tribe, no matter how dire things appeared to be.

But Desert Rose had long given up on faith, especially in the gods. They were the ones who had allowed her tribe to get torn asunder by warring nations around the desert, and the ones who had given her a magical ability she had never asked for. It was both a gift and a curse, just like her destiny.

If the gods truly were listening, they wouldn't have let Anar Zel be killed by the current Oasis emperor, Han. Nor would they have let her father be trapped in Ghost City in exchange for the tribe's safety, or let

Wei be murdered by his own brother, the very same person who had killed Anar Zel. If the gods were powerful and just, they wouldn't have allowed the desert to be ravaged by the kingdoms surrounding it, or the world to be thrown off-kilter with magic falling in the wrong hands.

But Desert Rose knew it was pointless to blame the gods or anyone else. The fate of the realms was much bigger than her or her tribe or the warring kingdoms. She was just a chess piece in the game, and she had to play her role or perish.

She would not allow the gods to make a plaything out of her.

She would find a way to survive and evade the prophecy. Her destiny would not lie in the hands of the gods, only her own.

'They have room,' Windshadow said from behind her, snapping her out of her reverie. The other desert girl came over and nudged her. 'Come on.'

It was a last-minute arrangement, and by a small stroke of luck they had managed to find an inn with a spare room for the night. They had been travelling for the past two weeks to finally arrive at Yeli Mountain, switching inns and aliases and doing odd jobs in exchange for lodging and food along the way. This far away from the Capital, their reputation did not precede them. To the locals, they were simply two girls from out of town, here to do odd jobs and eke out a living.

Yet, the closer they got to the mountains, the difference in the locals' attitudes towards them grew more noticeable. Wary gazes lingered on them as they passed; people whispered behind their backs. The tension was as thick as curdled milk, and the girls tried their best to ignore the unwanted attention, keeping their heads down and never staying at any place long enough for anyone to get too close.

Desert Rose was no stranger to Yeli Mountain, having been here on a mission to track down a mercenary once. She had ended up meeting Wei's half-sister and her *shouren* family, finding out just how many of those beast-people remained in hiding, in fear of persecution for being what they were in a society intolerant of magic.

And yet, here she was with Windshadow, two Elementals, descendants of a love child born from two immortals, back in the Oasis Kingdom now ruled by a war-hungry emperor. If it weren't for the fact that the Earth Elemental was said to be residing in these mountains, she would not have stepped foot in this kingdom ever again.

All eyes fell upon them when they entered. Windshadow seemed unbothered by the attention, forging ahead as the busboy led them up the stairs towards a sparse, utilitarian room at the far corner of the inn. Desert Rose could tell that Windshadow made the young boy nervous, given the way he kept casting furtive sidelong glances at her and scurried away as soon as Windshadow paid him.

Once they were left alone, Windshadow set about checking every corner of the room, then peered out the window to survey the surroundings. Desert Rose was too exhausted to take any of the necessary precautions; all she wanted to do was sink into bed and shut out the constant anxiety of getting caught by Emperor Han's men, of the poison still flowing through her veins and the antidote Meng had procured for her tucked in her tunic, and of the niggling sense that Oasis Kingdom was no longer the same.

Everything had changed ever since the magic-resistant Wall was torn down during the battle at Danxi Plains. The Oasis Kingdom no longer had protection against magic from the outside world, and the energy inside felt chaotic, as though tangled in different skeins of wild magic. It drifted in through the windows on an early autumn breeze. In the distance, winds howled from the mountains, mingling with the vague cries of what Desert Rose could swear were the beast-people, whom she now knew for certain lived deep in the heart of Yeli Mountain.

Windshadow closed the window and tossed her belongings onto her bed after she was done with her checks. 'Glad you're making yourself useful,' she said, shooting Desert Rose a pointed smirk.

Perched on her bed, Desert Rose offered only an apologetic smile. It had been two weeks since she and Windshadow had snuck back into Oasis Kingdom, two weeks since the battle at Danxi Plains, and she could feel her hope and resolve waning by the day. Her sorrow sat like a growing stone in her chest, weighing her down with every step forward she tried to take. It seemed like she had barely processed each loss and separation before another hit her. Anar Zel's death in the Darklands.

Parting with her father again after finding him at last. Leaving her tribespeople again as they sought refuge beyond their ruined camp. Watching the Metal Elemental being murdered by the Fire Elemental.

And Wei. Watching Wei fall to his death.

The last thought snagged at her heart, cutting clean and deep like a freshly sharpened blade. She reached for the double knives he had gifted her. She kept them close to her these days, tucked in her waist belt, while the ones her father had given her were stowed in her boots. They were each a reminder of how far she had come, and of the long road that lay ahead of her that she now had to travel alone.

She missed him. She missed how he could sense her mood with one glance, how he always seemed to find the right words to quell the storm inside her. She missed the comforting timbre of his voice and warmth of his hands when they wrapped around hers. She missed how his gaze softened when he looked at her, how they would lean against each other and trade stories through the night. She had grown so accustomed to his presence, solid and unwavering, that his absence now felt like a gaping hole inside her.

'Stop pining, Rose. It's not going to bring back the dead,' Windshadow's voice cut through her thoughts again.

Desert Rose felt a prickle of irritation at her callousness. The Wind Elemental had been this way for as long as she had known her, scoffing at bleeding hearts and pretending as though nothing tied her down. But Desert Rose knew better. She had witnessed the change in her desert sister over the past year, even back when they were assassins-in-training at the House of Night in the imperial palace. She had seen how Windshadow had doubled back for her when she was in danger and given her the last of their rations (though pretending like she couldn't care for the stale bun), and she had heard the way she talked about her tribe from which she was estranged. Windshadow liked to pretend she didn't have a heart, but Desert Rose knew better, and it annoyed her whenever the other desert girl behaved as though she was above all worldly attachments.

'You're a real comfort, Windshadow,' she snapped.

Windshadow only shrugged. 'The sooner you realize there's no point lingering on what's gone, the sooner we can focus on what we came here for.'

As much as she hated to admit it, Desert Rose knew Windshadow had a point. They hadn't come all this way to mope over the dead and the lost. They were here to hunt down the last Elemental, the Earth Elemental, and kill him before the spring was awakened, or before any of the remaining Elementals could kill them. Lazar, the boy who wielded fire, was particularly intent on eliminating his competition, and him being at Emperor Han's side meant he had advantages that the rest of them didn't.

'How can you be sure he's even here?' Desert Rose asked. How could they trust what the Fire Elemental told them? Desert Rose had watched him roast the Metal Elemental alive without batting an eyelid. For all they knew, this could be a ploy to trap them both in the Oasis Kingdom so that he could kill them both at once.

'Of course he's here,' Windshadow said. 'Lazar wouldn't gather us all here if he didn't intend to kill us in a kingdom where he has backing from the emperor himself. Not only will he be able to kill us with the help of the emperor and the Imperial Army, but he can also do so under their protection.' She arched her back and settled into her bed. 'He can be rather predictable sometimes, once you have figured him out.'

'Do you think he lured us here on Han's orders?'

'That's one thing I can't figure out about him—where his loyalties truly lie. Sometimes, he seems to operate on his own. Other times, he is foolishly devoted to Han.' She folded her arms under her head and stared up at the ceiling. 'Either way, they'll come for us soon, drive us out of hiding. In the meantime, we find the Earth Elemental and get rid of *that* threat.'

Windshadow seemed entirely too comfortable with this life of running and hunting. Perhaps this was the life she was used to, the life she thrived on.

Desert Rose couldn't help but recall a conversation she had had with the Wind Elemental not too long ago. The latter had seemed to anticipate the prophesied end, where the sole surviving Elemental would ascend to the heavens after eliminating the rest and unlocking the spring. Desert Rose felt a twinge of pity for Windshadow—she had no emotional ties to her life on earth and would rather meet her end sooner rather than later.

Yet, Windshadow hadn't killed her yet. They had been travelling together for weeks; she had had plenty of opportunities to do so. Desert Rose had been certain the other desert girl would slit her throat while she was sleeping or poison her drink, but sometimes, she was not so sure. Sometimes, she would catch Windshadow looking at her with just a hint of atypical affection whenever they shared a lighter moment. Windshadow had said—rather defensively—that on their own, they were no match for Lazar and the Earth Elemental, so she would not kill Desert Rose until the other two threats were removed. But a part of Desert Rose still felt that the Wind Elemental who prided herself on her lack of any sentimental streak was perhaps capable of mercy, if not love.

Later, at dinner, they found a seat in the far corner of the restaurant that gave them a clear view of everyone. Diners here were a varied bunch, travellers from nearby provinces and local merchants travelling with their wares. They were mostly humble folk, unlike the foreign merchants and high-calibre officials Desert Rose had seen in the Capital. Many already seemed to know each other, while others befriended one another with far less reserve than the inn patrons in the Capital.

A group of at least ten people were huddled around a table in the centre of the inn, where a spread of dishes was laid out for sharing. But the patrons were far too engrossed in their conversation to tuck into the food.

'Another unexplained death in the village? That's the third one in a week,' one of them said.

'Some say it's supernatural work from the mountain shamans and black magic is involved,' someone else replied in a voice so hushed Desert Rose had to strain her ears to catch. A conversation involving shamans and black magic was grounds for arrest in a kingdom as intolerant as this one, but paper could not contain fire for long, and there was no stopping the rumours from spreading.

They didn't know, Desert Rose realized. These villagers and patrons had no idea that the Wall had been torn down, that the kingdom was now susceptible to all sorts of magic flowing from the outside world that the old Oasis emperors had been desperate to shield the kingdom from.

'This emperor is as legitimate as my father's old donkey,' one of them spat. 'Word is, he was exiled by the Fifteenth Emperor for treason. How can a treasonous son become an emperor? He must have pulled some dirty tricks to get on the throne.'

Everyone at the table shared nervous glances but their interest in the topic made them stop short of silencing the man who spoke.

'What about the other son?' a young man dressed in the ethnic robes of what Desert Rose guessed was the Mci tribe asked. 'The one who ascended because their father was murdered? Think he did anything dirty too?'

'I'm sure he did,' the first man replied. 'They all do. None of their hands are clean. But among all of them, he seems to at least give two donkey's farts about us, the people. Too bad he was chased out of the kingdom by the current emperor.'

It was treasonous talk; all of this, if overheard by any authorities, would guarantee prosecution, if not death. But out here in a little village five *li* from Yeli town, they were confident that no one would bother censoring them.

Windshadow shot Desert Rose a look. The man might just have been speculating about Prince Meng, but his guess wasn't far off. Meng's hands weren't entirely clean—even though it was technically Windshadow who had murdered the Crown Prince, Meng was the one who had hired Windshadow to help him secure the throne by eliminating the competition. Emotionally bound and manipulated by the Empress Dowager, Meng had planned for the Crown Prince's murder right down to the last detail, making sure that it would leave him free of suspicion while Windshadow did the dirty deed.

While Desert Rose knew it was common for the imperial family to engage in internal power struggles, the revelation had jarred her and changed her view of the gentle Fourth Prince for good. She still didn't know whether to trust his intentions—the sting of his betrayal last spring lingered—but he *had* attempted to make amends ever since they crossed paths again in Lettoria. A tiny part of her also still believed that his heart was in the right place when it came to ruling the kingdom. At the very least, he was not brutal and selfish like his father and Han . . .

'Do you suppose he's the Rebel Prince?' one of them asked in a hushed voice.

At that, a buzz went around the table. Even the innkeeper's ears pricked as he attended to a couple of new guests.

'The Rebel Prince,' Windshadow snorted. 'Looks like Meng's campaign in the west is working.'

Desert Rose wasn't so sure. Ever since they had parted ways in the Darklands, she had heard nothing about Meng, whether he had chosen to return to Lettoria and continue his alliance with the duplicitous King Falco or whether he had left with Bataar and the Dugur clan leaders. Yet, word of the Rebel Prince had travelled across the desert. She had caught wind of it on the way here but couldn't say for certain that it was Meng.

In any case, she had no desire to concern herself with Meng's decisions and the fate of this kingdom when her own tribe was still stranded and her father was trapped in Ghost City. The sooner she found the other Elementals, the sooner she could get this prophecy business over with and release her father from the deal he had made with the Ghost King.

That night, Desert Rose's dreams were haunted by the dead. She saw Wei plunging from the city walls, her father's soul amongst the souls of other men trapped in Ghost City, the remains of Anar Zel and Wei's mother in the Darklands. She saw the Metal Elemental and his brother parting ways, never to reunite again. She dreamed of Meng, the gentle, scheming prince she once knew, now supposedly a rebel out to regain the throne. It seemed like all she had done since she was forced to flee from her tribe that night on the White Moon Festival was lose the people she loved. When would this all end?

All this while, her magic continued to twist and roil inside her like a distressed animal, a constant reminder of the poison that remained in her.

At dawn, fervent knocking came at the door.

Desert Rose sprang awake, shaking off the remnants of her stupor. Windshadow was already heading for the door. She slid it open just a crack and peered out through it, then opened it fully to reveal the innkeeper standing at the door, looking irate and panicked.

'There are officials on their patrol, and I can't have you both staying here without official papers,' he said.

'I thought you said it wouldn't be a problem,' Desert Rose said. *Officials don't bother patrolling these parts*, was what he said when he allowed two desert girls to stay as long as they managed to cough up the money.

'That was before someone got murdered down the street last night. Now everyone here is a suspect and you two being here will implicate me. Now scram before the authorities arrive.'

Windshadow was about to put up a strong protest, but Desert Rose held her back. 'Someone was murdered here?'

'It's happening everywhere in this county now, it's terrible for business,' the innkeeper grumbled. 'I suggest you leave unless you wish to be investigated.'

But they were too late. The pair of officials and their retinue stormed up the narrow dirt path towards the inn before Desert Rose and Windshadow could make their escape. The girls snuck to the front of the inn and watched from the second-storey window at the end of the corridor. Dressed in their embroidered black and vermilion uniform, they looked exceptionally out of place in this humble village, and exceptionally obnoxious.

Apart from the two officials, however, the rest were dressed in identical black tunics with crimson trimming. Desert Rose had had enough experience with imperial scouts to recognize their uniform and the way they operated. They were given free rein to destroy and intimidate, a power they happily abused too often. The last time she came face to face with them was in an inn just outside the Oasis Capital, where they had destroyed the place just to capture Wei, their wanted rogue prince.

The officials riding ahead of the pack came to a stop before the inn and dismounted. Behind them, the scouts did the same and joined the officials at the entrance of the inn. The clomp of their heavy boots indicated their arrival before their imperious voices did.

'Hide,' the innkeeper hissed at Desert Rose before scurrying downstairs to meet the scouts.

Desert Rose and Windshadow crouched on the stair landing to observe the goings-on below. With everyone downstairs and their attention transfixed on the new visitors, the second floor was deserted, allowing the two to watch without being noticed. They exchanged a look when the officials sauntered in, torn between the need to flee and their desire to stay and satisfy their burning curiosity. What could this group of people possibly want with a humble inn like this in the middle of nowhere?

'Everyone in a single row, with your hands behind your heads,' the leader bellowed, his hand resting on the hilt of his sword tucked by his waist.

A hiss came from behind them, where a man peered out from a room near them. He was the one who had spoken at dinner the night before, comparing Emperor Han to his father's donkey. Up close, he appeared to be a northerner, with his craggy sun-worn face, burly physique, and rough-spun clothing.

'Best to stay inside,' he whispered, gesturing for them to retreat.

Desert Rose remained where she was. 'What's happening?' she whispered back, as though she had no clue. She had learned that asking the simplest questions could sometimes garner the most insightful answers.

'Patrol, I suppose. They happen from time to time in these parts, with the'—his voice dropped to a barely audible pitch—'Ling rumoured to be living in the mountains.'

Desert Rose possessed only rudimentary knowledge of the Ling, but what little she knew of them made her empathize with them. The Ling, as she had learned during her time in the House of Night, were a collective but diverse group of magical beings and practitioners who were supposed to have been killed during the Great Purge—and the subsequent ones over the centuries—but were rumoured to be living on in the kingdom, spending their days in hiding in the Yeli Mountains. The Ling also included the shouren, for whom Wei's father harboured a mortal hatred, given that his daughter, Princess Qiu, had eloped with one of the beast-people.

Persecuted and driven into hiding for their magical abilities, the Ling continued to be denizens of the Oasis Kingdom, their name now only uttered in furtive whispers that sent a chill down everyone's spines. Desert Rose might not have met another Ling apart from the shouren, but her own encounters with the beast-people had shown her that they were no different from any other person from Oasis Kingdom, struggling to eke out a living within the confines of society.

'But as long as you don't practise magic or have it in your blood, *ticha* is harmless, isn't it?' the man went on, continuing to eye them both.

Not to them. Both Desert Rose and Windshadow each had personal experience with the special herb that could detect magic. While drinking ticha-infused tea would temporarily disable magic on top of delivering pain akin to having knives down one's throat, direct contact with ticha leaves brought about greater anguish and even debilitation to the magic carrier.

'If the place is clean and they find no illegal persons, they'll be on their merry way,' said the man.

'What happens if they find illegal persons?' Desert Rose asked.

'Then they'll round up everyone and take them to the Capital for questioning.' He peered closer at them. 'You two are clean, aren't you?'

'As clean as *you* are,' Windshadow retorted. The man pursued the topic no further.

Downstairs, the pair of officials surveyed everyone gathered there. 'This inn is under investigation for the homicide down the street,' he declared in a booming officious voice. 'By the Seventeenth Emperor Han's orders, anyone under suspicion of harbouring or abetting the Ling will be fined and taken in for questioning.'

This mountain town was small, with no more than a hundred people living there, excluding inn patrons. Why would Han bother inspecting a tiny countryside village like this one when he had just ended a devastating battle with Lettoria?

'He knows we're here,' Desert Rose murmured. It seemed presumptuous to think that the scouts were here to seek them out, but she and Windshadow had come suspiciously far without being detected or captured. Desert Rose couldn't help but wonder if they were walking deeper and deeper into a trap each day. Perhaps this was where the scouts would corner them at last.

'The emperor has more than the Ling to worry about, with the Rebel Prince coming to challenge his reign,' a voice piped up among the inn patrons.

A deadly silence crept into the inn. The patrons shuffled nervously, exchanging tense glances with one another. It was one thing to speak of the rumoured Rebel Prince among themselves, but with authorities around, that could get him executed.

'Who speaks?' one of the officials demanded, glancing around for the guilty party.

It was a young man in his twenties, if his friend tugging on his shirt sleeve to shut him up was any indication. The man had a stare that simmered with defiance. But perhaps having gained a sense of self-preservation at the last moment, he did not repeat himself.

'Does everyone here believe in the Rebel Prince as well?' the other official challenged.

The crowd shook their heads, fervent and fearful. The innkeeper bowed. 'Certainly not, good sirs. That is but a baseless rumour intended to disrupt the peace of our great kingdom. We wouldn't dare to challenge the Seventeenth Emperor's legitimacy in any way. We are just humble mountain folk trying to scrape by.'

The officials seemed mollified by the innkeeper's assurance. He headed to the end of the line and waved for the scouts to proceed with the ticha testing.

Windshadow nudged Desert Rose. 'We should talk to that man. Get some information on this Rebel Prince they seem to worship.'

One of the scouts glanced up just as Desert Rose and Windshadow were about to retreat into their room. His gaze fell directly upon them. 'There's more of them upstairs,' he called out. Behind them, the northerner ducked back into his room and shut the door tight.

The scout squinted. 'It's her!' he cried. 'It's them!'

Her suspicions were right—Han knew they were in the Oasis Kingdom and he was searching for them. That was why he had allowed them to enter through the gates with no one stopping them after the battle at Danxi Plains, and why they had come this far unscathed.

Assuming Lazar was still on his side, he would therefore have known that Lazar had told them the Earth Elemental's rumoured whereabouts and led them here to Yeli Mountain, making it easier for him to track them down.

They had known this could be a trap of sorts and chosen to walk right into it for the sake of finding the Earth Elemental, but now that they were cornered in this dingy inn by imperial officials, the threat of capture seemed awfully close.

'Run,' Windshadow hissed. She wasted no time dissipating into a gust of wind and slipping out the nearest window, leaving Desert Rose at the stair landing scrambling to her feet.

Desert Rose didn't have a convenient ability like Windshadow's, nor was she able to use her magic. Ever since the Metal Elemental shot her with a poison dart in defence, using her magic would only debilitate her.

The only option now was to fight the scouts head-on.

As they charged up the stairs towards her, she whipped out her double knives, the ones Wei gave her. In a way, it felt as though he was there fighting alongside her, just like old times.

The first scout came at her with his *dao* without a moment's hesitation. The meaty blade sliced through the air and narrowly missed her arm. She flung her knives against the scout's dao when it came for her again, staggering backwards against the weight. The other scouts burst out of the inn, most likely to chase Windshadow, but the remaining half pressed closer and closer, cornering her.

She glanced out the window at the end of the corridor, which would take her out through the front of the inn. It wasn't a high drop—just two storeys. Should she make a break for it?

A brown fox skittered up the stairs before anyone could stop it. It moved with calculated intent as it dodged among the scouts. Then, so quickly it seemed like a trick of the eye, it shifted in and out of human form, tripping scouts and disarming them before they could react. His face remained that of a fox, but human limbs shot out to snatch their weapons and toss them to the ground floor.

'Shouren!' one of the scouts cried as he picked himself up.

They lunged for the fox, but it was too quick for them, skirting across the floorboards and down the bannisters before anyone could grab it.

Desert Rose slipped down the stairs when the scouts spared a moment to decide whom to capture, whether a shouren—rarely sighted but declared a threat to the kingdom—was worth giving up an Elemental for.

The scouts gave up on the fox and turned their focus back to Desert Rose. They barrelled down the stairs after her, their heavy boots thumping on the wooden floorboards.

Downstairs, the inn had erupted in chaos. Inn patrons ducked out of the way as the fox knocked over stools and wove around table legs. It didn't seem interested in the food laid out on the tables, almost as though its only intention was to wreak as much havoc as it could.

Desert Rose tightened her grip on her daggers and slipped between an incoming pair of soldiers, slicing her way through them before ducking under a dining table, emerging just in time to hack at the sturdy legs of another pair of soldiers. Duelling with Windshadow in the House of Night had taught her not to underestimate the element of surprise in a fight, and that tip served her well this time. The soldiers went crumbling to the ground, the pained cries almost drowned out by the commotion in the inn.

With four of the soldiers felled, the path was clear. Here was her window of opportunity to escape.

As she charged towards the front door, a willowy, masked girl in a roughspun man's tunic appeared out of the crowd of patrons and grabbed her hand. Hers was cool and slim, but her grip was firm as she tugged Desert Rose towards the back.

'This way,' the girl hissed.

Her voice sounded familiar, but Desert Rose couldn't quite place it. She let the girl lead her out of the inn anyway. Behind them, the fox was ducking around tables as a pair of scouts tried to reach for it.

'Don't worry, he'll be fine,' the girl said, sensing her glance back.

They raced down a narrow dirt path behind, where a dense forest lay just a stone's throw away from the back of the inn. Thatched-roof houses flanked the path, where a few chickens roamed in the backyard and housewives peered curiously at them. Ahead, the forest loomed, canopied by scarlet and amber autumn leaves, and empty for as far as Desert Rose could tell—a welcome sight.

The deeper they wound, the more unruly the undergrowth became. They crashed through it clumsily, stumbling over moss-covered rocks and getting caught in broken twigs, not bothering with stealth as it was hard enough to navigate this untrodden part of the woods. Behind them, the sounds of the commotion died away, giving way to melodic bird calls and the urgent rustle of leaves.

When they seemed to have lost sight of the scouts behind them, they came to a stop and caught their breaths against an oak tree. The crisp autumn air offered reprieve from the stuffy inn, and Desert Rose inhaled deeply as her racing heart tapered to its regular pace.

'Why didn't you use your magic to fight?' the girl asked. 'You could have defeated all of them at once and escaped.'

'It's a long story . . .' Desert Rose frowned. 'How did you . . .?'

A glint shone in her eyes. 'Don't tell me you've forgotten me.' She removed her mask. Her grin was at once recognizable, infectious.

Desert Rose blinked. 'Qiu?'

The Lost Princess threw her arms around her in a hug.

Two

Windshadow

The scouts were more persistent than she gave them credit for. Two pairs of them were already waiting for her outside the inn, and when she blustered out the window, they felt her breeze and gave chase.

She became one with the autumn wind, relishing the moment she shed her mortal skin and blended into her element. The liberating feeling never got old—she felt free and weightless as her Elemental self, unencumbered, and sometimes she could even forget the weight of her destiny that she carried.

A wild peal of laughter escaped her. These mortals thought their human senses and primitive weapons could trap a Wind Elemental? Then again, she *had* been captured before—twice—thanks to the ticha. *Don't underestimate them*, she reminded herself. Especially not Han. The First Prince had more tricks up his sleeve than he let on.

She had barely gotten more than one li away from the inn when a searing pain hit her. The sensation—like a wildfire tearing through her—was familiar. She had experienced it before at the hands of Han, when he captured her using ticha-infused water, and in the imperial prison, where they rammed ticha leaves down her throat.

She swore as she felt the human weight of her body again. No longer was she airborne; she was now a tangle of limbs as she crashed to the ground.

She might be an Elemental, but these scouts were trained and prepared to defeat the likes of her. They had the one weapon that could maim and even kill an Elemental. Her thoughts snapped to

Desert Rose. If the scouts could capture a Wind Elemental with ticha, what hope did a Water Elemental with poisoned magic have?

You're not responsible for everyone's safety, she reminded herself. Desert Rose would find a way out like she always did. Windshadow's job was to save herself. Since when did she start caring about others anyway?

The ticha leaves this time were thankfully not wet, and therefore didn't linger on her skin. But they got her on her knees long enough for two pairs of gloved hands to grab her roughly by the shoulders and pin her against a tree. Windshadow twisted her face to the side before it slammed against the trunk.

The Fire Elemental stepped into view on her right, wearing his customary smirk. It was the smirk of someone who knew he had the upper hand. Windshadow felt a feral urge to ram a fistful of ticha leaves down his throat.

'You made out alive, *azzi*,' Lazar said breezily.

'I could say the same for you,' she replied, delivering as much snark as she could in her disadvantaged position.

The last time she had seen the Fire Elemental, they had been engaged in a bitter duel at Danxi Plains, where Lettorian forces had clashed brutally with the Oasis Army. But after the sandstorm whipped up by the Ghost King in his attempt to aid Desert Rose, she had lost sight of Lazar. Windshadow was neither foolish nor optimistic enough to believe that Lazar was dead, but the sight of him back in his glory in Oasis Kingdom rankled her.

'I thought I might find you in one of these mountain villages,' he said. 'The Earth Elemental is a tough one to track down.'

It would be easy for Lazar to kill her on the spot. Windshadow knew how hell-bent he was on ascending to the heavens (if that was truly the fate of the surviving Elemental—for all they knew, the survivor would end up being punished by the gods). And now he had her pinned against a tree before him, weakened by ticha. He could burn her to the ground without blinking an eye and eliminate a competitor.

He seemed aware of that fact as well.

Yet, for all his bravado, something was amiss. Windshadow peered at him, squinting past the glare of sunlight streaming through the canopy of leaves. His face wore a grey pallor, as though the shadow of death hung over him. He appeared, for the first time since she met him, much older than his age. There were shadows under his eyes, a certain sombreness that tugged at the corner of his lips despite his smirk. He wasn't even toying with a ball of fire in his palm the way he usually did.

'What's wrong with you?' Windshadow demanded.

Lazar gestured for the soldiers to release their grasp. They obeyed and stepped back, giving him a wider berth than usual. Windshadow massaged her shoulder where they had gripped her, sending them a doleful glare.

Lazar's smile was wry this time, no longer a smirk. 'Apparently, our qi is limited. Using too much of it too soon will make us go out quicker than a flame.'

Windshadow understood at once. His magic was starting to eat him alive.

She felt it within her too. As the days wore on, her magic morphed into a ravenous creature that seemed to draw out bits of her life every time she used it. She was simultaneously fuelled and drained by it, as though she and her magic each sustained itself by consuming from the other. It was a different relationship from when she had first discovered her magic, when it had fed and served her.

In some versions of the prophecy, the Elementals were predicted to be consumed by their magic on their way to finding the spring, if they hadn't killed each other first. Windshadow certainly felt as though she had aged over the past couple of years from using her magic intensely.

For Lazar, perhaps due to how much he harnessed and used his magic, he appeared to be ageing much faster.

'Well, your end seems to be nearer than mine,' she said, gesturing at his face.

He shrugged. 'That's why I'm not going to kill you now, even though I very well can.'

Windshadow raised her brows. 'You're saying you need my help to eliminate the other Elementals.'

'I'm saying we need each other,' he corrected, prideful as ever. 'At the rate we use our magic, we won't last till the end. The more qi we can steal from the other Elementals, the longer we can last.'

Windshadow imagined herself killing Desert Rose and stealing her qi. She imagined how much stronger she would feel, like she had when she first discovered her power. It was a thought she had considered more than once in the last couple of weeks, when she and Desert Rose were both desperately drained of energy. Yet, Windshadow had resisted the urge each time, telling herself that the timing was not right, not because she couldn't bring herself to.

But even though she hated to admit it, Lazar was right. If they didn't kill each other first, their magic would. And she would do better to keep her enemy—and biggest competitor—close to her.

'Our end is near, azzi,' Lazar said, as though he had heard her thoughts. 'The sooner we find the Earth Elemental, the sooner we can put this all to rest. The Water Elemental is weak, given to sentiment; killing her would be a stroll in the garden.'

Windshadow felt a snap of irritation at the way he dismissed Desert Rose. He didn't know how resilient and tenacious she could be—nor did he care. To him, she was merely a lesser rival, barely worth his concern.

'What about Han?' she sneered. 'Didn't he hire you as his little errand boy? Even if you decide to abscond, don't you think he will hunt you down? This is his kingdom now.'

Up went that cocky smirk again. 'You assume we need to work against Han in order to get what we want.'

Windshadow understood at once. 'He's sent you to look for the Earth Elemental.'

Lazar nodded. 'He wants me to capture the Earth Elemental—or, better yet, capture all the existing Elementals so that he can use us to build his personal army.'

Windshadow laughed. She couldn't decide if Han was delusional, ambitious, or simply entitled for thinking that he could get Elementals to serve him, a mortal emperor. Then again, he wasn't the first emperor who thought he could have the world at his feet.

'But what do his ambitions ultimately have to do with us?' Lazar went on. 'We could just get rid of the Earth Elemental and be on our way.'

Windshadow snorted. 'So you're using his agenda to fulfil yours.'

Up went that smirk again. 'It's nothing you wouldn't do, I'm sure. We are one and the same, after all. We'll do anything to survive.' A pause. 'You trust me, don't you?

It was a trick question, of course. Lazar had never been one she could trust, and she loathed how he kept claiming that they were alike. But a part of her knew he was right. They were good at staying in the game.

One could always count on a turncoat for betrayal, and the closer she stuck to him, the better tabs she could keep on him, for her own safety. It was no longer simply a matter of trust. They were running out of time too. For now, it made the most sense to team up with him while they hunted down the last Elemental.

Now, it was a matter of survival. And surviving was what she was best at.

* * *

Emperor Han kept Lazar on a long leash.

The imperial scouts tailed them all the way as they journeyed towards Yeli Town. Yet, none of them ever stopped or hindered them. As long as she was with Lazar, it seemed, she was untouchable.

Yeli Town, while bustling, carried a strange underlying current of fear and unease. It was much smaller than the towns in the Capital, and mostly filled with locals dressed in humble clothing, unlike the Capital where furs and silks were the common garb. Shoppers milled along the streets, going about their errands, but mothers pulled their children close to them, casting their wary gazes around, particularly at newcomers like Windshadow and Lazar. Even the merchants and vendors seemed reluctant to hawk their wares, as did innkeepers in soliciting customers.

It wasn't until they passed by the local town-crier making his rounds with his gong that Windshadow understood the reason for the tension in the town. 'Beware of the Ling! Beware of the shouren!' he cried, striking his gong each time he belted out a warning. 'Guard your homes!'

A wizened old lady dressed in a patchwork robe appeared soundlessly next to Windshadow, holding out a sprig of an all-too-familiar plant. 'Some ticha for you, miss?'

Windshadow jerked away from her on reflex, sending her the coldest stare.

'It'll protect you well from evil qi,' the old lady went on, oblivious to Windshadow's response. 'There's been too much of it around lately, I can feel it in the air. Just look at those sudden deaths in the last two weeks.'

With the Wall torn down by the mages from Lettoria, magic could now creep into the Oasis Kingdom and fall into the wrong hands. Windshadow was no fortune teller, but she had a feeling the number of unexplained deaths would increase in the coming days.

Lazar nudged her to keep moving. 'Too many peddlers in these parts,' he muttered as they shuffled along. 'If she could feel a change in qi, why couldn't she tell we're not entirely mortal?'

But Windshadow wasn't so sure. She and Lazar were walking beacons around here, in a mountain supposedly overrun with magic-practising folk. They left the old lady behind and rounded a corner into an adjacent street, then down another, and another, until the mountain loomed closer and closer. At last, they arrived at the final street that lay just before the mountain, with a narrow winding path at the end that led up to it.

Unlike the healthy bustle of the town square and marketplace, there was barely a soul around here. Silence crept up on them as they went deeper down the street, and a chill swept through the wide and empty pavements. Houses had their doors and windows shut, and most of the shops were boarded up. Save for a handful of them that were open, it almost seemed as though this northern corner of Yeli Town had been abandoned or shunned by the locals.

A prickle at the nape of her neck made her tense up. She glanced out of her periphery and spotted the flash of a tunic before it slipped out of sight.

'We're being watched, and it's not just by imperial scouts,' Windshadow muttered. Lazar agreed, though he hardly seemed bothered by it.

She had heard about the characters that lived here, the ones who dwelled in the deepest, darkest parts of these mountains, who lurked in the night and blended in among humans during the day. Had they detected them already, two Elementals walking about in broad daylight in a kingdom now destabilized by external magic?

The old lady was right. There was a strange qi lurking around the area, an energy that pervaded these streets and settled into its nooks and crannies. And that aura only grew stronger the closer they came to the foot of the mountain.

Windshadow had limited encounters with the shouren, but she guessed that they didn't leave behind scorch marks or dead livestock and plants along with a lingering bad qi.

It wasn't the shouren. Something else was at work here. And she and Lazar seemed to be walking straight into the tiger's den.

Three

Wei

Being part of the undead in Ghost City made one lose all sense of time. Wei had no idea how long he had been trapped here, or how long it had been since the battle at Danxi Plains, but it felt like an eternity.

The last thing he saw before waking up in Ghost City was Desert Rose charging towards him through the fray as he plunged from the watchtower. Had she managed to defeat the Fire Elemental? Had she found the last Elemental yet? Where had she gone after the battle? It was killing him to be stuck here, not knowing what was happening in the outside world and not being able to do anything.

But the Ghost King had declared him not dead when Wei appeared in Ghost City, a soul among the many trapped here. His words had kindled a spark of hope that everything had gone according to plan, that Zeyan and Beihe had found Wei's body and taken it to the Dugur tribe shamans who would reunite his body with his soul.

Yet, as much as Wei tried to maintain his optimism, a part of him was starting to lose faith in the possibility of him returning to the mortal world.

There was so much left to do—overthrow an emperor, avenge his mother and brother, save a kingdom—but he was stuck in this limbo, unable to execute any of his plans. How had Desert Rose's father stayed here this long—since last winter, when he was overthrown by the Dugur clan leaders—and not lost his mind?

Being without a physical body was disorientating. He was sentient and present, just unable to move like someone with a corporeal vessel was able to. He felt caught between being dead and alive, as though he existed but also didn't.

Scarbrow, the Dugur tribe chieftain, appeared next to him. Wei had met him once, when he and Desert Rose first found him here among the souls in Ghost City. Wei hadn't mentioned it, but he was humbled by how the chieftain had sacrificed himself by exchanging his soul for his tribe's safety (although that refuge was short-lived—half of them were now on the run after the imperial scouts destroyed Ghost City).

Desert Rose had told him much about her foster father, how he had adopted her as a child wandering the desert and taught her everything he knew. How he had protected her from suspicion from some of the tribe members with *mukh* water that concealed her magic, which had first manifested when she was eight years old. How he was the kindest, fairest, and gentlest person she knew despite his rough exterior.

Wei had his own early memory of Scarbrow, when he had gotten lost in the desert as part of an 'exercise' his own father made him go through, and the chieftain had taken him in for the night, essentially saving his life. He was forever indebted to Scarbrow, and meeting Desert Rose again had felt as though fate was taking him in a full circle.

'It takes some getting used to, being here in this state,' said Scarbrow, gesturing at both their immaterial bodies.

'Hopefully, I won't have to get too used to it.' Wei shot Scarbrow a wry smile. 'Although if I had more time here, I might be able to convince the Ghost King to help me.'

The undead ruler of Ghost City had soundly rejected Wei when he had enlisted his help to defeat his brother. He needed an army, one that could replace Han's loyalists when he finally came head-to-head with his brother, and there was none more powerful—that he knew of—other than the Ghost Army, consisting of undead soldiers that would be inexorable in battle.

'I have no interest in partaking in the wars of men,' the Ghost King had said. 'I am merely a reaper of souls, awaiting the day I am free of my servitude. The day the last Elemental can free us.'

The Ghost King had been the last ruler of the Hesui Kingdom until he was killed by Wei's ancestors. As a result, he was doomed to remain stuck in this purgatory until the last prophesied Elemental unlocked the spring and led the Damohai back to glory, which would free him and his ghost army. But while Wei knew it was brazen of him to enlist the Ghost King's help now, he also hoped that the agreement between the Ghost King and Desert Rose would be enough to galvanize him to aid Wei. His request for the Ghost Army's assistance wasn't simply to settle a score with his brother or wrestle for Oasis Kingdom, but to ultimately save Desert Rose. As long as Han—and his sidekick Lazar, the Fire Elemental—was still in the picture, Desert Rose was in danger.

The only agreement that the Ghost King was concerned with now was the one he had made with Desert Rose, whose father being trapped here gave her an unshakeable reason to fulfil her end of the deal. But Wei knew that the Ghost King would just as quickly switch alliances as soon as a stronger Elemental came by and struck another deal. The Ghost King held no allegiance to anyone, not any Elemental, and certainly not a mortal like Wei.

But for as long as he was stuck here, Wei would continue to appeal to him. Ending the wars between the kingdoms and overthrowing Han would help Desert Rose somehow, after all, and Wei would do everything he could to aid her in fulfilling her destiny.

'About this army you said you wanted to build,' Scarbrow began, breaking his train of thought.

It was an ambitious plan—how was a rogue prince, shunned from his own kingdom, going to drum up enough strength to fight the current Oasis emperor? Many in his home kingdom knew him as the black sheep of the imperial family, the one who had left home and abandoned his title, his family, and his country for the wild. Even if Han was the exiled prince, he now had the support of the Empress Dowager and the High Advisor, and had free rein to do whatever he wanted to remain in power.

Without the Ghost King's army of souls, Wei had nothing with which he could fight against Han. Would he have to return to the cunning King Falco with his tail between his legs and be at his mercy again, after Falco basically held Desert Rose hostage to ensure Wei held up his end of the deal?

'The Damohai,' Scarbrow said.

Wei blinked, snapping out of his thoughts. 'I'm sorry?'

'The Ghost Army is not your only option,' Scarbrow said. 'You can look for the Damohai, enlist their help.'

The Children of the Desert, descendants of the love child of the Sky Princess and Earth Prince, were the original guardians of the desert and the rulers of the Hesui Kingdom that was now carved up and assumed by surrounding kingdoms and mercenaries eyeing the territory for ages. The Damohai were a lost people now, scattered and weakened by what Wei's ancestors had used to disable their magic. How was he to find them, much less enlist their help?

'I thought no one had seen them for centuries,' Wei said.

'They're in hiding, but according to the prophecy, the surviving Elemental is meant to find the Damohai and unite them once again. The Damohai will pledge allegiance to the Elemental that is destined to lead them out of the darkness and back into the light. If Rose is the last one standing, her fate will lead her to them. From there, you can borrow the army you need to defeat your brother and end his campaign.'

The Damohai were Desert Rose's people by blood. Like them, she came from that immortal bloodline. If there was anyone she might turn to for help in searching for the Earth Elemental, it would be them. So if Wei could find them, he could most likely find her.

Wei's heart swelled with the anticipation of finding Desert Rose again. Wherever their fates took them in the end, for now, as long as he could find her, they could walk on the same path for a while longer.

He knew her. She would not linger at the same place for long. She would have gone in search of the other Elementals. As long as he could find them, he would find her too.

Scarbrow's gaze turned heavy. 'We all want the wars to end. We want peace back in the desert. If you believe you can see that through, then I will assist you in whatever way I can—as will my tribe.'

Wei nodded. 'My mother and brother never lived to see the day our kingdom flourished peacefully. I will see it through if it's the last thing I do.'

There was much to be done, and this was only the beginning. His plan to overthrow Han was a long shot, and it all hinged on his ability to leave Ghost City.

Trust in the timing of all things, his Snow Wolf Sect master used to say whenever Wei got impatient on a hunt. He had taught him about *wuwei*, of going along with the natural course of things rather than being attached to a specific outcome. For now, he would lay his trust in Zeyan and Beihe, and have faith that he would leave Ghost City eventually.

'How did you come to meet my daughter again?' the chieftain asked.

Wei was thankful for the change in topic. He had already thanked Scarbrow for saving his life in the desert years ago, but so much more had transpired the second time he met Desert Rose, when she fled the Dugur tribe last winter.

'She snuck into my tent the night she was persecuted by the clan leaders, then we fought off a sand hound together the next morning,' Wei said. He could feel the corners of his lips quirk as he recalled their first encounter, where he first caught a glimpse of her stubborn, prideful streak and dexterity with the double knives she had borrowed from him. 'She told me she was meeting you at the Oasis Capital, so I gave her a ride there . . .'

They had gone from strangers who barely trusted each other to allies to confidantes, and now his heart ached every time he thought about her. He had never allowed himself to grow attached to anyone precisely because he feared the possibility of losing them like how he had lost his family. But with Desert Rose, he hadn't been able to stop himself from falling, despite knowing that they were doomed to be apart, that fate already had plans for them to go in different directions.

'I'll find her again,' he heard himself saying. 'Not just for the Damohai, but . . . I *want* to see her again.'

He longed to hear her voice, see her wry smile, bask in her energy again. The thing with Desert Rose was that she threw her entire being into everything she believed was worth fighting for, everything she loved and cared for. Wei loved that the most about her.

Scarbrow was watching him, and he clearly understood what he saw in Wei's face while he was thinking about Desert Rose. 'Thank you for being by my daughter's side all this while. But I must remind you that her destiny is already determined by the gods. You cannot go where she goes in the end.'

Wei knew that. He had learned about the prophecy from the Dugur tribe matriarch, Anar Zel, when he first met her in Ghost City.

Whether or not Rose managed to be the last surviving Elemental, she would no longer belong to this world. She would ascend to the heavens and take her place among the gods.

Yet, he refused to believe that this would be their ending. He would not let the gods write their story.

A tug came at this chest, so gentle at first that he thought he had imagined it. But he felt it again in his gut, his limbs, until he could no longer deny the pull that compelled his entire body ceilingward. The more he resisted the force, the stronger it grew.

Scarbrow seemed to notice a change in him too. 'What's wrong?'

Wei found himself rising to his feet, called to the invisible force. A strange light filled the room. He glanced down to find his body glowing brighter than everyone else's in the chamber—even the Ghost King's—almost as though he was being imbued with new life.

Everyone crowded around him, staring and murmuring. Scarbrow watched him with concern and a tinge of cautious joy.

From the middle of the horde, the Ghost King drifted towards Wei. 'Go,' he intoned with a permissive wave of his hand. 'The mortal world calls for you.'

Wei nodded, relief washing over him. Zeyan and the rest had succeeded with the ritual after all. 'I look forward to your assistance in the plan.' With a parting glance at Scarbrow, he gave in to the sensation, letting it tow him away.

Darkness clouded over him, and he felt himself drifting into an abyss. It was impossible to tell how much time had passed—he seemed to float on for eternity, until the stale air inside the chamber gradually eased into something light and cool. He felt it fill his lungs, felt the even pace of his heartbeat again, the rise and fall of his chest as he breathed deeper.

Sensations hit him in quick succession. When he opened his eyes again, sunlight streamed in, flooding his vision. The tugging on his body had ceased, and he lay prone on what felt like a soft warm rug, staring up at the roof of what appeared to be a tent. He felt the warmth of a fire nearby, heard the murmur of voices a few feet away. Then the sound of footsteps heading towards him.

Zeyan's face came into view. 'He's awake, he's awake!'

Beihe appeared in his line of vision next. 'Give him some room, Zeyan.'

The glare of sunlight intensified as they shifted away. Wei felt the reassuring weight of his fingers as he attempted to move them, the sinews in his arms as he clenched them, the heaviness in his head as he tried to sit up. He was back in his corporeal body, though after all that time as a spirit, it was slightly disorientating to fit back into his mortal form.

More familiar faces came into view. The Dugur tribespeople—Yanda, Qara, and Khum—stepped closer to him, though maintaining a respectful distance.

They had done it. His Snow Wolf Sect brothers had come through for him, just as he had trusted them to. Wei felt the urge to throw his arms around them in gratitude, but his body felt as though it had been trampled by a horse and he could barely lift an arm.

Zeyan and Beihe understood his intention anyway and pulled him into a tight hug. Wei winced, but his relief overshadowed the pain in his body.

'How long has it been?' His voice came out a little hoarse. Yanda handed him a mug of water immediately, as though she had been prepared for this moment. He gulped down the drink gratefully.

'Almost two weeks,' Zeyan said. 'We came here as fast as we could. There were Oasis soldiers still scouring the vicinity for survivors after the battle.'

Here was the makeshift tent where half of the Dugur tribe had taken refuge in a small desert town two days' ride from Mobei, a region on the north-western border of the Khuzar Desert. Mobei and Monan were two adjacent regions that lay on the border between the desert and the western colonies of Lettoria and Sorenstein. Were it not for the warlords that guarded these highly sought-after regions, the Lettorians and Sorensteins would have encroached further upon the Khuzar Desert.

Still, Wei knew that the warlords only had as much power as the western kingdoms allowed them. Their peace agreement stood only for as long as both parties got what they wanted from the other—resources in exchange for safety.

Being in Mobei was not the safest option for the Dugur tribe, especially when its chieftain was still trapped in Ghost City. As long as there was no peace between the kingdoms surrounding the desert, the Dugur tribe would never have a place to land. And Wei knew Desert Rose's biggest wish was the well-being of her tribe. No matter where she went, her heart lingered on them.

The unrest would never end unless men like King Falco and Emperor Han were no longer in power.

Wei threw off the covers around him. There was no time to waste.

'What do you think you're doing?' Zeyan said, pushing him back into bed.

Wei fought against his friend's insistence at keeping him in bed. 'We need to get moving, strike while they are still weak.'

He had already spent two weeks out of action. Han would have been rebuilding his campaign, his army, and hunting down the Elementals. There was so much lost time to make up for.

With a firm push, Zeyan forced him to lie back. 'Relax, things need time to simmer. We've already set things in motion. Now, let's get you back in shape before we rush on to the next step.'

Wei ignored Zeyan's suggestion. 'And what news of Meng? Where is he now?'

His half-brother's intentions remained a mystery to him even until now. Some days, Wei pitied him for being a victim of circumstance; on others, his revulsion for Meng and the measures he took to survive and succeed overshadowed any shred of pity or kinship he felt towards his half-brother born on the same moonless night as him. He used to resent Meng for being the favoured child—even though they shared the same birth star—while Wei was declared by High Advisor Mian to be a potential threat to his father's rule. Now, he was no longer convinced that his own fate was worse than Meng's. They were each forced to survive in different ways.

Zeyan shook his head. 'Last we heard, he found the spring with Desert Rose's help and the Dugur clan leaders made the shamans awaken it. But without the Elementals, an awakened spring remains ineffectual.'

All their hope now lay in finding the Elementals. But where could they begin? Even if Desert Rose and Windshadow had likely gone to the Oasis Kingdom in search of the Fire Elemental, whom Wei assumed had survived the battle at Danxi, they could be anywhere in the kingdom. It would be like searching for a needle in a haystack.

'If I may,' a voice spoke up. Everyone turned to look at Yanda, who gestured at the group of five shamans behind her. 'Anar Zel used to do this ritual with the shamans whenever we migrated between seasons. It's how we gather the whole tribe and make sure we leave no one behind. Perhaps we could try to find Rose that way.'

Wei had met the Dugur tribe matriarch when she rescued them in the Darklands last spring. She was immensely powerful and skilled in the natural arts, and her healing powers had nearly restored Wei's mother back to health before the imperial scouts' attack at Ghost City caused their untimely deaths. Despite all her skills, she had been caught off guard by the ambush and died trying to save Wei's mother. Wei hadn't even gotten the chance to thank her for helping them.

'But I thought those were only for shorter distances,' Qara said. 'Can the shamans do it across the desert?'

'It's worth a try,' Wei said. 'The Wall is down, so that's one less barrier. We'll get as close to the Oasis Kingdom as we can for them to perform their ritual.'

'And then?' Beihe asked.

'And then we sneak in at dawn.'

Four

Meng

When Meng was little, when he didn't know any better, he would often ask High Advisor Mian what he was destined for. Everyone seemed to make a huge fuss over his birth star and expected him to amount to great things. His brothers each fought for their own calling—be it power or freedom—but all Meng wanted was to read books and drink tea in the imperial library. He didn't have Han's ambition or Wei's wanderlust or Yong's discipline and sense of duty. He had nothing and no one to fight for. What then was his purpose and what did everyone expect of him?

Now, having discovered the Immortal Spring, he understood at last what it was he sought, what ignited his soul and propelled him forward. Not adventure or power or duty, but knowledge. Discovery of that which eluded rationality and reason and pushed the boundaries of human imagination.

And now he had learned that the mythical spring existed. And after decades—no, centuries—of searching, he was the only one in his lineage to have found it. He could study it, understand it, unlock its mysteries like no one before him had.

Yet, a strange hollowness remained in his chest. It had persisted ever since he had parted ways with Desert Rose and Windshadow to rejoin the Dugur clan leaders. Now, stuck in a desert town with the clan leaders, none of whom he could trust, he was struck by a strange sense of homesickness, for the familiarity and comfort that reuniting—albeit briefly—with Desert Rose and Windshadow had brought. They were the closest to friends he had ever had.

But it seemed as though he was destined for a life adrift and alone now that he was stranded between two kingdoms, unable to call either home.

He no longer had his destiny laid out for him, having abandoned it the moment he fled from the imperial prison with Windshadow last spring. And now he found himself unmoored—heart, body, and soul.

'I still think we should stay with Lettoria for a while longer,' said Gan, one of the clan leaders, his raised voice snapping Meng out of his thoughts. 'There is more we can do there than in Oasis Kingdom or the desert. Falco doesn't know that we have found the spring.'

Meng held back a sigh, wishing he was anywhere right now but stuck in this dingy room in a desert tavern with the clan leaders who were debating on their next steps.

'But now that we know the location of the spring and King Falco is none the wiser, I say we take this knowledge back to the tribe and cut ties with Lettoria from here on,' Huol argued.

'Falco is no fool,' Gan said. 'He would have anticipated our betrayal, and to abandon this alliance now will only leave us stranded before the time is ripe.'

'Falco is a lying, scheming turncoat himself,' Erden piped up. 'He would just as quickly sell us down the White Jade Sea the moment we lose our value to him.'

'Enough,' Blackstone bellowed, looking rather torn himself. He turned to Meng. 'Prince Meng, what do you suggest?'

Meng's impression of Blackstone had changed since their first meeting, when Meng first forged an alliance with them for the Spring Ceremony coup. The clan leader constantly tried to assert authority with the use of brute force, such as how he overthrew the Dugur tribe chieftain last winter, but he had neither the command nor true respect of the other clan leaders. He lacked strategic wit and was easily swayed by his emotions and desire for power. It was only a matter of time before he lost whatever power he had stolen from the tribe chieftain.

'I am now a wanted man in Oasis Kingdom, according to my brother. And now that I no longer have anything to bring to the negotiating table, Lettoria has no place for me. My number of allies runs low,' he admitted. 'But fate favours he who persists. My intention to regain the throne remains unchanged, and there is still a way to be forged forward.'

Han thought he could return to the Oasis Kingdom and turn everyone against Meng, take what he had worked so hard for. He thought he could make use of their mother's favouritism and claw his way to power, that Meng—who had never come to physical blows with anyone in his life—would be too weak to fight back.

But an emperor did not need to employ brute force to remove his enemies or instil fear in his people to win their hearts. He could rule with wit and fairness, and Meng would show his brother just how wrong he was to underestimate him, he who would make a better emperor in the end. There was still much to be done for the kingdom, and Meng would keep trying until his last breath.

While Lettoria might have technically won the battle at Danxi, having torn down Oasis Kingdom's Wall and weakened the Oasis army, it had also suffered its own losses. Both sides were recovering from the battle, and Meng and the Dugur clansmen had the upper hand now that they had located and awakened the spring, with King Falco in the dark since none of his soldiers had made it back to Lettoria to inform him.

But Meng knew better than to think he could control the spring the way his father had intended to. The Immortal Spring, a relic of the gods, was no mortal's to control, and he had no delusions of power over it, much less the desire to use it as a weapon in biological warfare. What he did have was knowledge and information about it, and those things were stronger currency than military might.

Their victory would depend on what they did next with that advantage. Meng and the clan leaders had wanted the same thing—to find the spring—but for different reasons. The clan leaders wanted to use it to gain control of the desert and make the Dugur tribe the strongest of these sands; Meng wanted his kingdom back. As with the partnership with Windshadow, this one with the clan leaders was mutually beneficial.

'King Falco must not know that we have found the spring and awakened it,' said Meng. 'I will seek an audience with the desert lords to rally their support—every bit counts. In the meantime, I need you to be my eyes and ears in Lettoria. Gan is right—Falco has more secrets than we know, and the more of those we unearth, the more we can use that to our advantage.'

Blackstone nodded. 'If they have another secret army that they intend to unleash across the desert on Oasis Kingdom, we will send word. We will also keep an eye on the spring. For too long have we subjected ourselves to exploitation by the likes of Lettoria and the others. This is the one leverage we have over the surrounding kingdoms.'

He didn't utter it, but Meng knew he was referring to the Oasis Kingdom as well. His father had consistently pressured and even plundered the desert tribes in his attempt to gain control of the desert and expand his territory.

This alliance would work only if all of them held up their end of the bargain. Meng didn't know how much the clan leaders could be trusted, but they had come all this way standing on the same side. He would just have to lay his faith in them for a while longer.

'We also need Rose,' Bataar piped up. 'We need to help her survive the prophecy so she can unlock the spring.'

The mention of Desert Rose made Meng falter as his mind churned out a plan. Last he saw her, she still had poison running through her veins, just enough to corrupt her magic without fully killing her. Had she taken the antidote? Did she even survive the battle at Danxi Plains? Meng feared he would never be able to atone for his mistakes towards her. He would much rather find her than meet with the desert lords, but they were set on different paths for now and he could only hope to get the chance to make it up to her someday.

'I'll ask the tribe shamans to help us locate Rose. She's the key to helping us all, and we need to help her succeed,' Bataar went on. He seemed to be convincing his father more than anyone else.

'You said she doesn't trust us anymore,' Blackstone said, making no disguise of his scepticism.

'I believe she will come around when she sees what we're doing for her.'

Blackstone appeared ready to contest that, but he nodded at last. 'You know her best. Do what you deem necessary.' To the other clan leaders, he said, 'We set out at dawn.'

That night, Meng slept soundly for the first time since leaving Oasis Kingdom last spring.

He had a plan now, a renewed sense of purpose and direction that anchored him. He might have been blindsided more times than he should have been—both by his family and his temporary ally—and he might not have Windshadow by his side now or an alliance with Lettoria. But he and the Dugur clan leaders were the only ones who knew where the awakened Immortal Spring was, and he could always forge new alliances.

His methods might have changed, but his goal remained the same. To take back the throne, to reclaim his position as a son of Oasis Kingdom, and to prove that he was the worthiest of all.

* * *

Located on the north-western and south-western border of the Khuzar Desert, Mobei and Monan were strategic cities that served as a buffer between the desert and the western countries, Lettoria and Sorenstein. While they had flourished from the trade between the east and the west via the Red Tea Road, they were often also caught in the precarious position of being allies with both the western countries and the desert tribes.

Meng certainly did not fault Mobei and Monan for playing nice with their neighbours. They were simply looking out for themselves, securing the resources and support they needed from both sides to ensure their own security and prosperity. He had met with the desert lords several times when he served as Oasis Kingdom's ambassador, and found himself sometimes empathizing with their predicament as mediators and liaisons, until he was reminded of how mercenary they were.

This time was no different. The desert lords had long grown weary and frustrated with Lettoria and Sorenstein over issues like trade deficits, labour exploitation, and territorial skirmishes, and with Oasis Kingdom growing stronger economically, their allegiance was starting to shift east as they sought a more equal partnership with the kingdom. Yet, Meng knew that as soon as his kingdom lost its pragmatic value to Mobei and Monan, the desert lords would easily return to Lettoria and Sorenstein's side.

Han might have already branded Meng as a traitor and would likely have his head as soon as he returned to the Oasis Kingdom, and Meng's brief dalliance with Lettoria had shown him that King Falco was not a friend, only a convenient temporary ally. But he was not out of options yet.

He now sat at the tea table in the Mobei lord's living room, aware of how keenly the two desert lords were eyeing him. Here was a rejected son of Oasis Kingdom seeking their assistance, though he called it a *partnership*. With their roles as intermediaries, they had the intel that Meng needed about Lettoria, Sorenstein, and the desert tribes. They had the connections he could tap on to rally the descendants of the Old Kingdom and make his comeback.

But *he* had knowledge of the spring. And that was all anyone ever wanted. No amount of tea or carved gold mirrors or spices was worth what one could derive from the Immortal Spring. Meng knew when he had the upper hand, and also to not give it away too quickly.

He also knew that one was only as strong as the friends he kept, just like a country was only as strong as its allies. And the way to weaken the latter was to cut off its connections and leave it stranded.

'You want us to cease all trade with Oasis Kingdom and Lettoria?' the Monan lord repeated, his perfectly groomed brows raised.

'With Oasis Kingdom under Emperor Han's rule, temporarily,' Meng corrected.

'Oasis Kingdom is our largest trading partner, and Lettoria provides military protection. Ceasing trade with either will greatly cripple us, what more both,' said the Mobei lord. 'What do you propose to compensate for our losses in the meantime?'

Meng could divulge his knowledge of the Immortal Spring. After all, every man who aspired towards power and wealth sought it. The spring was the biggest leverage he had that would certainly make the desert lords agree to an alliance against Han. Yet, any good strategist would know not to reveal his hand all at once. His aim was to gain their support and trust first, before revealing what was in store for them.

'I cannot promise a compensation now,' Meng replied. 'But you have my word that Oasis Kingdom under my rule will offer a fair and beneficial trade with the desert cities.'

'Unfortunately, Prince Meng, your word does not count for much now that you are no longer the ruler of Oasis Kingdom.'

Meng leaned forward on the table and levelled his gaze at them. 'How long do you foresee my brother being on the throne, with the famine and border wars that have been going on ever since my father's rule, and now having lost the recent battle with Lettoria? The Wall is down, and the tide is shifting. Rebellion is brewing within Oasis Kingdom as we speak; it is only a matter of time before Han loses control.'

And even though the Oasis Kingdom's Wall was down, Lettoria had suffered a debilitating loss too—according to the Dugur tribe's scouts, Chryso had met his end on the battlefield at the hands of the Fire Elemental. King Falco would loathe having lost his cherished Metal Elemental. Both the warring kingdoms were now at a stalemate, which made this the best time to strike.

'And you believe you alone can defeat your brother?' the Monan lord asked.

Meng had had encounters with a handful of rebel groups in Oasis Kingdom, one of which was the shouren, whose aid he had employed for the Spring Ceremony coup. They might sometimes be a recalcitrant bunch divided by different agendas internally, but the passionate ones were willing to do what it took to support a cause, especially if it concerned their fate, and they had come through during the Spring Ceremony.

'I have an army,' he said. 'It just needs to be assembled.'

Army was a generous term for what the shouren—the Night Beast Sect—could be. They were a scattered group of various beasts and creatures with varying strengths, abilities, and vulnerabilities. Furthermore, they lacked a leader to unite them, which made them all passion and purpose without strategy.

But now that the Wall was down and magic was pervading Oasis Kingdom, a rebellion—or even a revolution—was on the horizon. The shouren—and certainly the Ling, who had always held the belief that they were robbed of their kingdom—would now have more purpose and faith in their ability to turn the tides. They were aligned in their goal to overthrow his brother.

'Oasis Kingdom is a significant trade partner of ours,' said the Monan lord. 'Emperor Han, in particular, has been importing large amounts of magical arms. Our economic partnership has never been stronger.'

Meng's ears pricked. Magical arms. What was Han doing smuggling large amounts of magical arms into the kingdom? Could he be building an army to rival Lettoria?

'Should I remind you that magic is still outlawed, even though the Wall has been taken down?' Meng said, quelling his excitement at the unintentional discovery. 'Any import of magic—what more magical weapons—is considered illegal and will have to be smuggled in.'

The lords exchanged a glance, shifting in their seats.

'Emperor or not, treason of the highest order is a sure-fire way to lose the throne.' Meng took a sip of his tea. 'I just need time to rally against Han and find the opportune moment to charge him in court. Meanwhile, your cooperation is very much appreciated and will be repaid when I take back the throne.'

He didn't mention his final weapon against Han: the scroll. The one that Desert Rose and Windshadow had retrieved from the White Crypt last winter, the one that contained *Duru-shel Minta*, the clue to unlocking all the dormant magic within the kingdom. The less people knew about the scroll, the larger the advantage—and element of surprise—Meng possessed.

His mother had disapproved of his intention to unlock the magic in the kingdom when he was emperor, instead focusing more on bringing back Han and solidifying their control of the court. Now, he could do all that he had meant to do without the burden of his title. Now that he was known as a rebel son who had defected to the enemy, no one was expecting him to stand on a moral high ground anymore.

All this while, being dutiful had never gotten him anywhere; it had only allowed others to betray him and cast him aside as soon as he had served his purpose. Even his own mother had forsaken him in favour of her elder son, despite everything Meng had done for the family.

At times, he wished he possessed Windshadow's callousness, Desert Rose's dogged passion, or even Wei's impulsiveness. Perhaps then, no one would underestimate him, and no one would doubt his capabilities.

It was never too late to change their minds.

He could still make a comeback, one that was beyond Han and his mother's expectations. He no longer needed to play nice or play by the rules. If taking the throne back meant he had to start a rebellion and overthrow his brother, then he would start building his own army now.

Keep your plans deep and unfathomable for them to strike as hard as a thunderbolt.

—The War Handbook, Lu Cao

Five

Desert Rose

Desert Rose never thought she would see Qiu again, though it shouldn't have come as a surprise that Qiu would appear around these parts. The Lost Princess had made Yeli Mountain her home, together with the fox-man she had eloped with.

Mostly, Desert Rose was just relieved to see her alive. After the disastrous uprising during the Spring Ceremony in the imperial palace, a good number of shouren had been captured and likely imprisoned or executed. Qiu hadn't been personally involved in the operation, but her brother-in-law, Zhong, had been a part of it. And given that the uprising had been instigated by the Dugur clan leaders, the very ones who had overthrown her father last winter, Desert Rose somehow felt responsible for the shouren's current predicament.

She glanced behind her now, half-hoping to see Windshadow sweeping through the dense foliage to catch up with them. After weeks of travelling together, her absence now felt jarring. But no one was behind her—no desert girl or stray gust of wind. Wherever Windshadow had fled, it was far from where she was now.

Ahead of her, Qiu deftly picked her way through the undergrowth with a broken twig. The sound of a flowing brook in the distance guided them through the forest, coupled by a lone bird call. Desert Rose had first met the princess on this very mountain, when she had snuck into her house to hunt down her mark, Golsha, for a House of Night mission. Qiu seemed perfectly at home in these parts, as though she had grown up here all her life instead of in the palace.

'Come on, we mustn't dawdle. They might still catch up with us,' Qiu said with a brief glance over her shoulder.

Desert Rose hurried to catch up with her. 'What were you doing at that inn?' As far as she knew, Qiu and the shouren rarely ventured out of the mountain for fear of capture. Perhaps with magic now seeping back into the Oasis Kingdom, it was harder for the shouren to be detected?

'There's been a spate of murders lately in Yeli Town, and some villagers are starting to organize a shouren hunting party,' Qiu said. A crease settled between her brows. 'We were there to investigate for ourselves.'

The shouren were a scattered bunch united mainly by their frustration at being persecuted for centuries. For them to emerge from hiding meant that this was a matter of grave importance. Qiu herself ventured down the mountain only to sell the herbs she picked to earn a living. They had been scapegoated for many of the crimes around the kingdom—with the most recent one being the murder of the Crown Prince Yong last winter—but never had they shown themselves in public the way Qiu's fox husband had today at the inn.

'We can make it back by nightfall if we take the shortcut.' Qiu peered at her face. 'But you don't look like you're up for it?'

Desert Rose was quite certain she wasn't. It wasn't just the journey or the dramatic getaway from the scouts earlier that had depleted her; it was her magic, sitting inside her like a firecracker waiting to be ignited. Back in Lettoria, King Falco had deliberately ordered for his physicians to leave enough of the poison inside her so that he could continue holding her hostage and make Wei obey him.

The antidote Meng had acquired for her sat tucked in her tunic, still untouched. From the battle at Danxi to journeying through the Oasis Kingdom undercover, she hadn't had time to think about taking it. Further, she wasn't sure if she could trust an antidote that King Falco had provided.

'I'm fine,' she said anyway in reply to Qiu.

But Qiu shook her head. 'We could rest for a night at an inn along the way—that might give us more time to investigate the deaths too.'

Desert Rose shook her head. 'It's too risky, with the scouts still on our trail. We should get to shouren territory as soon as we can.'

Qiu gave a tentative nod. 'If you're sure you're up for it . . .'

'I am.' She would push herself for the remainder of the way if she had to. Every moment she was out here with Qiu, she was putting her in danger too.

Qiu was watching her as though contemplating her next words. 'By the way . . . Wei didn't come back with you?' It sounded as though she had been waiting to ask that question for a while.

A fresh wave of pain washed over Desert Rose as the memory of his falling body made nausea rise in her throat. She had been powerless to save him. If only she had gotten there sooner . . .

She shook her head in response to Qiu, unable to utter the words. That he would not be coming back. That she had come for him too late.

The princess understood right away, her eyes already welling up with tears. 'How did he . . .?'

'Han pushed him off the watchtower.'

Rage gathered in Qiu's eyes at once, hardening her gentle features. Desert Rose recalled how happy she and Wei had been to reunite last winter in Yeli Mountain, how easily they teased each other, and the pride in Wei's eyes when he looked at his sister. She wished more than anything that he was here now to see his sister again.

'Han will pay for this. It's only a matter of time.' Qiu seemed almost certain about his eventual downfall, almost as though she knew something was in store for him. Were the shouren planning another coup? Who were the ones backing them this time if Meng was no longer in the Oasis Kingdom?

'Come,' Qiu said, as though she had heard her thoughts. 'There are some people you might want to meet.'

They forged ahead, this time mostly in silence as they each processed the loss of Wei. Desert Rose forced herself to concentrate on her surroundings—she would not give in to her grief, not now when there was so much left to do.

Covered in fall foliage, the forest was now a riot of colours. The dappled morning sunlight turned the leaves amber, scarlet, and gold, and the sounds of a running brook and distant bird calls made her forget her natural aversion to the mountains. For some reason, she could appreciate how peaceful it was here this time, despite still being on the run from imperial scouts and having poisoned magic inside her.

Perhaps her limited time on earth made her more appreciative of the fleeting beauty around her.

They arrived before a dirt road just as Qiu announced that they were a quarter of the way up the mountain. The road wound towards a copse of trees, behind which stood a three-storey roadhouse with a crooked roof.

Desert Rose halted in her tracks just as she stepped out onto the road. Something niggled at her. A force, an energy that lingered in the forest like a silk blanket trailing behind her.

She inched forward in the direction of the force, quickening her footsteps as it grew stronger. Faint footprints tracked through the mud, leading her to a maple tree surrounded by a bed of its own fallen leaves.

Remnant qi rose in wisps from the damp earth. Desert Rose could feel the energy emanating from the ground, almost as though it was calling out to her. But something about it felt sinister, twisted, almost like dark magic. It hung heavy in the air, much like the poison sitting inside her.

She glanced at Qiu, who had caught up with her and now peered at her in concern. 'Something's not right here.'

Qiu gasped and pointed at something at the foot of the tree, where a hand was peeking out. They went around it and found the corpse of a middle-aged man perched against the tree, his lips already blue and his face ashen. There were no noticeable wounds or injuries on his body, or any indication of distress before he passed away. He seemed to have simply sat down by the tree and died. Yet, his position appeared to be too carefully arranged for it to have been accidental.

'Another one,' Qiu murmured, checking his pulse. She sighed. 'Dead.'

Desert Rose inspected the body from head to toe. The remnant energy buzzing off it reached for her, pulling her in. She could feel her magic answering its call, roiling inside her like an animal riled up. She was reaching out to it before she realized what she was doing, until a wave of nausea rose in her throat, threatening to engulf her.

She snatched her hand back and staggered away from the corpse. Her skin continued to buzz, leaving her shaking and her breaths shallow, hindering her attempt at appearing unaffected. Qiu was watching her, uncomprehending and unable to help, but she probed no further when Desert Rose stepped away from the tree.

They left the body behind and took off down the dirt road without a backward glance. Still, the oppressive qi continued to tail Desert Rose like a mournful soul she couldn't shake off.

Something else was at work here, something powerful that was not the shouren. And they were getting closer to it.

* * *

The trek up Yeli Mountain was a treacherous one, filled with vine-strewn dirt paths and lichen-covered boulders that they had to sidestep, often at their peril since the paths lay right next to the edge of the cliff.

Desert Rose's breathing grew laboured as they went higher and the paths grew slicker and narrower. The mountain was still and silent, laced in fog so dense that it was nearly impossible to tell where they were. But Qiu cut through it with the confidence of someone who had trekked down this path countless times, glancing back on occasion to make sure Desert Rose was close behind her.

When they came to a stop at last, the sun was well overhead and the fog had cleared to reveal an outcrop—the very same one Desert Rose had been to last winter that concealed a cave deep enough for Qiu and her husband, Heyang, to make a surprisingly cosy and adequately furnished home.

But the cave was apparently deeper than Desert Rose realized, extending to a larger area behind the kitchen and storage area where Qiu stored her herbs. That area was now packed with an assortment of humans and animals—wolves, cougars, boars, deer, foxes, hares, and more milled about, some tending to minor injuries, others jittery and pacing in circles.

The shouren.

Qiu scanned the crowd anxiously before finally spotting her husband. 'Yang,' she cried in relief, dashing into his open arms. The fox-man appeared to have emerged from the earlier tumult in the inn unscathed. Desert Rose exchanged a glance with him, conveying her gratitude for his help in distracting the scouts, and he nodded back. Next to him, his younger brother, Zhong, watched her with a sceptical eye.

Unsure of what to do, she remained by the entrance, surveying each shouren, who in turn eyed her with unnervingly steady gazes. Her last encounter with the shouren had involved a fire that had destroyed their home, leaving them stranded in winter. Given that she clearly looked like a desert-bred foreigner, she stood out amongst the shouren like a sore thumb.

Qiu came over to her and sat her down in a chair. The cave looked just as Desert Rose remembered it, right down to the jug of milk on the dining table in the living room.

'We found another body,' Qiu said, glancing at Desert Rose, as though expecting her to supplement more information.

'I felt its qi and . . . something else,' Desert Rose said, recalling the ominous energy she felt tangled up with the remnants of the dead man's soul.

Heyang exchanged a look with his brother Zhong. A collective murmur buzzed around the other shouren.

'Soul snatchers,' Heyang said at last.

'Soul snatchers?' Desert Rose echoed.

He nodded. 'They belong to the Black Lotus Sect, we believe—dark magic practitioners who harvest souls for their qi. Of course, there could be other sects at work, but the pattern of attacks seems to point to the Black Lotus Sect.' A furrow worked its way between his brows. 'Something is different lately. More and more sects seem to be crawling out of the woodwork now, and they're becoming bolder in their operations.'

'The Wall is down,' Desert Rose supplied. 'The Lettorians tore it down two weeks ago in a battle.'

A stunned silence seized everyone. Someone gasped. Some shifted back into human form, their faces grim; others fell completely still, pausing their fidgeting or pacing.

For as long as these people had probably known, the Wall had guarded the kingdom from magic; now that it was gone, the energies of the kingdom were in flux, and the dynamics had shifted. The ruling class, decidedly mortal, no longer had absolute power over those with magic running in their veins. What was to happen now?

'That explains the growing audacity of the sects,' Heyang said, breaking the silence. 'The Ling have always kept a low profile until now. They must have felt a shift in the energies when the Wall came down. My hunch is that they are starting to prepare.'

'Prepare for what?' Desert Rose asked.

Heyang's face was the grimmest Desert Rose had ever seen. 'The rebellion. To take over the throne.'

'Then we must leave,' a woman said, clutching her young rabbit-pawed son close to her. 'I don't want to be part of any rebellion. Not if it means endangering my family's life.'

'I agree,' another man with stag ears replied. 'We are helpless against the more powerful sects. I'm not sitting around waiting for them to come and steal my qi or drag me into a war with the Imperial Army.'

'Are they powerful enough to fight an Elemental?' Zhong said. He turned to Desert Rose, his gaze even more challenging now. 'That's what you are, aren't you?'

Every pair of eyes fell upon her. Desert Rose's voice died in her throat.

'She saved us from a fire before, using her magic,' Zhong went on. 'If there's anyone powerful enough to fend off the other sects, it would be her.'

'An Elemental?' someone said, eyeing her up and down. 'What would a desert-born Elemental be doing here on Yeli Mountain?'

She could tell them the truth. That she was here to find the Earth Elemental and could use some help. That she intended to fulfil the prophecy to save her father and her tribe. That she had been poisoned and that using her power now could kill her. But how much of it would the shouren believe? And why did she have to explain herself to a group of people she held no allegiance to?

Furthermore, she knew nothing about the Black Lotus Sect and had no idea what to expect. How could she begin to fight them off and protect the shouren?

A murmur had risen from the shouren as they considered Zhong's proposal. They were afraid, Desert Rose realized. The beast-people had spent so long hiding in the shadows, fearing persecution, and after the defeat during the Spring Ceremony, where several shouren were captured for the uprising in the palace, they no longer had the gall nor fervour to take on another strong adversary.

Qiu shifted closer to her and addressed the crowd. 'Let's be reasonable here. Rose has no obligation to help us, nor can she fight against the other sects alone. We just narrowly escaped imperial scouts. We can all get some rest first and then come up with a plan. The snatchers won't attempt to take on all of us so soon after the last attack.'

But before anyone could consider her suggestion, a hare scurried in, skirting past legs and dashing straight to the middle of the living room, where he morphed into a gangly teenage boy. His eyes were wild with panic as he glanced around at everyone.

'They're here,' he panted. 'The snatchers got one of us.'

The Ling (灵)

Little is known about the Ling, Children of the Moon. This esoteric group of magical beings and magic practitioners have lived in hiding within the Oasis Kingdom ever since the Great Purge that the First Oasis Emperor ordered upon the establishment of the Zhao dynasty.

Many believe that the Ling descended from the last ruling family of the Hesui Kingdom before the Oasis Emperor defeated them and came to power. Others believe that the Great Purge had caused the magic to go out of balance within the land and infused regular mortals with magic by accident. Yet others believe that the Ling are distantly related to the Damohai, the descendants of immortals. After all, the Damohai consist of various beings from beast-people to shamans, soothsayers, and mediums.

Whatever their origins, it is widely known that the Ling's magic is derived from nature to form their qi, the life force that they spend years cultivating. Their magic and their qi are intrinsically tied together; one cannot exist without the other. Therefore, to steal or remove (for energy cannot be destroyed) a Ling's magic is to kill them. This has naturally led to hierarchies and constant infighting, for even the Ling are not exempt from greed and lust for power.

The Ling have been scattered for centuries, splitting up into many factions and organized into hierarchical sects, each with their own set of rules, customs, and practices. Sect order is distinguished by colour. For instance, the White Ling Sect (白灵教) is the highest sect that rules over the entire Ling population, including the Yellow Star Sect and Blue Mountain Sect. The colour within the name may indicate the sect's rank, but there are also various other smaller sects at the bottom of the hierarchy, such as the Night Beast Sect consisting of the shouren.

Most sects generally do not have much to do with one another, partly because of their differences in customs, beliefs, and such, and partly to avoid congregation and the notice of non-magical folk. In the magic-intolerant Oasis Kingdom, to possess or display magic is to seek a death sentence, and the Ling are too weak and scattered to bring about a revolution to overthrow the imperial family.

In general, sects within the Ling fare differently due to their inherent magical capabilities or prowess.

The White Ling Sect is said to comprise the remaining descendants of Hesui Kingdom's last ruling family, making them a group of royalty among the Ling. They also include high-level sorcerers, making them the strongest and most self-sustaining sect.

Lower-level sects like the Three Stone Sect may have to resort to petty crime and trickery to get by or to blend in with the locals, while mid-level ones like the Red Moon Sect and the Blue Mountain Sect may compete to get into the good books of the White Ling sect for more protection or resources.

Ling sects are constantly evolving, growing, or shrinking as a result of their rivalry, territorial wars, and shifting alliances. Yet, despite the numerous factions within the population and their internal divisions, the Ling are believed to share one common goal: to take back their kingdom and regain their place as the ruling class.

That, however, appears to be a pipe dream for as long as magic within Oasis Kingdom remains locked up. Until then, the Ling continue to live in the shadows of Yeli Mountain, waiting for the day the moon turns the tides in their favour.

—Excerpt from *Tales from the Old Kingdom Vol. I: Myths and Magic,* by Lu Ji Fang

Six

Windshadow

Yeli Mountain spoke its own language, one that Windshadow had no knowledge of. All her life, she had only known the desert, until she came to the Oasis Kingdom and grew familiar with the inside of the palace walls.

The mountains pressed close around them, bellies full with secrets and history. It had seen things, centuries upon centuries of tumult, rebellions, and persecution. The prosperity of a kingdom and the moral decay of its leaders. It had seen men try to take the place of gods and now it was about to see the descendants of the gods try to take back the world.

They were barely a fifth of the way up the mountain, and the dense, overgrown forest made their climb slow and riddled with obstacles, especially since they had chosen the shortcut. An unsettling silence sat upon the forest like a woollen blanket. Even the cries of wild animals in the distance were muffled.

Windshadow glanced at Lazar trekking next to her, holding out a little ball of flame for warmth and light in the fog. She could kill him now. They were alone in this deserted forest, and she had the advantage here—she could disguise herself in the fog and gain the element of surprise if she attacked, while Lazar's power would only make him stand out.

But as tempting as the idea was, she knew that they were stronger together. On their own, their energies were still weak from the battle at Danxi Plains. If they were to hunt down and destroy the Earth

Elemental, who likely had his qi intact from not being involved in the battle, they needed to draw on each other's strength for now.

Lazar glanced over at her, smirking as though he had heard her thoughts. 'We lost them.'

'What?'

'We've shaken off the emperor's scouts. We're no longer being watched by them.'

Windshadow could no longer catch the telltale flash of vermilion and black uniform behind them. Yet, she couldn't shake off the feeling that they were still being tailed.

A movement out of the corner of her eye made her pause and hold her breath. Adrenaline rose in her, sharpening her senses. Was it an animal? One of the shouren living in this part of the mountains? But no, the form and movement were distinctly human. Did an imperial scout somehow manage to track them down after all?

She shared a look with Lazar, who seemed to have noticed the extra company too. He gave her a subtle nod and they pressed on, readying their magic.

Three steps in, a faint rustle came from their left.

They were being followed. And whoever it was, they were watching them now, biding their time. It was easy to stay hidden in this fog, but unless they had abilities like hers, no attack would go undetected.

As though on cue, a whoosh of wind on her right sent her swerving away on reflex. The gleam of a blade cut through the gloom, just inches away from her neck. Mortal weapons—good. Anything mortal could be killed. She grabbed the attacker's arm and wrenched it towards her, then elbowed him in the gut and the face. He gave a grunt and rolled away, just as another figure in black descended on her from a nearby fir tree.

There were five of them, each clad in identical black tunics and masks.

Three feet away from her, Lazar was fending off the third attacker with a fireball that he lobbed viciously at him. Aflame, the attacker's cries trailed into the distance as he stumbled away, leaving the other two to swoop in on Lazar.

Windshadow's own duel with her attacker was not over. This one was female, she realized when she reached for her neck and grabbed her shoulder instead. The girl's agility and speed were almost comparable to hers, a Wind Elemental. Whatever she lacked in brawn, she more than made up for it.

Who *were* these people?

It wasn't until they got close enough for Windshadow to catch a whiff of the girl's aura that she understood. Her body was mortal, but her energy was more elevated than a regular mortal's. She had no supernatural powers, but she could draw energy from nature to enhance her abilities. She had to be a magic practitioner, most likely one of the Ling.

Yet, something was different about her qi. It felt denser than that cultivated through nature, as though weighed down by an ominous force. This was dark magic, potent and coagulating, drawn directly from the earth. Was this a sign that the Earth Elemental was indeed in these parts?

Before she could strike out at the girl or shift into her elemental form, a shout came from one of them. Almost immediately, a pungent scent crept into the air, a heady mix of rotten eggs, nectarines, and something else Windshadow couldn't pinpoint. A black cloud convened right above her, pulling close like a fast-gathering storm.

It took less than three heartbeats for the toxic gas to knock her out.

* * *

The crackle of a fire made her jerk awake. She roused to find herself lying on a bed next to a fireplace in a rather spacious bedchamber. The noxious gas still left her light-headed, but she felt physically intact otherwise. She struggled to sit up, then took a moment to regain her bearings.

As far as she could tell, she was alone in the chamber. Where were her attackers? Had she been rescued? What happened to Lazar?

The bed was hard, with a thin cotton sheet that barely provided any warmth. As soon as the dizziness wore off, she threw off the covers and got out of bed to survey the room. It was adequately furnished, with utilitarian furnishings and no personal effects to provide further information about its owner—a small table in the middle of the room upon which a pewter pitcher and two clay cups sat, a wooden chest of drawers, and a dressing table with a grimy bronze mirror.

She slid the door open and peered out. Night had just set in . . . how long had she been unconscious? A smattering of stars was sprinkled across the sky, and the lonely silence indicated that she was still in the mountains. She recalled, amid her stupor earlier, being in an open-top carriage and going over a bump at a fork in the road. One path led towards a steep trail that would lead them further up the mountain, and the other towards a flat road that wound into a wall of trees. The carriage had veered right, into the wall of trees that clearly led them into this far-flung, isolated manor.

The manor seemed like a traditional *siheyuan*, though it sprawled larger than the ones in the Capital, with generous courtyards bordered by widely spaced one-storey buildings. Yet, despite being situated in the middle of the rural mountains, this manor—albeit nondescript—seemed well maintained, nothing like the dilapidated huts of the countryside.

Who owned this place? More importantly, why was she brought here?

She would find out.

The tip of a sword approached her throat just as she was about to step out of the room. She froze and levelled her gaze at the newcomer. He was slightly older than her, with sharp brows that pulled together as he appraised her, a hooked nose that made him look extra hawkish, and a scar that ran along his left jaw. His black tunic was stark against the overcast sky and grey eaves behind him, and a tuft of loose hair flapped in the chilly mountain breeze.

He took a step forward, forcing her to take one back into the room. Only when both of them were fully inside did he lower his sword.

'What a warm welcome,' Windshadow said, eyeing the blade as the boy sheathed it by his side. 'You shouldn't have rescued me if you didn't trust me.'

'Who said I was rescuing you?' he said. 'You forget we were the ones who assailed you in the forest earlier.'

'You wouldn't have tucked me in bed if you didn't have use for me. So quit beating around the bush and tell me what it is you want.'

The boy smirked. 'You are just as mouthy as the other Elemental.'

She ignored him. He didn't know for certain that she was an Elemental yet—she hadn't revealed her abilities in the forest—and she was not about to confirm it. 'Where am I? Who are you? Why did you bring me here?' she demanded.

'Just as inquisitive too.' He headed over to the table in the middle of the room and poured her a cup of what appeared to be water. Windshadow was parched, but she refused to drink it when he offered her the cup. The boy shrugged and set it down. 'Follow me then.'

They stepped out into the courtyard. Save for the usual stone lion statues there were no other embellishments to the manor. Apart from the fact that it was the only one in these parts, it appeared to be just another common housing compound, except that its blackened roofs and weathered stone statues standing on guard made it look more austere than usual.

'This place used to belong to an old imperial physician who came here to provide his services to the poor after he retired from court. After he died, this place was abandoned. The Black Lotus Sect decided to take over and spruce it up.' He knocked on a sturdy looking pillar next to him. 'Nothing too elaborate, but it's cosy enough for all of us.'

'The Black Lotus Sect?' Windshadow raised a brow at him.

She had heard a lot of things about the Black Lotus Sect, many of which involved black magic, ruthless guerrilla attacks, and human sacrifice. In fact, she wouldn't be surprised if they were the ones behind the recent spate of grisly murders. The boy seemed too young to be a formidable black magic sorcerer, but Windshadow knew better than to underestimate him.

'Isn't the Black Lotus Sect supposed to be a myth?' she said instead, making sure her condescension came through.

His gaze sharpened at her. 'All myths came from some form of truth. *You* are supposed to be one too.'

Again, she refused to rise to the bait.

'You can continue to play dumb all you want, but we're trying to build a rebellion here,' said the boy. 'So either you help us overthrow the emperor or find us someone who will.'

In the distance came a faint, low chanting, filling the compound with a constant urgent buzz. It was distracting, to say the least, and Windshadow had the sense that the chanting wasn't some sort of religious prayer. The boy offered no explanation for it and continued eyeing her, waiting for her response.

Windshadow surveyed him back. So the Black Lotus Sect did intend to seize power, but they were still too weak to do so. 'What makes you think you can overthrow them?' she asked at last.

'The Imperial Army has been weakened after the battle. And with the Wall taken down, Emperor Han's control over the kingdom is tenuous at best.'

'How do you know about the Wall coming down?'

'We can feel the shift in energies, of course. That, and our scouts have been tracking the situation in the Imperial Army. Emperor Han did not just inherit the throne, he also inherited the border wars and the famine and the growing unrest in various parts. Coupled with the shift in energy, the kingdom is slipping quicker into chaos by the day. Now is the time to strike, and we need all the help we can get.'

'So you think you and your Black Lotus friends are up to the task?'

'The emperor is building his own special army, according to our scouts. If we can destroy that—along with the Imperial Army—we can deliver a huge blow to his sovereignty.'

Windshadow had no doubt that Han was fortifying his personal guard now that the Wall was down and Oasis Kingdom was vulnerable to magic from the outside. Underneath all that sharp-toothed belligerence, he was deeply insecure, and sought protection and power to maintain his chokehold on the kingdom.

She glanced at the boy askance. 'You think a little sect like this is able to take on the entire Imperial Army?'

'The good news is, we're not alone in this. Almost all the Ling sects are coming together for the cause, which is quite a miracle, if you are aware of all the infighting that's been going on all this while.' He nodded at her. 'And then, of course, we now have two Elementals on our side, one of whom was the emperor's right-hand man.'

'I wouldn't be so sure about his loyalty to the sect,' Windshadow said. 'What is it the sages say? "Capture a man physically, and you will have a slave for a day; capture his mind and you will have a servant for life"?'

Lazar certainly belonged to no one, not even Han, who had thus far provided him with the protection and support he needed to survive in this kingdom. Windshadow did not trust him to stay true to any person or course of action, much less an agenda like overthrowing Han that hardly benefited him.

The boy nodded. 'The Fire Elemental is indeed unpredictable, but he has his uses.' His expression turned sombre. 'My parents and grandparents were part of the Black Lotus Sect, and my sister and I will continue their legacy and finish their life's work. This kingdom will experience true justice one day. We will fight for our place in it, and we will make them pay for what they did to us.'

Windshadow understood vengeance. She herself was fuelled by it and had relied on it many times in her life to survive.

'For centuries, we have been weak and oppressed, shunned and persecuted. Now that the kingdom is in flux, this is the best time to strike,' said the boy.

'That's all well and good, but I have no interest in the fate of this kingdom or whose hands it falls into,' said Windshadow. 'I only have one purpose for coming back here—'

'To find the Earth Elemental.' He chuckled, as though amused by her foolishness. 'He is not someone you can hunt down if he chooses not to reveal himself. He is more powerful than you can imagine.' He turned to stare at the snow-coated face of the mountain looming in the distance over the roofs of the siheyuan. 'The mountain stands tall because of him. The forest remains verdant despite the many fires and droughts it has experienced. And all the inhabitants—all the Ling sects, including us—have been concealed and protected thus far because of him. He draws life from the very earth we stand on, and in turn nourishes it, imbuing in it his magic.' He glanced at her. 'He has spent years in isolation cultivating his magic while you and the other

Elementals were out there fighting meaningless battles and wasting your qi. You think you and your fiery friend can take him on in your current state?'

'No more than you think your little sect can overthrow Emperor Han,' Windshadow retorted, refusing to concede to the doubt that the boy had sowed in her mind. Indeed, she had spent all these years being Prince Meng's spy and expending her magic on petty duels and battles that did not take her closer to her goal of becoming the last Elemental.

'We're not just going to overthrow the emperor, silly,' the boy scoffed. 'What would be the point of that? They're just going to find another emperor to replace him, and the system will remain the same; we will continue to be oppressed by the mortals in power.'

Windshadow bit back a note of irritation. 'Then what? What's the plan?'

His eyes gleamed, looking almost otherworldly in the grey gloom. 'We're going to annihilate the entire imperial family and end the Zhao dynasty.' He held out a hand. 'Join us, and you can be sure the Earth Elemental will reveal himself to you.'

Seven

Desert Rose

Desert Rose had no knowledge of the Ling beyond what Qiu and the shouren had told her. Nothing had prepared her for a face-to-face encounter with the snatchers. Even if she was able to employ her magic, they still had the element of surprise on their side. But it beat sitting ducks inside the cave and waiting for the Ling to surround them. If nothing else, she could let herself be taken and find out what their affiliations were, whether they could lead her to the Earth Elemental.

Most of the young and able-bodied shouren had already shifted into their animal form, ready to face the snatchers. Desert Rose whipped out her double knives and headed out the cave with them. Whatever was coming next was anyone's guess. Wei had once shared a teaching from *The War Handbook* with her—*to know neither one's enemy nor oneself is to succumb in every battle.* And she was walking into this blind—quite literally.

The vicinity was clear, though cloaked in a thick fog that made it hard to see beyond ten feet away. It was evident the enemy was trying to divert them further away from the cave to launch an attack on them. But they followed the hare-boy anyway, moving in packs of four since it was easier to travel in small groups to avoid being noticed than having the entire group compromised.

Desert Rose advanced alongside Heyang and Zhong, both padding stealthily as brown and black foxes, barely making a sound in the thick silence. Qiu had insisted on coming along as well, despite having no special advantage apart from the stash of poisonous herbs tucked in her pocket to use as defence.

They ventured far enough for Desert Rose to start wondering if the hare-boy had made a mistake and imagined the threat. How could he be sure they were snatchers? This part of the woods was so desolate it seemed as though no one had been here in decades. The undergrowth had flourished, creating a plush blanket riddled with moss-covered rocks and revealing no tracks in the ground. The fog, so dense it almost stifled her senses, wasn't helping either.

A rustling of leaves made them come to a dead halt. Footsteps—several pairs of them—raced around the clearing, making it hard to tell which direction they were coming from.

Desert Rose shared a look with Qiu. As discussed, they split up instantly, diving in opposite directions so that they wouldn't both be targeted at once.

The snatchers seemed to swoop down from the sky, though they had likely only been perched on the trees. They moved with unnatural stealth, going undetected until they had the four of them surrounded. There were five of them, all dressed in identical black tunics and masks, and wielding weapons varying from bows and arrows to daggers.

They were skilled with their weapons, but they didn't seem to need them anyway. They positioned themselves in a circle around them and, with a collective wave of their arms, dispersed the fog. As soon as the fog dissipated, Desert Rose could sense their qi. This was why they hadn't noticed them earlier—the fog had masked their energies and obscured their physical presence. Their dark, heavy energy seemed to come directly from the earth, as though the snatchers were drawing from the mountain's ancient, bottomless source of magic.

Had the other packs of shouren ventured far? Could they count on them for backup? There was no way the four of them here—two foxes, an Elemental with poisoned magic, and a mortal princess—could take on these Ling.

Qiu was the most vulnerable one here. The shouren could shift whenever they needed to and rely on their keen animal instincts to save themselves. Desert Rose had her double knives, at the very least. But Qiu was only human, and untrained in combat.

'Heyang,' Desert Rose murmured to the brown fox next to her. 'Take Qiu and leave. I'll handle these people.'

Heyang spared only a moment's hesitation before shifting into his human form. 'You cannot defeat them on your own when you don't know the extent of their abilities,' he said.

'There she is,' a familiar voice drawled, interrupting them. Desert Rose spun around, her hackles raised.

Lazar. He sauntered through the fog in his usual cocky demeanour. Gone were the vermilion and black robes that he used to wear as part of the imperial guard. Now, he was dressed in a black tunic like the rest, though he was unmasked.

Somehow, it didn't surprise Desert Rose to learn that the Fire Elemental was a turncoat who had now hopped from Emperor Han's side to the Ling's. His loyalties seemed to always lie with the highest bidder who could offer the most protection at any point in time.

The last time she had seen him was at Danxi Plains, where he had literally cooked the Metal Elemental alive in his armour. Fire was a naturally destructive element, but Lazar's power seemed to be the strongest out of all the Elementals she had encountered. She was no match for him in her current state.

'Nice to see you again, azzi,' Lazar said.

'Can't say I agree with that sentiment,' Desert Rose retorted. 'I quite enjoyed thinking that you died at Danxi Plains.'

He nodded, as though agreeing with her opinion on the mountain air. 'It must have been comforting to think that you have one less competitor.' He threw out his arms and sent twin bursts of flames her way. 'Sorry to disappoint.'

She dove out of the way, trying to catch a glimpse of the others. Who were these snatchers and why had Lazar decided to team up with them?

Zhong shifted back on his two human feet too, wearing his usual irritable scowl as he turned to Desert Rose. 'If you're going to reminisce about old times with your friend, then the rest of us will get going.'

One of the snatchers waved a hand, gathering the fog into a dense cloud that turned a putrid shade of yellow and launched it at Zhong. It obscured his entire head at once, stopping him in his tracks before he could leave. In no time, Zhong collapsed to the ground, his fingers scrabbling at the dirt as he choked.

Heyang turned to the snatchers. 'Please. My brother means no harm.'

A couple of the snatchers relented, but the others remained unyielding. Zhong's choking eased enough for him to speak. He grabbed Heyang's arm. 'It's not us they want,' he rasped, his face still obscured by the cloud. 'They want the Elemental girl.'

Qiu stepped closer to Desert Rose, but as the cloud shifted closer to her, Heyang pulled her out of the way.

How were they to fight against a weapon like that? Desert Rose glanced at the double knives in her hands. Would she be able to drive them into Lazar's heart? Even if she were, what hope did they all have of escaping the snatchers? They all had magic on their side; without using hers, she might as well surrender now.

She would just have to give it a shot. Hopefully, she could buy the rest some time to flee. She stashed her knives back to her waist belt and threw out her hands. Multiple jets of water struck each of the snatchers in the chest. The cloud around Zhong dissipated as the snatchers flew backwards and crashed to the ground, unconscious.

It worked. Her magic still worked. It didn't feel like it used to, as though it filled up every corner of her soul and made her feel alive, in her element. Just like back at Yarshe Valley, it felt like a foreign creature writhing and snapping inside her.

'Go,' Desert Rose urged Heyang and Qiu as Zhong scrambled to his feet. '*Now.*'

Heyang nodded once at her, then grabbed Qiu's hand and towed her away despite her protests. Zhong was already sprinting through the forest, back to where they came from.

Twin whips of fire lashed out at her, singeing her sleeves. She spun away, just barely escaping the attack, and ducked behind a fir tree. She scanned the clearing for Lazar. Now that the fog had cleared, he stood in stark contrast against the trees just five feet in front of her, flanked by two Ling. The remaining three Ling had scattered, likely going after Qiu and the shouren.

Lazar flashed her his usual smirk and threw out his hands again, flinging the fiery whips at her. This time, one of them caught her by the wrist. White-hot pain ripped through her, driving every thought out of her mind until all she felt was the sensation around her wrist. She had the vague sense of being reeled towards Lazar, but no amount of struggling worked.

'Do you know how easy it would be for me to finish you off right now?' Lazar hissed against her ear. 'You are the weakest among all of us.'

Don't give in, Rose, she urged herself. She might not be as powerful as Lazar, nor had she spent as much time as Windshadow in honing her magic, but she wasn't the weakest. All the elements were equal—they could complement each other as much as destroy each other—and her element was exactly the thing needed to put out a fire.

She mustered every bit of moisture she could find around her—from the gentle mist to the distant running brook, the dewdrops on the leaves, the sheets of ice on the mountaintops—and even from inside her, and willed it to fight against the Fire Elemental's attack. A cool blanket seemed to flow over her skin, and when she glanced down at her wrist, she found it coated with a shimmering layer of water, protecting her against Lazar's fire.

Lazar stumbled back as though the contact between her water and his fire physically hurt him. The whips retracted as quickly as they had been flung out. She seized the moment to duck out of his reach.

A grunt came from Lazar, and the last thing she saw was someone crashing into him and knocking him off his feet.

Then came the blowback. She had experienced the torture of her poisoned magic back at Yarshe Valley, after she had raised the water level of the river under King Falco's orders, and it had felt as agonizing as ingesting ticha, if not worse. This time was no different. Her magic seemed to have a life of its own as it ripped its way through her.

Somewhere in the distance came a third voice—also male, though this one was deeper—but Desert Rose could barely make out the words over the roaring in her ears.

The forest spun above her—a blur of canopy and sunlight—until her legs gave way. Her magic thrashed like a furious creature inside her, threatening to tear her apart. If only she had taken the antidote . . .

The last thing she felt was a pair of arms catching her. The voice murmured to her, but all she heard was a string of muffled words. She caught a glimpse of a shadowy face hovering above her, faintly silhouetted by sunlight, and then the world melted into darkness.

* * *

The faint hum of voices made her stir.

She cracked open an eyelid, taking a moment to adjust to the glare of a lamp on the table near her. Her limbs ached from stiffness, as though winter had settled into her bones and joints.

She was back at the cave. Qiu's home. She recognized its cool comfort and the gentle scent of herbs in the storeroom. The familiarity of her surroundings calmed her racing heart, and she deepened her shallow breaths.

'You're awake.' The familiar timbre of the voice sparked hope among the ashes of her heart. It sounded just like him. Could it possibly be?

His face shifted into view, half illuminated by candlelight. The other half remained shadowed—making his features starker, the planes of his face keener—but there was no mistaking it. That face had filled her thoughts and dreams of late, giving her the strength to keep going whenever her spirit broke, almost as though he had been with her all the way back from Danxi Plains to the Oasis Kingdom.

Wei.

He was dressed in a simple dark blue tunic that made the gentle slope of his shoulders stretch further. In his eyes was the stoic kindness that always managed to ease her racing pulse. It was the gaze he reserved only for her, one that she had grown so accustomed to seeing, even in the period of his absence.

She was fairly certain she was not dreaming now. He was sitting right in front of her, very much alive and warm, if his hand, tightly wrapped around hers, was any indication.

'Hello, stranger,' he said softly, a small smile playing at the corner of his lips.

She ignored the protests of her embattled body and scrambled to sit up. He helped her up, propping her against the bed frame with his usual careful, quiet strength.

'You're alive.' The words escaped her in a breath. She reached for his hand again, then laid her hands on his shoulders, against his cheeks. Save for a scratch on his face, he appeared intact, unscathed. She frowned, scanning his face. 'How . . . how is this possible? I thought you were dead.'

'So did I.'

'But I watched you fall . . .'

'If Zeyan and Beihe hadn't managed to retrieve my body, I would have died there, at the foot of the watchtower. But after Han pushed me off, the last thing I saw was you on the battlefield, and then nothing. When I woke up, I was in Ghost City, but the Ghost King was unable to reap my soul because I wasn't dead yet.'

'So Zeyan and Beihe found your body?'

He nodded. 'The plan was for them to take my body back to the Dugur tribe if I were slain during the battle—'

'For the shamans to heal you,' Desert Rose murmured. Of course. It was a smart plan, given that Zeyan and Beihe—Wei's most trusted brothers from the Snow Wolf Sect—had spent the last two seasons with half her tribe ever since she and Wei left them to go to Lettoria. The shamans couldn't bring back the dead, but they could restore a person's energy and soul using the natural arts. As long as Wei had a fighting breath, there was still hope.

Yet, the plan was not failproof. So many things could have gone wrong. Had Han been a little more thorough, had Zeyan and Beihe not managed to find Wei's body, had they not taken him back to the tribe in time, Wei would have joined the other souls at Ghost City—for good.

'Why didn't you tell me before? I could have aided you in your plan.' She felt the threat of tears warming her eyes and brushed them away before they could spill out. 'I thought you were dead all this time, even though I tried so hard to convince myself you weren't.'

He reached out and took her hand, running a tender finger across the back of it. He was always gentle with her, even during their first encounter in the desert, when he had drawn out the poison from her blood where she had been bitten by the sand hound. 'It was safer for you not to know. You were already watched by King Falco, and he could activate the poison in you. Besides, I didn't want to distract you from your mission with my own agenda.'

'You are *not* a distraction,' she said hotly. 'Your agenda would be my agenda too.'

Wei only shook his head with a sad smile, but she could hear what he was not saying. Their agendas had set them on different paths, which would only diverge further from here. They both knew it, but neither of them wanted to be the first to utter it and make it irrevocably true. A part of her wanted to believe that she could still fight fate, that they both had agency in determining the course of their lives. But on quiet nights, another part of her would give voice to her doubts, telling her that she was but one mere Elemental against the will of the gods.

'How did you find me?' she asked, attempting to change the topic.

'You left a trail. Well, not *you* specifically. Now that the Wall is down, I imagine your magic is like a beacon to every shaman and sand hound, ghoul and magical creature imaginable. You're an Elemental, after all. They're all hungry for your magic, and they've left a trail of destruction behind you. I traced your route by following the trail of murders, starting from the village you stayed in all the way to this mountain, to where I found you.'

His words took a moment to sink in. 'So the villagers died because of me?'

He shook his head. 'Not exactly. The snatchers have been going around stealing people's qi for a while now, even before you came to Yeli Mountain. But the Ling sects have been watching you ever since you entered Oasis Kingdom. It's a miracle that you managed to come all this way unscathed . . . mostly.' There was that familiar wry smile again, the one that made her breath catch every time.

She massaged her temples, struggling to recall what she last saw. 'Lazar was with them. What happened to him after I passed out?'

It seemed unlikely that the Fire Elemental would retreat at the appearance of Wei, but Wei said, 'He fled after you used your magic against him. Maybe you got some of that poison in him too. We can only hope.'

'So you came to Oasis Kingdom alone? What about the rest of them?'

'Zeyan and Beihe are with your tribe. They're all putting up at a desert town ten li from the Palamir Mountains. They've been . . . adjusting to the new life, but they're still waiting for you and the chieftain to return.'

His gaze was loaded with more that he wasn't saying. It seemed to loom over them now—her destiny and the eventual, inevitable end, should the prophecy play out as it was meant to. Her father's return to the tribe would mean that she had succeeded in fulfilling the prophecy. It would mean she was never returning to her tribe either way—whether she was eliminated by the other Elementals or she eliminated them and ascended to the heavenly realm.

'Qiu is in the kitchen making you a tonic,' Wei said, cutting through her thoughts. 'She said something's amiss with your energy.' He peered at her face. 'It's your magic, isn't it? It's still poisoned.'

She pulled out the vial with the antidote that remained tucked against her chest all this while. 'Meng acquired it from King Falco. I haven't quite dared to take it.'

Meng had gone to great lengths to procure the antidote for her, even giving up his only leverage over King Falco. Even if he had only done so to assuage his guilt for betraying her, she would be wasting his efforts if she chose not to take it. But it wasn't Meng she didn't trust. Meng—who had once betrayed them and let them down immeasurably—had, for the briefest moment in Lettoria, stood on the same side as them after being deserted by his kingdom. Falco, however—how could she believe that the cunning Lettorian king would simply hand over the antidote that would save her life and free her from his control?

'We will find another way. Qiu's brewing a tonic for you as we speak. We're hoping it can mitigate the adverse effects of your magic so you're not debilitated every time you use it.' A crease had burrowed its way between his brows. She reached out to smoothen it with a finger.

His face softened under her touch. Something passed between them. The realization that even after everything they had been through, they were sitting in front of each other again.

He caught her hand in his. She found herself leaning closer to Wei—and him doing the same—until she could catch a whiff of his familiar scent. The scent that reminded her of home. That made *him* home.

Wei's hand brushed her cheek as he cupped her face. She tipped her head back, almost dizzy from his proximity again after all this time apart.

A shuffling noise, like someone hurrying away, made them both pull apart. They turned to find Qiu at the entrance of the chamber with a tray laden with a piping bowl of pungent-smelling medicine, caught between entering and leaving the scene.

She shot them a sheepish smile. 'I didn't mean to interrupt.'

'Not at all,' Desert Rose said, despite her own flaming face. She beckoned Qiu in and shifted away from Wei, but Wei remained where he was, unfazed by his sister's interruption.

Qiu set the tray down on the bedside table. 'Wei told me about your magic, what the Lettorian king did to you. And I couldn't help but overhear about the antidote you have. This tonic can help to neutralize poisons, but it may not be potent enough. Taken together with the antidote, though, it just might completely neutralize the poison in you. It's a risk you have to decide if you want to take. It's strong, though. Try some first to see if your body responds well to it.'

Desert Rose nodded.

Wei took the bowl and blew gently on a spoonful of the medicine before bringing it to her lips. The tonic grated against her throat, as hot and bitter as bile, but she forced herself to swallow it. The roiling in her gut eased almost instantly, as though a wave had subsided inside her, a wild creature showing signs of being tamed.

Qiu and Wei were peering at her face, watching for her reaction to the tonic. Qiu broke into a relieved smile upon seeing Desert Rose grimace at the bitterness but otherwise displaying no other adverse response to it. 'Told you it was strong,' she said apologetically.

Heyang and Zhong entered the room as Desert Rose contemplated whether to take the antidote with the remaining tonic.

'We've got good news and bad news,' Heyang announced.

Qiu took a deep breath. 'Let's hear them.'

'The good news is, the others have scattered away from here. We figured it's better that way than to gather everyone in one prominent place,' Heyang said. 'The bad news is, the villagers are on a witch-hunt. They think it's us who are going around killing the locals, so we're basically being scapegoated again, this time by the snatchers from other sects. The locals are leaving out ticha traps around the forest, and a few of our people are severely ill or injured.'

Qiu sighed. 'And it's only a matter of time before the other sects come for us too. We are too small and too weak compared to them. Should we gather everyone in the cave for now?'

'How long can we hide?' Zhong said. 'The snatchers will be back, for sure. And they can hold out longer than we can. I'm pretty sure they're from the Black Lotus Sect, and we're definitely no match for them.' Zhong shot Desert Rose an accusatory glance. 'It's not us they want though—not primarily, at least.'

'You're right. It's clear who they are targeting, and I cannot stay here and put all of you at risk,' Desert Rose said, attempting to get off the bed. Wei and Qiu stopped her at once, making her lie down again.

Zhong rolled his eyes. 'You'll be as good as dead if you go out there and fight them on your own, even with your magical powers. They're not regular bandits, you know.'

'That much is clear,' Wei said, shooting him a warning stare. 'I don't reckon you have a plan to propose?'

'I'm sorry, rogue prince,' Zhong said, folding his arms and glaring at Wei. 'My brother and I were busy trying to save *our* people and haven't thought up a plan yet. Maybe you can make yourself useful here.'

Qiu sighed in exasperation. 'Enough, both of you.'

Zhong jabbed a finger in Desert Rose's direction. 'How's this for a plan? We use her as bait and lie in wait for them. The snatchers tend to strike at night, so we won't even have to wait long. The sun's already setting.'

'You mean like . . . setting a trap?' Heyang asked.

'Out of the question,' Wei piped up. 'She's still recuperating, and we don't know the extent of their abilities.'

Desert Rose watched them squabble, growing more aware, with each passing moment, of the antidote sitting in the vial in her hand. She hated how powerless she was now. After experiencing the extent of her powers, this inability to use her magic felt torturous. She couldn't stay here and continue to be a liability. Since she had tried Qiu's tonic and it had worked just with one mouthful, then perhaps, as Qiu had said, taking the antidote with the tonic could finally neutralize the poison in her.

She uncapped the vial and retrieved the antidote. The unassuming brown pill sat in the palm of her hand. Should she leave this to fate? It beat sitting here doing nothing. If the Ling truly were after her, then she couldn't put Qiu, Wei, and the shouren in danger too.

She popped the antidote into her mouth and swallowed it while the rest of them were still arguing. Wei stopped and turned to stare at her.

Other than a faint bitterness that lingered in her mouth, the antidote seemed to have no effect on her. There was no telling if it worked. She finished the rest of the tonic. This time, the aftermath shook her right down to the bone. Her body thrummed, the blood in her veins rushing like a river behind a broken dam. She could feel Wei's arms around her, and a strange culmination of energy in her gut that folded in on itself, smaller and smaller, denser and denser, until all at once, the sensation vanished, and she was able to rise to her feet.

She glanced around at the room, where everyone present was watching her—Wei, Qiu, and Heyang with varying degrees of concern, and Zhong with no little amount of suspicion.

She raised a tentative hand and closed her eyes, pulling the moisture in the air towards her, then gathering it in the palm of her hand. When she opened her eyes again, a tiny orb of water was hovering above her palm, shimmering like a lake on a cloudless summer's day. She waited for the blowback, for the pain to rack her body, for her body to revolt against her. But all was still; only a gentle warmth spread through her.

It felt as though something had returned to her, settling into its usual nook, and she was once again whole. No longer did her magic feel like an enemy to her; it was now her friend and trusty weapon, ready to fight alongside her.

A grin broke out on her face. 'It's back. My magic is back.' She knew that with utmost certainty.

Wei let out a breath, then threw his arms around her. When they pulled away, she looked up and met Wei's gaze. This time, her voice did not waver. She was ready.

'I guess it's time to meet the Ling.'

Eight

Meng

It took Meng almost a week to persuade the desert lords to be on board his plan to take the throne back from his brother, but that, he realized, was the easiest part of all.

Harder still was ensuring he made the journey back to Oasis Kingdom in one piece. King Falco was still hunting him down, and so were the imperial scouts his brother had sent on his trail. Han still believed Meng was alive, and he was leaving no stone unturned.

In just one season, Meng had gone from an emperor to a refugee, a wanted man sought by both his own kingdom and its rival. And what wrong had he really done? It was by a mere twist of fate that the tides had turned against him. The injustice burned, spurring him on in his search for the one person who would understand this feeling.

The Wind Elemental was intent on seeking out the only other Elemental that hadn't revealed himself so far, and the word on the street was that he remained hidden in the Yeli Mountains in Oasis Kingdom, among the Ling. With the Wall taken down by the Lettorians, the Ling would likely be emboldened to seize back their power. His home kingdom was in flux now, and it was only a matter of time before it descended into chaos. This would be the best time to throw Han off his precarious perch on the throne, and Meng wanted to be there to witness—no, *orchestrate*—it.

Windshadow would understand; she would be on his side, as long as they were empathetic to each other's causes. For an opportunist like her, she had been surprisingly loyal so far.

Although perhaps Windshadow was not the only person who understood vengeance. His brother Wei had been through his fair share of injustices in the imperial court, scorned by their father from birth and always receiving the shorter end of the stick among the brothers. No wonder he wanted nothing to do with the throne, opting for a life out in the wild and forging his own fate.

Meng's own fate was now unwritten as well. It was up to him alone to take back control of his life and write his own ending. He would make sure it would be one for the books.

The further back east he got, the closer the brushes he had with the imperial scouts. He travelled now in a wagon driven by a merchant from Mobei, sitting amongst rolls of handwoven carpets and woollen rugs. The desert lord had suggested this method of entering Oasis Kingdom, calling it 'unbefitting for an ex-ruler of a kingdom, but it would get the job done'. Meng wasn't bothered about being packed among the carpets and rugs, or that his legs were cramping up from staying in one position the entire journey; what mattered was that he entered the kingdom without being detected.

Security at the kingdom gates was a lot more stringent these days. With the Wall gone, the guards were doing double the work to screen visitors and ensure that 'undesirables'—those who had no purpose or right of entry—were kept out. Meng peeked out from under the hemp covers, making out the pair of guards who had stopped the merchant.

'What business?' one of the guards demanded as he eyed the wagon.

'Trade, sir,' the merchant said in heavily accented Oasis language. Meng held his breath. This was where things got tricky. Before, everyone had to show their paperwork and proof of business in Oasis Kingdom, have their belongings checked, and then go through the cleansing ritual by drinking ticha water to certify that they were non-magic. What would the regulations be now and what would the punishment be for breaking them?

'Trade,' the guard echoed, eyeing the wagon. He patted the bulky load, ripping off the top cover to peer in. Meng pressed as close as possible to the back of the wagon, letting himself be obscured by two massive rolls of rugs.

'Also, please accept this,' the merchant said in a conspiratorial tone as he leaned towards the guard surveying the wagon. A pause. 'Just a token for your hard work, good sirs.' The guard abandoned the wagon, his attention diverted. When Meng peeked out from a tiny opening in the covers, he spied the merchant handing the two guards a small perfume box each. 'Mother-of-pearl. Worth a fortune,' he whispered.

The wagon soon began trundling along again, heading through the gates and into the town.

Meng released his bated breath. Who knew it would be this easy? His father had been staunchly against corruption (though, of course, he had happily exempted himself from that moral high ground), and any instance of bribery—especially at the borders—would be stamped out.

Meng laid his head against the back of the wagon, his breathing eased now that he had made it back into the kingdom. This homecoming was a far cry from his last one, when he had returned through the Capital gates as ambassador and Fourth Prince, in a carriage drawn by servants. He now returned as an outlaw, a wanted man, an emperor who had been overthrown and then fled the kingdom on the back of an Elemental. There was no fanfare this time, only notoriety, dishonour, and shame if he was caught.

A moment later, doubt struck him. Had it truly been that easy for him to return? Or was Han expecting him and luring him right into the tiger's den? Did he have guards lying in wait to nab him; was he waiting to humiliate him and have him hanged as turncoats were?

No, he was overthinking it. His brother was chasing bigger things now; he wouldn't even regard Meng as a threat to guard against. He had a throne to secure, wars to fight, and more riches and power to seize. His ambition—and complacency when it came to his younger brother—would be his downfall. Meng would make sure of that.

The wagon rolled to a stop at last. Meng waited for the merchant to pull back the covers before emerging from his hiding spot. They had arrived at the mouth of an alley just after the Lan County entrance. Two streets down stood a simple arch with the words *Pingyi Town* etched on it. Several other trade wagons made their way into the town as the odd errand boy navigated the footpaths with his day's load.

'This is as far as I can take you,' the merchant said as Meng dismounted.

'Thank you for your assistance,' Meng said. He had little to give, but a small jade pendant as a token of his gratitude. The merchant refused at first, but accepted the pendant upon Meng's insistence.

Lan County was large enough to disappear into and far enough from the Capital for Meng to not be recognized among the people. It was also the county where Yeli Mountain was located, where the Ling were said to be in hiding.

Almost out of habit, Meng mentally recited 'The War of the Realms' again.

> *There was a time when heaven met earth*
> *through the sacred Celestial Pool.*
> *Gods and monsters worked together,*
> *each with a task to do.*
> *They guarded their realms and upheld the peace,*
> *kept the magic flowing through.*
> *But when two immortals broke the rules,*
> *gods and demons took to war.*
> *The Pool dried up and magic fell*
> *into the inept hands of men.*
> *And so lies the world, sickened by greed*
> *until the Pool flows free again.*
> *Only the essence of the gods can free*
> *that which has been contained.*

He had committed *Duru-shel Minta* to heart after Desert Rose had decoded the scroll for him last winter during the Trials. This was the key to unlocking all the dormant magic in Oasis Kingdom. The incantation was buried in that song, but it would take a Ling—a magic being or practitioner—to activate the magic in the land.

And he who held the key to the magic of Oasis Kingdom held the key to the Old Kingdom. There was so much untapped potential in the ancient kingdom of Hesui, which his forefathers had suppressed and buried over the centuries just because they were afraid of the magic it contained.

Meng believed that magic was inherently neither good nor evil. It was the wielder of magic who imposed his intentions on it and corrupted it. Under a fair and just ruler, Oasis Kingdom could prosper and stand on its own, no longer fearing enemy attacks, or suffering from famines and droughts at the whims of the gods, or relying solely on trading partners for key resources.

But if that magic fell into the hands of Han, that could mean the destruction of the kingdom as they knew it.

A pushcart wandering down the street pulled him back to the present. Meng scanned his surroundings, grounding himself. He needed to blend in—no one could recognize the Fourth Prince or report that he was in Lan County before he found the Ling.

The market was strangely deserted for this hour of the day. The autumn chill was starting to creep in, but the streets felt exceptionally colder. Apart from a handful of stragglers and errand boys he had seen at the entrance, there was hardly anyone around town, while those around seemed to be in a hurry to get off the streets. Where were the mothers doing their shopping in the market with their children, the street vendors, the delivery boys?

He stepped into a spice shop, one of the few that had their doors wide open.

'Pardon me,' Meng called, scanning the shop for anyone.

An elderly man Meng presumed was the shopkeeper hobbled out from one of the aisles with his walking stick. He appeared to be the only person in the shop. 'How may I help you, good sir?'

'I'm just here in Lan County on a visit,' Meng said. 'Is it always so quiet around here?'

The shopkeeper shifted his nervous glance out the door and back to him. 'There's been a chain of murders leading all the way up to Yeli Mountain. The locals are terrified. County magistrates and imperial officials, even livestock, have been killed. Everyone is staying indoors until the culprits are caught.'

Meng frowned. 'Are there no leads at all, since there has been a string of cases?'

'As far as I know, the culprits have left absolutely no traces behind and there are no witnesses. They're very methodical and operate during the wee hours of the night.' He seemed about to say more but stopped himself.

'Go ahead,' Meng urged. 'I'm just a lone visitor, you won't get in trouble for telling me things.'

'Well, it's not my place to talk about this. But you'd best watch out for yourself while you're here. There's a shift in the air these days, and there's talk about'—his voice dropped to a hoarse whisper, and Meng leaned so close to the old man that he could count the lines on his wizened face—'magical folk roaming these parts. They're becoming more brazen now. Some suspect it's dark magic practitioners responsible for the killings, but no one has any proof.'

'Dark magic practitioners?'

'It's very underground business, but I've been around long enough to hear about all the secret sects that lurk within the mountains. Never got around to witnessing them, thankfully, but these bizarre cases never used to be so frequent or blatant.'

A chain of murders leading towards Yeli Mountain. Secret sects of dark magic practitioners that lived in the mountains. It seemed there was only one way to go if Meng wanted answers—or to find the people he was looking for.

He exited the shop, lost in thought, absently crushing the packet of sour plums he bought from the shopkeeper. In the distance, Yeli Mountain loomed over the town, its craggy grey peaks stark as a warning.

No gains without risk. He had made it all the way here; he was so close.

He headed in the direction of the mountains, ignoring the foreboding feeling sitting in his chest.

Nine

Wei

Wei watched the gentle rise and fall of Desert Rose's sleeping form. It felt surreal to be sitting next to her again, taking turns to keep watch like all those nights they had been on the road together.

He hated Zhong's idea to use Desert Rose as bait, but he knew as soon as she took the antidote that there was no talking her out of it. Her compassion and humanity were some of the things he loved most about her, but she could also be exasperatingly stubborn and self-sacrificing at times. For someone who once claimed to not believe in destiny, she sure seemed to take her responsibility seriously.

Wei kept his ears peeled for the slightest sound, but the mountain's silence was as thick as its evening mist, concealing any traces of stealthy prowlers. They were out in the living room, where Desert Rose was waiting on the chair near the fireplace and Wei sat in a dark corner five feet away, waiting with her. It was easier for the snatchers to find her this way, Desert Rose had said, insisting that the others retreat into the safety of the bed chambers located deeper inside the cave.

'You don't have to keep staring at me,' she murmured now, cracking open her eyes and peering at him from across the room. 'I'm not going to disappear into thin air.'

'Just making sure the antidote didn't kill you,' he said.

The crackle of the fire filled up the silence that stretched between them, laying bare the unspoken shared understanding that they were not out of the woods yet. That the possibility of the antidote not working remained to be seen.

When she spoke again, her voice sounded far away. 'Why do the Ling want me? Why now? I've been here at Yeli Mountain before, and they didn't hunt me down then.'

Wei tried to recall everything he knew about the Ling. Growing up sequestered within the palace walls, he had little to no knowledge of the magic practitioners other than what Matron had told him in secret— that they descended from an ancient line of shamans that once ruled the Hesui Kingdom, and were driven into hiding in the mountains after the Great Purge that cleansed all magic from Oasis Kingdom. Some believed all that remained of the Ling were dark magic practitioners, resorting to using their cultivated magic for petty crime to scrounge a living. Others believed that they were just biding their time, awaiting the day someone strong enough could help them take back the kingdom they believed was stolen from them. Someone like the last Elemental with all of heaven and earth behind her.

Desert Rose shook her head when he was done sharing what he knew. 'So they're after me so that I can help them stage a rebellion?'

'I can't say for certain, and no one knows how they operate, or the extent of their abilities and network,' he said. 'They're underground, but they're clearly organized. My guess is, now that Han's lost the battle and the Wall is torn down, the Ling are seizing this moment to stage an uprising.'

'Well,' she said with a wry smile. 'You're probably not opposed to the notion of overthrowing your brother.'

'Not if it means sacrificing you.' The words tumbled out before he could stop himself. But he no longer wished to hold back his feelings, not when their time together was limited. Not when they would soon be on separate paths. He would choose her, over and over again, even if it meant giving up his kingdom for now. Vengeance remained in him—he would not rest until he sought revenge for his mother, for Matron and Yong—but he would not sacrifice the living for those he had already lost.

Desert Rose stared at him, her gaze inscrutable, but he never got to hear her response because in the next moment, she froze. Her eyes flicked to the cave entrance. 'Someone's coming,' she hissed before shutting her eyes and going slack.

Wei followed suit, forcing himself to remain where he was instead of closing the distance between them like he longed to.

The snatchers slipped in with barely a sound, the four of them leaving only a gust of wind in their wake. A grunt from Desert Rose disturbed the silence.

Wei leapt to his feet at once. Someone grabbed him from behind almost immediately, locking him in a chokehold and pinning his arms against his back. He climbed up the cave wall and used his weight to flip overhead, throwing off his attacker and crashing into the dining table next to them.

A shimmering stream of water hit one of the snatchers in the chest, throwing him backwards against his partner. Desert Rose had her hands outstretched, keeping the snatchers at bay.

'Rose, behind you,' Wei yelled, dashing over to her. But the snatcher knocked her out with a quick blow to the neck. Her stream of water died as she collapsed against him. Wei charged towards them, but the other three snatchers erected a floor-to-ceiling energy field that walled him in. Wei threw himself against the force field repeatedly, getting flung back each time despite his efforts. He could only watch as one of the snatchers threw Desert Rose over his shoulder and carted her away, flanked by his companions.

By the time the wall disappeared, the four of them—and Desert Rose—were out of sight.

Qiu came rushing into the chamber, lamp in hand, with Heyang and Zhong right behind her. She glanced around wildly. 'What happened? Where's—'

'They've taken her.' Wei grabbed the lamp from her. 'Stay here. I'll get her back.' He raced out of the cave in the direction the snatchers had gone, leaving Qiu's calls behind him.

Night had fallen, and in this part of the mountains the darkness was deep and almost impenetrable. Wei held the lamp close to the ground and kept his eyes peeled for footprints or stray boulders and roots. The trail began from the outcrop in front of the cave, extending through the forest where the mud was thick and damp. Wei cursed at his slow progress, ignoring the branches snagging at his clothes.

He had no idea how much time had passed, but the footprints finally came to an end at the foot of a massive oak tree, just before a root as high as his knee. At the base of the root, half covered by a pile of twigs and dead leaves, was a hole, just large enough to fit a grown man. Wei surveyed the vicinity. There was no other trail that led anywhere else. All signs pointed to this tree.

Could they possibly have gone into that hole in the ground? It wasn't unfeasible. Wei had, after all, entered one before in Ghost City with Desert Rose and discovered a whole undead army there. What might this one lead to?

This could be a trap. Wei pushed away the thought. If it was a trap that led him to Desert Rose, then so be it.

He stepped through. The fall was immediate, almost as though the ground was pulling him in. He tumbled through the air for what felt like several li deep, amid a darkness as gentle as the silence, as though everything was muted by the soft earth around him.

When he finally landed, it was on a ground as cushy as a pile of dry leaves.

With the air knocked out of his lungs, he lay sprawled on a platform in the middle of the subterranean cavern, an underground chamber several times larger than the one the Dugur tribe had camped in at Ghost City—except that this chamber was aglow with paper lanterns that hung off its walls in neat rows, emitting an almost hypnotic scent that made him drowsy at once. Several footpaths radiated out from the centre platform, leading to lit tunnels that he couldn't see beyond.

He shook his head and picked himself off the ground. Somewhere in the distance he could hear the slow drip of water off the walls. A strange low murmur echoed throughout the cavern, though the words were unintelligible. He almost suspected he was dreaming until a dart careened towards him. He swerved just in time for it to brush past his shoulder.

'Not bad, rogue prince,' a female voice said.

Wei spun around to see a woman dressed in a flowing white robe that seemed far too impractical given that they were deep within the earth. It was hard to determine her age—she appeared to be in her twenties but carried the stateliness of an older woman.

She strode towards him, her back ramrod straight, making her seem taller than she actually was. 'Your reflexes are far sharper than the other idiots who dared to venture into our realm.'

'I see my reputation precedes me here,' Wei said, matching the woman's insouciance.

'You're the one the others are pinning their hopes on, the wild horse who went out of the kingdom to seek his fortunes.' She cocked her head. 'You look far less impressive than they described.'

'I live to disappoint,' Wei said dryly.

She smirked. 'I know what you're here for. Do you really believe she will make it out of here alive?' Her tone was far from menacing—in fact, it sounded almost conversational—but Wei found himself ready with a retort. 'You might have come all this way to find her, but she will not be able to leave this place. You are but a mortal—a prince, but just a mortal one—and she's an Elemental. She will fulfil the prophecy here either way, and you will not be able to stop it.'

Either way. Which meant there was someone here who could take her closer to the final point. Realization dawned on him.

'I take it that the Earth Elemental is here then,' he said. The only Elemental left, the one Desert Rose came all this way to hunt down. 'He sent those people to capture Rose?'

'*Capture.* How crude, your choice of word. The White Ling Sect is a respectable one that has no need to resort to such measures, but the shouren—and you—are ridiculously protective of her. It was the only way His Highness could reach her.'

Wei snorted. 'I don't recall *His Highness* inviting her in for some tea.'

She was unfazed by his sarcasm. 'You mock, but deep down you are intrigued. You want to know more about us, and potentially how we can be of use to you and your agenda. Indeed, we can help you overthrow the current emperor and get you on that throne.'

Wei stared at her, keeping his face still and giving nothing away. The Ling couldn't possibly know that he had created the rumour of the Rebel Prince coming back to take the throne. No one else but Zeyan and Beihe knew. Everyone was supposed to think it was Meng since he was the more legitimate son. No one was supposed to guess that Wei was the one stoking the flames of rebellion.

The woman raised a brow at him. 'You have intentions of taking the throne, do you not? That's what you've wanted ever since your mother was imprisoned and your brother murdered.'

She was a mind reader, Wei realized. She could hear every one of his thoughts running through his head now and read his entire history.

'You catch on fast,' she said, looking almost impressed. 'This is why they stationed me at the entrance—so I can suss out the intentions of visitors and trespassers. You may call me the Priestess.'

'I'm here just for Rose,' he said. 'I'm not interested in your job here.'

'You shouldn't concern yourself with her fate anymore. What happens to her from hereon is not within your control—it never was. And I know you didn't come here just for her.'

There was no point denying his intentions in front of a mind reader. 'You say you can help. Don't you think you're overestimating your abilities? Your people have been hiding away in this mountain for centuries.'

'We know the Wall has been destroyed. The incoming energies from outside have strengthened ours. These are unprecedented times, and now is the moment we can turn the tides in our favour.'

'You mean take over the throne.'

The Priestess scoffed. 'The throne is just a symbol of power. We have no use for such an illusory thing.'

'What then?'

'True power is capturing the minds of the people. Make them see that magical and non-magical folk can coexist. For that, we want someone on the throne—someone we can work with.'

Wei understood at last. 'You want me to be a figurehead while you hold the reins to this kingdom.'

The Ling had no interest in being on the forefront, after spending so many centuries in convenient obscurity; they wanted someone to perch on the throne while they pulled all the strings from the back. What good had come to those in prominent positions of power, after all? His brother and father had been easy targets of many assassination attempts, the last of which succeeded. The Ling, rather wisely, would instead have a puppet they could control as they took back the kingdom that Wei's ancestors had stolen from them. And perhaps with time, as the Oasis emperor's reign weakened, they would end the entire Zhao dynasty and establish their own.

He supposed it was poetic justice from their point of view, that the descendant of their enemy should pay for those crimes.

Yet, why should he become their puppet? Why should he pay for his ancestors' crimes by sacrificing his own life and freedom? There were other ways to right these wrongs; he was not obligated to negotiate by their terms.

'Do you have any other choice, rogue prince?' the Priestess asked. 'You have neither influence nor power, neither allies nor an army— except us. We can rally behind you, help you unseat your brother. In turn, you return us the rightful control of this land.'

It sounded like an absurd proposition. Wei was certain that Meng, a schooled strategist, would never agree to such terms. But he was not Meng, and his method of getting ahead involved understanding the motives of everyone involved.

'Word has it that the emperor has been building an army, a special personal guard equipped with magical abilities,' the Priestess added.

Wei snapped to attention. His first response was to deny this possibility, but a part of him had expected this. Lettoria's attack with the Ferros—the magical army built from metal forged by the Metal Elemental—would certainly have given Han the idea to build his own army, one that was just as formidable. He would be hungry enough for protection and power to do just that.

The Priestess nodded, having heard his musings. 'We believe Han is using the Black Ling to build this army. Our aim is to stop him before that happens—or at least build a White Ling Army powerful enough to destroy his.' She began pacing. 'If he is indeed working with the Black Ling, then it's most likely that he is working with the Black Lotus Sect. They have long been a thorn in our side.'

Wei had no interest in the enmity between the White and Black Ling. They could tear each other apart for all he cared. If Han was building a magical army, it would be nearly impossible to defeat him without a counter-army just as powerful. A counter-army like what

this Priestess was proposing for him to lead, as long as he played by
their rules.

'And where does Rose fit into all this?' he demanded. 'You
kidnapped her to force her to become part of your rebellion?'

'Still preoccupied with her,' the Priestess scoffed, shaking her head.
'The Water Elemental is destined to be part of the prophesied battle
among all the Elementals. She is therefore instrumental in *our* battle,
even crucial to it.'

Wei did not respond. Something heavy sat in his chest, not simply
because this was yet another group of people looking to use Desert
Rose, but because he knew he was powerless to protect her.

'You cannot protect her forever,' the Priestess said, reading his
mind again. 'Eventually her destiny will catch up with her, and you
will have to let go.' Her voice was neither stern nor kind, simply
matter of fact.

The rational part of him knew he could not fight fate, nor hold
Desert Rose back from facing her end, whatever that might be. Yet,
another part of him wanted to rage against fate, derail from the paths
that had already been laid out for him and Desert Rose respectively.
They could still take back control, leave all this tumult and struggle
behind, find a corner of the world that belonged to them. Couldn't they?

'What you can do now,' the Priestess went on, 'is join hands with
us. We help you get on the throne, and you can exact your revenge on
your brother . . .'

This time, Wei neither questioned nor denied how she knew, deep
down, that the reason for him wanting the throne was primarily for
vengeance on Han. He had never lusted after the throne or political
power the way Han—or even Meng—did. Yet, this was something he
had to do, even if it was the last thing he did.

'And in turn, you help us regain influence on this land and piece
back our kingdom,' the Priestess finished.

Our kingdom. Did she mean Oasis Kingdom or Hesui Kingdom—
the one they had ruled over centuries ago that had been carved up over
the years?

It seemed like a fair proposition, where they each achieved their aim.
Yet, something niggled at him. He had been thoroughly manipulated by

the Lettorian king last summer, who had held Desert Rose hostage to achieve his aim. Wei had revealed his weakness once, and this Priestess too must have discovered it within the first moment of meeting him. He could just as easily be walking into a trap again this time. After all, he was no mind reader.

Could he truly trust the Ling? Were their intentions simply to back a puppet emperor? How committed were they to backing Wei and Desert Rose, who was essentially the Earth Elemental's rival in fulfilling the prophecy?

The Priestess was watching him, no doubt listening to every single one of his thoughts.

'First, I'd like to see Desert Rose,' he said at last.

Darkness and Light

The Ling is generally split into two categories—White and Black—based on the type of magic they perform.

To preface this topic, there is in fact no inherent inclination for magic to be white or black, light or dark. Magic is magic. It is the intention of the wielder that determines its nature.

The White Ling have historically been associated with white magic—that is, magic that exists in its natural state and is used for good—while the Black Ling practise magic for immoral or selfish purposes. Given that their intentions are directly opposing, the White and Black Ling sects are natural enemies.

Ever since the Immortal Spring was blocked by the Celestial King after he found out about the moonlight tryst between his daughter, the Sky Princess, and the Earth Prince, magic has been in the hands of these magical beings; once men, who cultivated their powers either by harnessing that which nature provides, or by deriving the qi of other living beings. The White Ling practises the former, and the Black Ling the latter.

Given that sect politics are constantly evolving, particularly at the beginning when the hierarchy was unstable and various factions were constantly fighting for power, disagreements among the Ling soon led to a group of them breaking away to form their own sects.

The Black Lotus Sect is one such dark magic sect that steals the qi of others to enhance their own. This corrupt form of magic has sustained the sect for centuries now. Like the White Ling Sect, the Black Lotus Sect is said to be one of the oldest sects living in Yeli Mountain, comprising sorcerers and spellcasters who were once part of the White Ling Sect, which encompassed many of the other sects, including Blue Mountain Sect, Yellow Star Sect, Red Moon Sect, and more.

Shifting loyalties and turbulent sect politics mean that one can hop from one sect to another once the nodes of power change, so a White Ling Sect member can become a Black Ling Sect member—and the reverse is true—as long as they prove their worth.

Yet, both factions are alike in their efforts to exist in a kingdom that shuns and persecutes them, armed with its inexorable stores of ticha, the only known weapon against magical beings. While they fare differently in terms of practical survival, their determination to be the ruling sect of the Ling have led them to seek their fortunes and power in ironically similar ways sometimes. In fact, a few Oasis emperors have even gone down in history because they were found to have formed secret alliances with either the White Ling or Black Ling—while the crime is lesser for the former, either way, it is treasonous to ally with anyone associated with magic in Oasis Kingdom.

The Ling have, over the years, gone into hiding. At the same time, these magic-practising sects continue to exist among us, hidden in plain sight. Their magic continues to pulse through Yeli Mountain, where the Ling are said to dwell in obscurity. And the day when magic is allowed to run rampant in Oasis Kingdom might just be the day the Ling takes over the reins.

—Excerpt from *Tales from the Old Kingdom Vol. I:*
Myths and Magic by Lu Ji Fang

Ten

Windshadow

The Black Lotus Sect was deviant, unpredictable, and unapologetic—everything that Windshadow herself was, and she felt more accepted by them than she ever had by her tribe. Within just three days of meeting them, starting with the boy she first spoke to (who later introduced himself as Yujin) and his twin sister, Yan, Windshadow found herself slowly lowering her guard against them.

Lazar, on the other hand, remained scornful of the Black Lotus Sect and their capabilities. Windshadow still could not figure out his true motives in being here, or where his loyalties truly lay. How much free rein was Han giving him, and why was he allowed to join the Black Lotus Sect? Did Han trust him with this group of rebels? One could never trust a turncoat to stay loyal, so Windshadow knew Lazar had to have other plans up his sleeve.

Whatever the case, she hardly saw Lazar around the siheyuan, and what glimpses she caught of him was when he was deep in conversation with the sect elders.

The sect moved swiftly and collectively, stealing the qi of livestock, of members of other weaker sects, and even of imperial officials, at a rate that drew the attention of local authorities. Yet, they evaded capture time and time again, and even managed to plant evidence that implicated the shouren. They left no trace of themselves, and their attacks on imperial officials advanced their agenda of disassembling the imperial court and causing chaos within.

Windshadow followed along on their missions, sticking close to the twins, who took her under their wing after her first day at the sect headquarters. They were just a couple of years older than her but were seasoned in the way they eliminated rival sect members and any officials who had affiliations with Emperor Han. Windshadow was even convinced that they could pass the Trials at the House of Night and join the Black Cranes.

Yan was the older twin, though Yujin regarded her with the protectiveness of an older brother. They shared a profound bond, a dynamic cultivated from years of relying on each other as orphans and training together in the sect, and Windshadow secretly wished she had that kind of connection with someone. It was easier being a lone wolf, but her brief lifetime in this mortal world would carry far more meaning if she could find a home in someone.

That was when she would usually stop to chide herself for getting sentimental. No sense growing attached to anything or anyone when she was only here for a short while.

The Black Lotus Sect were not the only ones going around stealing qi, although they had the upper hand, being the oldest and most powerful Black Ling sect. Other Black Ling sects were doing the same, and soon it became a race to see which sect could get stronger faster. The competition was aggressive, but the Black Lotus Sect seemed determined to stay on top.

'Even though the Black and White Ling are in a temporary truce and alliance, after we overthrow the Zhao emperor, all the sects—and by extension, all the citizens of Oasis Kingdom—will be looking at which sect is fit to rule them, the Black Lotus Sect or the White Ling Sect,' Yan explained when Windshadow asked her about the intense rivalry. 'The White Ling Sect has the Earth Prince leading it. We need to be as strong as them—if not stronger—to contend for the right to rule.'

'If you ask me,' Yujin quipped, 'I think what the Black Ling lacked was unity. The White Ling—the Blue Mountain Sect, Yellow Star Sect, and so on—are mostly loyal to the White Ling Sect, but here we are still competing among ourselves to be the biggest and baddest sect. At least having a common enemy now is helping to unite all of us, if only for a while.' His voice dropped to a conspiratorial whisper. 'After we've overthrown the imperial family, though, that's when things get exciting.'

His sister shushed him sharply.

Windshadow didn't care much about sect rivalry, but all this background information was useful in preparing her to meet the Earth Elemental. She had noticed how opaque the sect elders were in their business; even Yan and Yujin seemed to be out of the loop. For now, she would bide her time, learn what she could about the Earth Elemental and what the sect's strategy was before she decided whom to align herself with and how she would take on the Earth Elemental. Prince Meng would be proud of her for not being impulsive this time.

On their next mission, Windshadow killed a county magistrate who had been accepting bribes for a decade and was secretly using dark magic to forge coins. He was on an official visit to the neighbouring county, and they waylaid him on his journey back. Windshadow completed the deed and left the scene in less time than it took for his guards to arrive. She felt no remorse, only grim satisfaction at getting rid of him and gaining the approval of the siblings and the sect. From then on, the three of them moved as a pack, working seamlessly to cover each other as they operated around Lan County.

At night, after dinner with the rest of the sect, they would gather in Windshadow's room, where they would trade tips on their kills while cleaning their weapons and drinking rice wine.

'We should have found you sooner. You were born for this life,' Yan remarked one evening.

Windshadow wished she did too. She had never fit in with her tribe, or in the imperial palace, or at the House of Night. Desert Rose was a welcome addition, but they were destined to become enemies in the end. One had to die for the other to live . . . or ascend to the heavens, or however it was that the prophecy went. She would find out when she was the last Elemental remaining.

Yujin agreed with his sister. 'You should put that gift of yours to good use. Every ally and official of the imperial family we get rid of takes us closer to the throne.'

But what did Windshadow care about the throne? All she wanted was revenge against Han. It would be sweet vengeance to see him overthrown—or better yet, killed—but she was here only till the last Elemental was eliminated; the future of Oasis Kingdom beyond Han's downfall hardly mattered to her.

'How much longer do you suppose it would take for the Earth Elemental to show himself?' she asked.

'It's hard to tell. He's . . . selectively social,' Yan said.

Windshadow raised her eyebrows. 'I take it you've never seen him in person.'

'What, lowly sect members like us? He will only meet high-level people.' Yujin shot her a look. 'Like Elementals.'

'So you're using me to draw him out.'

Yujin shrugged. 'The sect elders have crossed paths with the White Ling elders before, but the Earth Elemental is a recluse. Too busy nurturing his qi or who knows what Elementals do.'

Windshadow smirked. 'Or he's just biding his time. Waiting for us to go to him.'

'He takes himself a tad too seriously, if you ask me,' Yujin said.

Yan shushed him. 'The forest hears everything.' She glanced around at the wall of trees surrounding the manor as though the Earth Elemental himself might swoop in and finish them all.

Windshadow shared a look with Yujin and they shared a chuckle. That moment—fleeting as it was—surprised her more than anything. Was this what it felt like to belong somewhere? To have inside jokes with friends, to experience calmness and ease rather than be permanently on edge? The feeling was brand new, unlike anything she had ever experienced. Even with Desert Rose, she felt on guard at times, wondering if her kindness was just a ruse to make Windshadow lower her defences.

A part of her wished that Desert Rose was here too, that she could share this moment with her desert azzi, the first friend she had ever made regardless of their eventual end. Those few weeks of travelling back to Oasis Kingdom with her had made Windshadow see her in a different light. No longer was she that sheltered desert girl who had to be schooled in the way of the world; she would probably appreciate Yan and Yujin just as much. For the first time ever, Windshadow felt a slight pang in her heart at the thought of Desert Rose.

Yet, as much as she had come to appreciate this rare camaraderie with the twins, something niggled at her. 'Why did the sect capture us, me and Lazar?'

'We didn't *capture* you; we took you in,' said Yujin. 'You're free to leave if you want, but how are you going to fight the Earth Elemental— and the White Ling Sect—on your own? So you help us overthrow the emperor, and in turn you get to meet the Earth Elemental—'

'The Earth Prince,' Yan corrected, 'as he's formally known.'

Yujin rolled his eyes. 'He's just a descendent of the original Earth Prince, not the actual celestial being himself. Everyone just treats him like he's royalty because he's an Elemental and a Damohai.'

'He's still more celestial than either of us, so show some respect or you might end up losing your tongue—or worse, your life,' Yan said.

Yujin turned back to Windshadow, who was trying to hide a smirk at Yujin's insouciance towards the Earth Elemental. 'As I was saying, you help us overthrow the emperor, and in turn you get to meet the Earth Elemental and settle your score with him. Win-win.'

'As for the Fire Elemental, despite his affiliations with the emperor, his loyalties have shifted to us,' Yan said.

'Do you really believe that?' Windshadow asked.

The girl shrugged. 'The sect elders seem to. He's been working closely with them on a secret mission, something about building an army. Perhaps they're preparing the Ling Army to attack soon.'

Lazar was helping the Ling build their army to overthrow Han? It made no sense. Why would Lazar attempt to overthrow Han when he had been benefiting from his loyalty to him up to this point? And wouldn't the imperial scouts who had been tailing him here report back to Han? What would Lazar get out of all this effort?

The following night, she snuck out for answers. Lazar had another reason for being in the sect, and it wasn't just to find the Earth Elemental. If he had an alternative plan, she would find out what it was before getting stabbed in the back by him.

The siheyuan, nestled among the mountains, was bathed in an almost eerie silence after dark. No bird call or howl of a wild animal, not even the rustle of leaves. Everyone had either retired to their rooms or gone out for missions. Windshadow waited until the twins were sound asleep before throwing off her covers and slipping out of the room. Outside, she shifted into her elemental form.

She drifted past the courtyard and slipped into every room looking for the Fire Elemental, but there was no sign of him, not in the common room or any of the chambers. A few of the sect members also seemed to be absent. Had Lazar left the sect? Was he on a mission tonight?

Then she heard the sound—the low chanting she had heard on her first day here. It sounded more urgent than the sort of prayers her tribe shamans chanted for special rituals and ceremonies.

In the distance, the faint glow of fire—a floating orb of light amid the gloom—caught her attention. She breezed through doorway after doorway, until the chanting grew louder and the flame grew brighter, revealing ten Black Lotus Sect elders gathered in a circle in the backyard, one of them being the sect leader, Huzun. Windshadow had seen him around the manor and heard about him from Yan and Yujin, but he had never spoken to her directly, trusting the twins to help her assimilate into the sect. To the Black Lotus Sect, she was just a powerful weapon, a means to an end, not a demigod to be revered or feared, and a part of her enjoyed that. Seeing him here now as part of this ritual made her realize just how little she truly knew about the Black Lotus Sect beyond what Yan and Yujin had told her.

In the middle of the circle stood a regular man in a ring of fire, his back erect and his hands curled into fists by his side. Flames lapped at his feet, yet his eyes were closed as though he were asleep, oblivious to the heat.

Windshadow shifted into her human form and ducked behind the wall. The elders detected nothing, relentless in their chanting. Beyond the backyard, the wall of trees swayed in the breeze, and Windshadow thought she saw the shadows of a throng of people in the forest behind the siheyuan.

This was a ritual. The sect elders were performing a night-time ritual on this man here, and perhaps on even more people beyond what Windshadow could see. But this wasn't how they stole qi. Windshadow had watched how the twins did it, capturing that little wisp of energy every time they killed someone or some beast. This ritual here was something else. The man seemed to grow stronger with each passing moment, his lean—almost scrawny—body swelling up into a muscular physique, the sinews of his arms tightening as though he was flexing . . .

'Night-time stroll, azzi?' Lazar's voice was warm against her ear.

Windshadow whipped around, ready to attack, but he only grabbed her wrist and placed a finger to his lips. Then he gestured for her to follow him, out of the elders' earshot. They headed down the corridors and back to the empty common room where scant moonlight slanted through the windows. Windshadow debated whether to continue observing the ritual, but perhaps it was easier to wring out an answer from Lazar directly and understand what part he played in all of this.

Lazar shut the door to the common room behind them, dimming the lamps until a lone one was burning in the corner. 'You seem to have questions,' he said at last, turning his attention back to Windshadow.

'You seem to have answers to my questions,' she replied.

'It is exactly like what you saw. They're building up their army. It won't be long now before they attack the imperial palace.'

'Is that the big secret that you and the sect elders have been harbouring?'

'It's hardly a secret that the Ling is preparing to overthrow the emperor. Han knows it, that's why he's making me keep tabs on them.'

'So you're here as a spy for Han.' She should have known he wouldn't switch allegiance so easily.

'I don't pick sides, azzi. I'm just here to find the Earth Elemental. But in the meantime, I have to keep up the charade if I want to survive. Being on the good side of the Ling and the emperor means I'm privy to information on both ends. As they say, knowledge is power.' He shot her a scornful look. 'You, on the other hand, seem rather content to just be hanging around your new friends.'

'It's called keeping a low profile. People reveal all sorts of things when you don't seem like a threat.'

'Well, have your fun here then. Meanwhile, Han is building his special army and stocking up on ticha to eliminate all of us.'

The memory of that blasted herb almost made her gag reflex kick in. How she would dearly love to get rid of all traces of ticha on earth!

'The imperial garden,' Lazar said as though he had heard her thoughts. 'That's where they're growing it. And the shed next to it is where they store it. Maybe I'll see you on your next mission there.'

'You're going back to the palace?' Windshadow said.

'The emperor expects updates from me now and then or he gets suspicious. Until the rebellion is over, we all have our parts to play. Knowing when to take action is the key to victory.'

'Thank you for reciting *The War Handbook* to me,' she said dryly.

He flashed her a smirk and turned to leave. 'I'll see you soon, azzi. May you find an opportune moment to strike soon.'

Aside from whatever army Han was building, ticha was the largest weapon he had against the Ling, against the Elementals. As long as he was armed with that herb, he could debilitate them all. After all, that was how the first Oasis Emperor had defeated the Hesui Kingdom.

The first way to defeat the enemy was to strip him of his advantages. She could start with that.

* * *

The following evening, Windshadow and the siblings set out on their next mission. She was growing used to this routine, this life of hunting down officials while scavenging for pocket money. Each kill—each imperial scout and official down—felt like a small revenge on her part against Han, like blowing holes in his wall of defence. Someday, soon, she would find him on his own without protection or armour, and he would pay for how he had once treated her.

'What's the plan tonight?' Windshadow asked the twins as they headed towards the town at the foot of the mountain.

Yujin shot Windshadow a conspiratorial smile. 'Our spies told us there's a special person in the mountains now, and there's a huge bounty on this person's head. If we capture him, not only will we get that bounty, we'll make a huge dent in the imperial family.'

They arrived at the rooftop of a nondescript three-storey inn at the town periphery, where most of the shops were either boarded up or had closed for the night, leaving the entire street in near-total darkness. The only light Windshadow could see was from the scant lanterns in the distant houses.

Next to her, Yujin let out a tiny hiss, then pointed at the window— the only lit one at this hour—right below him. He was perched on the roof, knife drawn, ready to break in through the window. Five feet away, Yan gave her a subtle nod.

Their target tonight was supposedly a high-ranking imperial official who, for some reason, was travelling alone and holing up in a rather ramshackle inn. This was clearly someone who did not want to be noticed, which made his agenda all the more suspicious.

Windshadow nodded back, then changed into her elemental form and slipped in through the window. The room was sparse, with a few personal belongings strewn about, and the bed was still made, the sheets smooth and clean, which meant the occupant hadn't been here long. A man stood behind a screen door, changing out of his robes. Windshadow ducked into a corner and waited for the right moment to attack.

But the man turned around, as though he could sense her presence. 'Who's there?' He got dressed hurriedly and pushed aside the screen door, his gaze roaming wild around the room.

Windshadow was so surprised to see Prince Meng standing before her that she almost slid back into her human form. The Fourth Prince was their target?

He seemed no different from the last time she saw him—sharp, observant gaze roving around the room, calmness in his movements— although he stood in sharp contrast to his shabby surroundings.

'W-Windshadow?' he called softly, almost hopefully.

Windshadow debated whether to shift back into her human form to meet him. Yan and Yujin were waiting for her on the roof, prepared to break in if they felt that she was in danger. But she had questions for Prince Meng. How had he managed to return to Oasis Kingdom? What was he doing here in Yeli Mountain? What was his next plan of action? He wouldn't return if he didn't have leverage over Han, or at least something that would give him a fighting chance. Even if he was the only one who knew where the Immortal Spring was, he would still need time—and an Elemental—to unlock it and reap its magic.

She shifted, revealing herself standing right before him. His eyes widened. This was, admittedly, a rather odd circumstance for them to reunite—they had only ever been partners, never assassin and mark.

'You're getting better at sensing my presence, Prince Meng,' she remarked.

'No thanks to all the times you entered my room uninvited,' he said as soon as he got over his initial surprise at seeing her.

'Careful, now. You don't want anyone hearing what you just said. Might cause a scandal in the palace.'

His reply was terse. 'We are no longer in the palace, and we both know I meant nothing of *that* sort.'

She smirked. 'Indeed. I should be asking you what you're doing in the middle of the mountains all alone.'

'Well, finding you is a pleasant surprise—'

'It is?' she blurted. No one had ever said finding her was a pleasant surprise.

'But I came here to look for the Ling.'

Windshadow took a moment to put the pieces together. 'You want to build your own army.'

He nodded.

'And you think the Ling will fight for you? They'll sooner kill you and bring your head back to do some ritual than lift a finger on your behalf. They want their kingdom back, the kingdom your forefathers stole from them.'

He chuckled, as though they weren't discussing the potential peril he was putting himself in. As though he wasn't aware that he was already targeted by the Black Lotus Sect.

'They can certainly kill me,' he said. 'But that wouldn't do them any good if they wish to take back full power over this kingdom.'

Windshadow frowned. What else did Meng have up his sleeve? It was hard to read him sometimes. He was still and deep as a lake, never revealing everything he intended to do or say. It made working with him frustrating, but a part of Windshadow was always intrigued—and impressed—by his mind.

'What do you have that they need?' she asked.

He watched her for a moment, as though debating whether to tell her. 'What you and Desert Rose retrieved from the White Crypt last winter,' he said at last.

The scroll. The one that contained the clue to unlocking all the dormant magic in the land. The old sorcerers who served the First Oasis Emperor had purged all the magic in Oasis Kingdom upon its conception and locked it up in that scroll. He who possessed it, therefore, possessed the land. That was why it was kept within the imperial palace grounds, although the sorcerers were smart enough to hide the scroll away in the bottom of a dry well in the White Crypt so that it was near impossible for anyone to retrieve it.

Anyone except two Elementals, apparently.

'In order to restore their magic fully, they need what's locked inside the scroll,' Meng said. 'I intend to negotiate for the best possible outcome for both—'

Yan and Yujin swooped in through the window and landed in tandem. Meng jumped, stepping back on reflex. As much as she knew princes would have had some level of self-defence training growing up, Windshadow had never seen Meng pick up a weapon. Against the siblings, he was sorely outmatched.

'*Don't,*' Windshadow said before either of them could make a move towards him. The siblings shot her identical looks of incredulity. 'Trust me, you'll regret killing him. Let's take him back.'

'*No,*' Yan said. 'Our orders are to kill him. We're already deviating from the plan, revealing ourselves like that.'

'Who are you people?' Meng turned to Windshadow. 'You're with them now?'

'Never you mind, Fourth Prince,' Yujin said. 'Windshadow, hurry up and finish the job already.'

'I'm telling you you'll want him alive,' Windshadow said.

'What will we tell Huzun?' Yan asked.

'Prince Meng has his use,' Windshadow said. If there was one thing the sect understood, it was that value was currency, and whether a person lived or died depended on what he could provide.

'He's a wanted man and has no political leverage. What use do we have for him? Even his own family doesn't care about him anymore.' Yan drew her arm back, ready to attack. Windshadow flung a sharp blast of wind, cutting her in the right arm. Shock registered in

Yan's eyes. Windshadow wasn't one for apologies and explanations, but she felt the need for both when Yujin joined his sister's side and the siblings attacked in unison.

Windshadow shoved Meng aside and threw out her arms just in time to fend off the wave of energy rolling towards her. 'I'm not going to fight you two,' she snapped. 'The Fourth Prince has something that the Black Lotus Sect can use to strengthen our forces against Han. And I can use that to lure out the Earth Elemental.'

That stopped the siblings in their tracks.

'The Black Lotus Sect?' Meng echoed. 'Dark magic?'

'What does he have that the Earth Elemental would want?' Yan demanded, still not easing her stance.

Meng stepped out from behind Windshadow, keeping his eyes on the siblings' hands. 'Something you need if you want to overthrow the emperor.'

'And you're willing to offer it to the Earth Prince? The White Ling Sect?'

'I believe we can come to a mutual agreement.' His voice had returned to the one that Windshadow was familiar with. It was the voice he used when negotiating with King Falco and the shouren.

She should have known. Prince Meng always came prepared. He wouldn't have dared to step foot into Oasis Kingdom if he didn't already have all the support and fallback plans in place.

The siblings exchanged a look, silently debating whether to take Windshadow and Meng's word for it.

'Trust me,' Windshadow said. 'This will make the White Ling Sect sit up and take notice. And then we can have some fun.'

Eleven

Desert Rose

She awoke to the cloying scent of incense.

Desert Rose cracked open her eyes and found herself lying on the ground in the middle of what appeared to be a massive cave dimly lit by pinpricks of light. It wasn't until she regained her full vision that she realized that the lights were lanterns, and the reason they appeared so small was because of how vast the cave was. Overhead, the ceiling lay far beyond what she could see, but she was alone on a stone dais.

Deep, sonorous chanting soon filled the cave, seeming to ooze from every crevice around her, making the ground reverberate. She picked herself off the dais, shaking the heaviness from her head likely brought about by the unrelenting smell of incense and ceaseless chanting.

She was underground, deep underground. It seemed as though the earth had been hollowed out below the surface and she had fallen into another world altogether. The walls of this subterranean chamber stretched above her for as far as her eyes could see, their craggy faces throwing ominous shapes across the ground on which she stood.

She ventured down the path, guided by the glow of lanterns. The chanting subsided the further she went, until a strangely peaceful silence was all that remained.

An imperious voice broke through the stillness. 'I've been waiting for you for a long time.'

Desert Rose whipped around, reaching for her double knives at her waist belt, but came up empty. The speaker was a young man who appeared to be her age or perhaps slightly older, like Wei, although he had the quiet confidence of someone who had been around for some time. He had the warm skin tone of someone desert-born, though his mannerisms were decidedly elegant. His silk forest-green robe seemed excessively lush considering that they were a hundred feet deep in the earth, and he moved towards her with an almost regal, slightly cocky air that suggested he was secure in his status here.

'Well, any one of you, I suppose,' the young man went on breezily, seeming oblivious to her reaction to him, 'but you especially. We came so close to meeting the last time you were on this mountain, but then you got distracted by the fire and we didn't get a chance to reach you.'

The fire on Yeli Mountain that the Fifteenth Oasis Emperor had ordered had nearly killed them all—her, Wei, Qiu, and Qiu's husband and brother-in-law. Back then, she had no idea that beings other than the shouren resided here as well.

'I was a little preoccupied then, obviously,' she said.

He gave a placid nod, as though he were agreeing with her about the weather. 'It's a pleasure to meet you at last, Water Elemental.' He cocked his head and held her in a probing gaze. 'Our paths were bound to cross at some point.'

It was evident by now who he was. The Earth Elemental was not quite what she expected. Instead of a much older person who had spent years in hiding, cultivating his powers, he was young and annoyingly handsome with refined features, which likely also played a part in his self-assured demeanour.

'Can't say I feel the same way,' she said, resisting the urge to massage her throbbing temples. 'Given that your people kidnapped me and dumped me here like a sack of potatoes.'

His lips twisted in amusement. 'You are far more valuable than potatoes. We have a mission to accomplish together, you and I.'

Desert Rose snorted. 'Aren't we destined to kill each other, you and I? Why are you wasting time chatting with me here?' Was this just a ruse to make her lower her guard against him? Had he planned an ambush where his people, now hidden from plain sight, were ready to attack her at his command?

He chuckled. 'Killing you would be foolish. Why should we waste our Elemental powers destroying each other when we could do so much more together? Mortals are destroying the natural world with their inventions and wars, and we are all the poorer for it. The world is ailing, unbalanced, and descending into chaos. We have to stop it from hurtling towards its own destruction. We, the chosen ones.'

Desert Rose let out a laugh. 'We were not chosen. Look at us— orphans and rebels and a boy who tries too hard to make himself important.'

The Earth Elemental seemed to take no offence at her words. 'Regardless of how you view it, the fact remains that we are different. Special. And we have a duty to perform.'

'My duty is to my tribe.'

'It is to more than just your tribe, and you know it. The fate of the world hangs in the balance, and it is up to us to fulfil the prophecy and set things right again. Look at how magic has corrupted this land and its inhabitants, how it has driven countries to war, to develop destructive weapons that can wipe out entire groups of people. Do we want *our* people to continue being subjected to this? The Damohai used to rule the largest and strongest empire in the world.'

The Damohai. The human-immortal race that descended from the Sky Princess and Earth Prince. Her people. Even the thought of it felt foreign.

'The *Dugur tribe* are my people,' she said.

He only smiled indulgently, as though he knew better than her. 'Your sentimentalism is quite mortal. You will soon see the futility of it.'

'Those snatchers. Are they your people? You've been making them go out into the villages and kill innocent civilians?'

He shook his head. 'Those are the Black Ling. We do not see eye to eye with them on various things, but we have agreed to put our differences aside for the sake of our cause. It matters not what magic they practise or how they survive aboveground, nor do trifling sect politics concern me. We are of the same kind. We are Ling, and we should not discriminate amongst ourselves. Instead, we need to work towards a common goal.'

'And that goal is to engage in rampant murder?'

He gave her a smile that could be interpreted as either patient or condescending. 'It is to become strong enough to rebuild our kingdom. The Old Kingdom, that is. Hesui. Not this bastard kingdom they call Oasis. We have been gathering our people over the years and it is only a matter of time before the Damohai regains its lost glory.'

The Earth Elemental's gaze drifted to something over her shoulder. 'Oh, good. He's still alive,' he remarked breezily. 'Well done, Priestess.'

Desert Rose spun around to find a stately-looking woman standing at the entrance of the chamber with—

'Wei!' she cried, dashing towards him and almost colliding straight into him due to the speed at which he was also coming at her. He appeared unharmed, as far as she could tell.

He scanned her from head to toe, also checking if she was injured. 'Are you hurt?' She shook her head, but he didn't let go of her hand. The Ling seemed to have kept them both intact, if a little shaken.

'Your Highness,' the priestess greeted with a bow, to which the Earth Elemental responded with a dismissive wave of his hand.

'We had to keep your friend alive,' the Earth Elemental told Desert Rose. 'I believe we can come to a mutually beneficial agreement for both parties, Third Prince. Or should I say, aspiring emperor?' He tilted his head.

Wei maintained his stoic demeanour, giving nothing away.

The Earth Elemental turned back to Desert Rose, unperturbed by Wei's response. 'I think it's time you met our people. They would be thrilled to meet you at last. Tomorrow, we will hold an official ceremony and induct you into the Damohai.'

Wei's hand tightened around hers. She squeezed his back. She might share the same blood with the Damohai, but they were as unfamiliar to her as the Lettorians and even Oasis citizens.

'The Damohai are our real tribe. Just because you were separated from them all this while doesn't make them any less family. They need us, just as we need them. Get to know them, and you will see just how alike we all are.'

She narrowed her eyes at the Earth Elemental. 'Why are you going through all this effort for me?'

'As I said, you and I have a mission to accomplish together.'

She sighed. 'So you keep saying. But what exactly do you want from me?'

His reply came without hesitation. 'Your hand in marriage.'

Desert Rose blinked. Wei's hand tightened around hers, and she had to tug on his hand to stop him from lunging at the Earth Elemental. 'My what?'

'Hand in marriage,' he repeated. 'A union, to be more precise. One between man and woman.' His gaze shuffled between her and Wei, and he let out a chuckle. 'Oh, don't look so aggrieved, both of you. Think of it as a marriage of convenience, if you'd like. One Elemental may not be strong enough to eliminate the rest *and* make it to the end, but a union between two complementing ones would make us twice as strong. Why kill each other and waste all this perfectly good energy when we can combine our powers, rebuild a kingdom, and ascend to the heavens?'

He was mad. Living in this underground world must have addled his mind so heavily that he had become delusional enough to believe such a hare-brained idea could work, that they could cheat fate and subvert the prophecy. There could only be one surviving Elemental at the end—the gods had willed it so. To imagine otherwise was preposterous.

Yet, he seemed wholly convinced about his plan.

'You are actually serious,' she said at last.

'Of course I am. I didn't go to all this length to bring you here if I weren't.

'I'm not going to marry you,' she said, in case it wasn't obvious to him. 'That's the last thing I would ever do.'

'I understand matters of the heart cannot be forced, but there are more important responsibilities you and I share. Our people have languished for centuries, waiting for the day we reunite them, restore their home and their glory. This is the best time to strike, while the Imperial Army is still recovering from the battle and the Wall is down. We must not delay.' He glanced at Wei. 'You and the Third Prince have no future together anyway, and you both know it. The least you can do is make good use of your limited time here to unite our people again.'

'You're insane,' Wei spat before Desert Rose could reply. He tugged on her hand. 'Let's go, Rose. We're leaving this rabbit hole.'

Desert Rose followed his lead numbly, her mind awhirl.

The Priestess appeared right in front of them, a menacing vision in white, blocking their way. 'You will accord the Earth Prince due respect,' she warned.

The Earth Elemental held up a hand and the Priestess took a step back. He circled around Desert Rose and Wei, his antagonistic gaze daring Wei to act out. 'Think of this as a mutually beneficial arrangement, Third Prince. You need your army, I need my Elemental partner. I can give you the backing you need to defeat your brother. All I ask is for you to let go of the Water Elemental's hand.'

Desert Rose shared a look with Wei. There was no question that neither of them would let go of each other's hand. Was there?

'I understand this must be a lot for both of you to take in. We can speak more in the morning. You are an esteemed guest in my abode, and so is your friend, so please make yourselves at home here. The Priestess shall show you both to your chambers.' He turned to leave, signalling the end of the conversation. 'Have a good rest tonight.'

'Wait,' Wei said, taking a step towards the Earth Elemental again before Desert Rose tugged him back. 'You can't just—'

'You have one night to make your decision.' The Earth Elemental turned around. This time, his gaze had lost all trace of amicability. 'But I will rebuild this kingdom if it's the last thing I do. Do not stand in my way.'

* * *

The silence in Yeli Mountain that night felt different, as heavy as the packed earth and as haunting as a lone wolf's howl.

As the Priestess led them through a series of tunnels in silence, sparing barely a backward glance, Desert Rose never once let go of Wei's hand. Its familiar warmth and sturdiness felt like the only thing anchoring her to the present, amid her worries about the future and all the lives on the line depending on her next move.

They came to a stop before two adjacent chambers with matching circular doorways carved into the rock. The air here, likely regulated by the Ling's magic, was cool and fragrant, threaded with an earthy scent.

Under different circumstances, this might have been an experience worth writing home about.

The Priestess turned to acknowledge them at last. 'At dawn, the bell will ring for all to rouse, and you will both proceed to the Grand Chamber. Everyone will be waiting there, including His Highness. Do not be late.'

She left before either of them could protest.

In the wake of her departure, Desert Rose and Wei stood reeling in the silence, their hands still interlocked.

'Well,' Wei said at length. 'This is an interesting turn of events.' He peered into the room next to him. 'Lodgings seem passable, at least.'

Desert Rose saw through his attempt at levity. He was avoiding the inevitable topic. The last time they had been manoeuvred into a corner was in Lettoria by the scheming King Falco. This time, it was an Elemental hungry for vengeance and power who would drive them apart from each other.

Yet, their paths were meant to diverge at some point all along. She was an Elemental destined to die either way, and he was a mortal prince fighting for the throne and his kingdom, one that they were about to bring a revolution upon. They were temporary allies who had fallen in love with each other in the brief time their paths had crossed, but gods, how she hated the fleetingness of this life!

'The Ling would make a formidable army . . .' she said slowly, peering at his face. 'You would want them on your side if you're going to overthrow Han.'

He stared at her in disbelief. 'Please don't tell me you're actually considering his ridiculous proposal.'

'Wei . . .'

'Because I would rather have no army if it means you have to sacrifice yourself and marry . . .' He struggled to find the right word to convey his scorn. '*Him*,' he spat at last.

Desert Rose gave him a sad smile. 'But you need an army. How are you going to fight against Han on your own?'

'I'll . . . I'll work with the shouren if I have to, gather a bunch of rebels, form my own army. We don't need the White

Ling Sect. We can find another sect to work with—this kingdom has no lack of rebel factions, I'm sure.'

'But the White Ling Sect rules over all the sects, all the Ling. They have influence, and they have power. They have the Earth Elemental with them, and shamans and priestesses . . . If anyone is able to overthrow Han, it's them.'

'I still have the Ghost King's support. We have the Ghost Army behind us too. They're still waiting for you to free them—so is your father. I'm not going to let some cocky mountain-dweller take you away. I made a promise to your father that I'll . . .' His gaze drifted away.

'You'll?' she prompted. He did not respond. 'Wei.'

He turned back to her. 'I promised him that I'll protect you till my very last breath, whatever the outcome.'

Heat rushed up her neck all the way up to her face. She and Wei had never been the sort who made grand proclamations of love or lofty promises of eternity. They both knew how their story would end.

'Don't marry him . . . please.' She could see that he hated the desperation in his voice, and she wished more than anything that she could turn her back on her destiny and walk out of here with him.

But she couldn't ignore her duty to her tribe, her family. Her tribe—and her father—was still waiting for her to reunite them. And she knew Wei had made avenging his family's death his life's mission now. He would take down Han if it was the last thing he did.

Marrying another Elemental seemed like a ludicrous idea when they were prophesied to kill one another. Could there possibly be another way to avoid that ultimate end? Her time was limited here either way. If she could help Wei *and* fulfil the prophecy, then perhaps this was the best solution for everyone—for now.

They had their roles to fulfil that would take them down separate paths. Perhaps the end was just coming sooner than they were prepared for.

She laid a hand on his cheek. 'Maybe this is bigger than both of us.' She stepped into her chamber before he could say anything more.

Twelve

Wei

He watched her disappear into her chamber. The distance between them seemed to be growing larger with time. It seemed harder to hold on to her these days; there was always something standing between them, be it the prophecy, a rival Elemental, or a power-hungry king and his political ambitions.

Sleep was near impossible that night. Every little sound made Wei tense. The earth seemed to hum in its own language, alive and sentient, and Wei was kept awake by the irrational thought of being buried alive in his sleep.

At dawn, he sprung up in bed at the first ring of the bell and got dressed. Desert Rose was at the entrance of his chamber, already dressed and waiting for him, when he emerged from it. He saw the same trepidation in her bloodshot eyes as the one he felt inside.

'I'm guessing you didn't get much sleep either,' she said, peering at his face.

'The threat of being buried alive was overwhelming,' he confessed.

A pair of Ling servants came to usher them down the tunnel they had wound through the night before. As they got closer to the Grand Chamber, the sounds of a convocation grew louder.

The Grand Chamber had transformed since the day before. The original lanterns were replaced with ornate ones that burned steadily and lit the chamber aglow, and yellow sashes ran down from chamber walls, cascading towards the ground. There, about two hundred people milled about, dressed in various displays of ceremonial robes. The White Ling Sect was a homogeneous-looking group, each tall and fair and almost ethereally beautiful. Even the children carried themselves with a stateliness that reminded Wei of the imperial family, except unlike his family members, the sect members here greeted one another like old friends. A young couple on the left were setting off a series of coloured sparks that enchanted a group of children. A trio of silver-bearded old men were speaking with a group of young people who bowed to them profusely.

Running down the centre of the chamber was a yellow carpet that ended at a dais upon which the Priestess stood, looking ethereal in her pristine white robes, her long ebony hair flowing behind her.

Wei almost let out a snort. People here sure loved their ceremonies as much as the imperial family.

The Priestess's gaze snapped over to him as though she had heard his thoughts. She stepped aside to reveal the Earth Prince lounging in an elaborately carved high-back chair on a podium in the middle of the platform, looking almost bored until he caught sight of Wei and Desert Rose.

He sat up at once, his gaze fixed on Desert Rose as he broke into a slow smile. Wei scowled, pulling Desert Rose closer to him as the Earth Elemental beckoned for them to join him.

The Earth Elemental rose and raised his hands. 'My fellow Ling.' His silky voice reverberated around the chamber, stopping everyone in the midst of their conversations.

They bowed in unison and chorused, 'Our exalted greetings to the Earth Prince.'

'We have with us two guests today, the Water Elemental and the Third Prince Wei.' He gestured for them to step forward again. Every pair of eyes fell upon them as they strode up to the dais. Whispers broke out amongst the crowd, and Wei caught snatches of conversations that involved the words 'rogue prince' and 'outsider'. He ignored them all, feeling a small vindictive sense of satisfaction when the Earth Elemental's gaze narrowed at his hand interlocked with Desert Rose's.

They came to a stop before the Earth Elemental, who seemed completely unaffected by the mutinous looks both of them were sending him. He pulled them apart and turned them around to face the crowd so that they were both flanking him.

'This is the moment we have been waiting for—another Elemental has come to join us,' the Earth Elemental announced, to which the crowd responded with unanimous cheers. 'And not just any Elemental, but the Elemental most compatible with me. Water and Earth, Fire and Air are the most complementary pairs. How lucky that the Elemental we found would be my perfect match.'

Wei shared a look with Desert Rose and resisted the urge to roll his eyes as the crowd erupted in cheers once more.

The Earth Elemental waved a hand and the crowd simmered down. 'And we also have the Third Prince from the imperial family.'

The response to Wei was significantly less welcoming. Murmurs rippled through the crowd and Wei caught several sideways stares as the crowd discussed among themselves. Here was a traitorous prince who had turned his back on the kingdom before, and now he was back with his affiliations and motives undiscerned. He had never cared for winning the hearts of the people, having wanted no part of the throne, but now that he was here to seek an army, he finally understood the need for the people's trust, if not support.

The Earth Elemental made no effort to dissolve the tension among the crowd, moving on to the next thing on his agenda instead.

'The Damohai had been severely weakened by the Oasis emperors after they took our land, dispersed us, and purged the kingdom of magic. But over the centuries, the Damohai have found each other and grown stronger. No longer are we as scattered as we used to be. No longer are we a weak tribe too scant to challenge the imperial family, the ones who robbed us of our kingdom. Today, we shall rebuild our people. We shall reclaim what was once ours.' He glanced at Desert Rose. 'Damohai, please step forward to meet the Water Elemental.'

About fifty of them proceeded to the front of the crowd, raising their hands as though thanking the heavens. A few weeks ago, Wei wasn't even sure that the Damohai existed. Now this legendary race of people stood before him in the flesh, proving that magic could never be destroyed no matter how hard his ancestors had tried to erase it from the kingdom.

The Damohai appeared no different from the others. Apart from their naturally warmer skin tones, they dressed and spoke like Oasis people. If he didn't know better, Wei wouldn't be able to guess that they were the descendant race of immortals. It was only until they collectively raised their hands to emit a warm glow that Wei noticed the telltale steel-grey hue of their eyes—the exact colour that Desert Rose's eyes turned whenever she used her magic too.

'Our exalted greetings to the Water Elemental,' they intoned.

'Together, the Water Elemental and I will reunite our people and restore the magic that has been purged from this land. We will rebuild this kingdom in our design,' the Earth Elemental declared. 'That shall be our legacy.'

The crowd roared their praises again. Wei couldn't help but think that the Earth Elemental enjoyed such validation, the pomp and pageantry, and the worship of these people. He glanced at Desert Rose, whose palpable discomfort made her avoid everyone's eyes and turn to him. Wei understood. The Damohai might technically be her people, but she felt no kinship with them, not like she did with her own tribe. She was here for them, not these people.

'How the Third Prince fits into our plans is a lot trickier,' the Earth Elemental went on after the cheering died down. 'Priestess, perhaps you would like to explain more.'

The Priestess took a step towards them, her movements so graceful it appeared as though she was gliding through the air. Wei narrowed his eyes at her, daring her to read his mind again. She only smirked and turned to face the crowd.

'The Third Prince has ambitions to overthrow his brother and take over the throne. Yet, given his history, he has little chance of becoming a legitimate emperor—at least, not with the current state of imperial affairs. What he needs, therefore, is an army.'

The murmur reached a fever pitch.

'It is time we take back ownership and control of our land, that which the Zhao dynasty has robbed us of for centuries,' the Earth

Elemental declared. 'We have waited long enough, gathered our forces. But we alone will not be enough to rebel. We need a figurehead, someone who will not only be the face of the rebellion but who also has intimate knowledge of the imperial family. The Third Prince, the dark horse of the family, will be at the forefront of the rebellion and assist us in overthrowing Emperor Han.'

'Wait just a moment,' Wei said. 'I never agreed—'

'Today also marks a special occasion,' the Earth Elemental continued, barrelling over Wei, 'where the Water Elemental and I are to be in union.'

Rage rose in Wei's gut. He had not come all this way here only to be strongarmed into an agreement. He wanted an army, but not if it meant that Desert Rose and the Earth Elemental would go into 'union' (whatever that meant), and not if he was going to be 'the face of the rebellion', a puppet on the throne controlled by the Ling.

His first instinct was to push the Earth Elemental off that dais and wipe that smug look off his face. But a glance from Desert Rose made him pause. He was the only mortal in this chamber. Assaulting the *Earth Prince* would ensure that he did not make it out of here alive. Worse, it might jeopardize Desert Rose's safety too.

The Earth Elemental was staring at her expectantly. How had they come from being manipulated by the king of Lettoria to being manipulated by an Elemental with delusions of grandeur? As much as he detested his ancestors' filthy deeds to establish Oasis Kingdom, Wei would rather give up his fight for the throne than lead a revolution just so the Ling could use him as their puppet emperor.

And Desert Rose . . . Would she really agree to marrying the Earth Elemental? She had said last night that she had to do what must be done, but why did it seem as though neither of them had any choice in this matter?

She spoke at last, her voice almost drowning in the vastness of the chamber. 'Will you lend all your might to Wei and support him in his mission to defeat his brother?'

Wei's heart sank. 'Rose, no . . .' But her gaze was fixed on the Earth Elemental.

The Earth Elemental beamed. 'Of course. You have my wo—'

A pair of sect members scurried up the platform, seeking the Earth Elemental's attention. Wei was grateful for the distraction—at least this would delay the decision or buy them some time to think this through—but his hand moved to his waist belt, ready to pull out his dagger.

'Speak,' the Earth Elemental ordered.

'Your Highness, we have found our target. He's travelling up the mountain now with a few companions who appear to be from the Black Lotus Sect.'

Wei's knowledge of the Black Lotus Sect was shallow, as was his understanding of the Ling. The history books he read in the palace never informed him about the goings-on in the underbelly of Yeli Mountain, nor about the politics and hierarchy among the Ling. All he had heard about the Black Lotus Sect was that they were a deviant faction of dark magic–practising Ling. Whomever this target was, he was crucial if he had the attention of both the Black Lotus Sect and the White Ling Sect.

The Earth Elemental's eyes lit up. 'Invite them over, please.'

'Our men are already bringing them in, Your Highness.'

'Perfect.'

Right on cue, the crowd parted below the platform, letting through three figures that edged through in a single file—a young man and a girl dressed in identical black tunics, and—

Desert Rose let out a small gasp. 'Meng.'

Wei stared. It was his half-brother Meng indeed. The last he saw him was in Lettoria, after Desert Rose was poisoned and Wei was about to head to the battlefield. Meng had promised to find the antidote to Desert Rose's poison and he had. Wei had assumed he would return to Lettoria to continue his political alliance with King Falco, but perhaps without their special army, Lettoria was no longer a worthy ally after the battle at Danxi Plains and Meng had returned to Oasis Kingdom to seek new alliances. Wei had never known whether to trust Meng. Even if their motives had been aligned for a while, Meng was still the person who had arranged for Yong's murder. Wei could never forgive him in this lifetime.

And now, whatever his agenda was, he was here in Yeli Mountain after the alliance with Lettoria fell through. Wei knew better than to let his guard down against Meng—his brother was the best strategist among them all, and he would not be back in Oasis Kingdom if he hadn't prepared any sort of leverage.

This only meant one thing: Meng still hadn't given up on taking back the throne.

Despite being overthrown by Han, who had the support of the Empress Dowager and the Council, Meng had chosen to come back and keep fighting for the throne—whether for the sake of the kingdom and the people or his own agenda, Wei did not know. But this meant that he and Meng would once again stand against each other, half-brothers born on the same night, under the same star.

Their lives had been determined by others at birth, when Meng had become the favoured son while Wei was accused by High Advisor Mian of being the inevitable bane of his father's existence. Now, here in the underbelly of the mountain, among a secret sect of sorcerers and magical beings, they would each forge their own fates, whether it meant continuing their family's legacy or putting an end to it.

'What a party we have with us today,' said the Earth Elemental, looking positively gleeful about the new company. 'Fourth Prince, how kind of you to join the White Ling Sect.'

Thirteen

Meng

The Ling. Meng could not believe his eyes. He was standing amongst the storied people who had, if his research was accurate, descended from the Damohai of the Old Kingdom. The original owners of this land. The land that his ancestors had stolen and built their own dynasty upon after weakening and purging all magic from it.

He felt as though he should apologize, first and foremost, but words failed him. He could only stare at the horde of people before him. The stories he had read from the restricted section in the imperial library were true. The Ling existed, not just as myths, but in the flesh, deep in the heart of Yeli Mountain. His excitement at the discovery made him almost forget why he was here, or the potential danger of being the only mortal amongst a whole throng of magic practitioners.

'Meng!' A familiar voice pulled him out of his thoughts.

'Rose,' Meng breathed. Wei had his eyes narrowed at him in suspicion, an expression that Meng felt almost grateful to see. At least he was not the only mortal in this place, and his half-brother still regarded him with the same suspicion, so familiar it was nearly a welcoming sight.

A lithe young man, clearly the leader of all present—which meant he was the Earth Elemental—beamed at him, his hands slightly raised as though he might pull out a weapon any moment. 'What a party we have with us today. Fourth Prince, how kind of you to join the White Ling Sect.'

Murmurs broke out upon the mention of Meng's identity. Desert Rose shared a look with Wei, likely wondering what Meng was doing here. Meng wished he had a good answer for them, but he was still catching up with everything that had happened ever since Windshadow broke into his room in that inn—being taken to meet Huzun and almost losing his life on the spot, convincing him that he had what the Ling needed to take back power, learning about the Black Lotus Sect's ploy to put out the word about the scroll in his possession and then use him as bait to lure out the White Ling Sect scouts, and finally being captured by the White Ling Sect members to stand among them now.

Every decision Meng had made ever since being dethroned by his brother had been more unexpected—and even ludicrous—than the last, but *this* had to top all of them. If word got out that the last Oasis Emperor was colluding with the the Ling, it would certainly hurt his chances of regaining favour in court.

But if he had his way, Meng would no longer have to seek approval from the council of corruptible yes-men who turned their backs on him as soon as the tides turned. He would revolutionize the imperial system and clear out every official who had betrayed him.

'I understand you have something of interest to us, and we would like to find out how we might come to an agreement.' The man's voice was light and silky, but somehow seemed to carry a veiled warning.

Yan and Yujin clasped their hands and bowed in greeting. Meng, from years of being in the palace, could detect a hint of nervousness—and fear—from the way they shifted on their feet. 'Exalted greetings to the Earth Prince.'

'We apologize for the intrusion,' Yan said, her head still bowed.

'It's hardly an intrusion if you were invited here.' He glanced at Meng. 'Specifically you, Fourth Prince.'

Meng realized he had remained upright the entire time, eyeing the so-called Earth Prince rather sceptically. He dipped his head. 'Greetings, Earth Prince.'

The Earth Elemental waved a hand, ushering him onto the dais where he stood with Desert Rose, Wei, and a woman dressed in a pristine white robe. Meng shared a look with Yan and Yujin, then stepped up onto the podium, trying to look more composed than he felt.

'Everyone, meet the Fourth Prince, Zhao Meng, of the imperial family,' the Earth Elemental announced to the crowd, which dutifully greeted him in unison. 'Most of us would know him as the Sixteenth Oasis Emperor just until recently when his brother dethroned him.'

Meng tried not to wince. The sting of the coup never dulled over time. For the Earth Elemental to bring this up right after introducing him to the crowd felt like an intentional slight, as though to remind him—and everyone present—who held the real power here.

The Earth Elemental paced around Meng, his gaze never leaving him. He appeared somehow to have been expecting him, if the thoughtful anticipation in his eyes was any indication.

Meng levelled his gaze, trying not to glance around for any sign of Windshadow. He couldn't sense her presence around him—the air here was still, almost heavy, and there was no trace of wind. Had she entered this chamber like she had intended to?

'Two sons of the imperial family in our territory,' the Earth Elemental drawled. It reminded Meng of King Falco, who had received both him and Wei in his kingdom last spring as well. But this man appeared younger than King Falco, perhaps around Wei's age. Surely Meng could be a match for him strategically? 'Priestess,' he called to the white-robed lady next to him. 'What do you read?'

'Indeed, he is here to make a proposition.' Her voice was throaty but commanding, making her seem more mature than her youthful appearance suggested. 'He believes he has what we need for the rebellion.'

The rebellion? It was true then, that the Ling intended to rebel. The scroll would unlock the magic in the land, which could make them strong enough to challenge the Imperial Army and Han's rule. The woman named Priestess was clearly a mind reader. Meng suddenly felt protective of his thoughts, but there was no hiding it from a Ling as powerful as her.

'He wants to know how we intend to revolt, Your Highness,' the Priestess said.

The Earth Prince raised his brows, looking even more intrigued this time. 'They say you have an inquisitive mind, Prince Meng, and a tactical one too. I would be remiss to not guard my intentions against you. After all, you were once an Oasis Emperor, and my people and I have long suffered under imperial rule.'

'I can offer an apology for my ancestors' actions, but I'm sure that's not what you seek. I can assure you, however, that if you assist me in taking back the throne, you and your people will never again have to live in fear of persecution.'

'That's very kind of you, Fourth Prince,' he replied coolly. 'I have heard about your reign, and I'm sure the Priestess can fill me in on the vision you have for Oasis Kingdom. But if we were to support either of you to ascend the throne, it would have to be on our terms. This kingdom belongs to us, and we intend to take back control of it'—he glanced at Wei—'regardless of which one of you dethrones your brother.'

Wei was here for the same purpose as him? Not just to dethrone Han, but to take over it? As far as Meng knew, Wei had never been interested in ruling. He had always aspired to living life outside the kingdom. But perhaps, after everything that had happened, his goals had changed—for better or worse.

'I have what you need to restore your magic to its full capacity,' Meng said. 'But until we can agree upon the specifics of this partnership, I'm afraid I cannot trust you with it.'

The scroll was the last bit of leverage he had. Until he had figured out Ling's plans for the rebellion, he would hold on to the last remnant of protection for *his* people—the citizens of Oasis Kingdom, the mortals who would be completely vulnerable should magic be restored.

The Earth Prince frowned, glancing to his side all of a sudden as though sensing something there. He threw out his hands, emitting a clod of dirt from his fingertips and striking something in mid-air.

A grunt next to Meng made him jump. The next thing he saw was Windshadow sprawled onto the ground unceremoniously before him. The Ling gasped, but the Priestess only stepped aside to give Windshadow and the Earth Elemental their space. Windshadow leapt back on her feet right away, her gaze fixed on the Earth Elemental.

'Wind Elemental, what a pleasure.' The Earth Elemental's eyes gleamed in excitement. 'Somehow you managed to evade my Priestess's Eye.'

'A convenient ability,' Windshadow said, matching his carefully measured tone, although she still appeared disgruntled about being caught off guard by the Earth Elemental.

They sized each other up like beasts in a ring, circling slowly, ready to attack any moment.

'I've heard you're hard to pin down,' the Earth Elemental said, stepping to the side pointedly.

'It is in my nature,' Windshadow agreed, mimicking his footwork.

The Earth Elemental continued shifting his position, biding his time. 'It must be nice not being anchored to the ground. Very liberating, I presume.'

She smirked. 'It certainly comes in handy in a fight with an Elemental pinned to the ground, if that's what you're worried about.'

Meng had seen what Windshadow could do with her powers. He had seen the destructive power of the wind, ferocious and invisible. Compared to the Earth Elemental, she had an innate advantage on the attacking front. Yet, the Earth Elemental had allegedly been in hiding for a long time, cultivating his magic. Meng had a feeling there was more to him than any of them expected.

The Earth Elemental waved his arm, as though taking his cue to display his prowess, this time raising the ground beneath their feet and making it undulate like waves. The ground roared to life like a rousing beast attempting to shake them off its back.

On the platform where only the Elementals, Wei, Meng, and the Priestess stood, only the Earth Elemental was able to maintain his balance. The rest of them toppled one by one, losing their footing. The Earth Elemental raised the ground higher until they were all on a precipice about twenty feet above the other Ling.

Wei and Desert Rose sprawled onto the ground at once and grabbed the edge so that they wouldn't fall off. Meng followed suit. Windshadow transformed into her element just as she slipped, turning into a gale that whipped around the Earth Elemental.

The ground trembled and shook, threatening to toss them all off. Meng clung on for dear life.

'Wei!' Desert Rose cried. Meng whipped around to see her fling out her hands to catch Wei as he slid off the edge. From her fingertips came a skein of water, elastic yet firm, that caught Wei by the waist and hoisted him back up. She threw her arms around him when he was safely by her side again.

Despite the pang he felt at the sight of Desert Rose embracing his brother, Meng was relieved to see her using her power again. She had taken the antidote he had acquired for her, and it had worked. That was all that mattered, he told himself.

Windshadow was launching herself repeatedly, relentlessly at the Earth Elemental, whose legs were now planted in the platform. He fended off each attack with explosions of dirt and earth that sprayed everywhere. The Priestess buried her face in her arms as she struggled to maintain her footing.

'A little help here, Rose?' Windshadow called.

Desert Rose threw out her hands and squeezed her eyes shut. Soon, the ground beneath them was moving again, this time like a tidal wave. Meng looked down. The earth, upon interference by Desert Rose's power, had softened and turned into mud. The platform dissolved and they flowed towards the ground again, back to level ground with the rest of the Ling. Everyone scrambled away from them as they got closer to avoid being caught in the sludge.

It was hard to tell who had the upper hand in this fight. All three Elementals—Earth, Water, and Air—seemed equally capable of staving off each other's attacks. They could wield the elements—they could move mountains and conjure storms and call on floods. They could bring down an entire kingdom if they chose to.

Right now, they seemed intent on tearing this place apart. The Earth Elemental was ripping up the walls and the very ground they stood on, threatening to bury them all alive. Windshadow tore through the earth, a vicious gale skirting around the deluge of rock and soil, lacerating anyone she got too close to, especially the Priestess. As Windshadow fended off the Earth Elemental's right-hand woman, Desert Rose drew her raised hands together and conjured up a massive wave that rose from her outstretched palms towards the Earth Elemental.

'Stand back,' she called to Wei, even though she came close to being smashed by a falling boulder had Wei not pulled her out of the way in time. The wave rose higher and higher, looming over them. 'Stand back!' she yelled again.

But just before she could send the wave crashing down on the Earth Elemental, a rumble overhead, low and insistent, made them pause in the middle of their fight. They looked up in unison, as did everyone else. Desert Rose lowered her hands and the wave dissipated, leaving behind just a telltale shimmer.

Confused murmurs broke out among the crowd. They were hundreds of feet deep underground, but the sound was loud enough to reverberate around the chamber. How would anyone be able to find them here?

The Earth Elemental turned to the Priestess, abandoning the fight with Desert Rose and Windshadow. 'Priestess, what do you see?'

'It's the Imperial Army,' she murmured. 'Their shamans blocked my Eye and launched a surprise attack.'

Meng frowned. Since when did the Imperial Army have a shaman?

The Priestess glanced at him, having heard his thoughts. 'The special army that the emperor is building has a shaman.'

The magical army Han was building. He was already sending it after the Ling in this impromptu attack.

'Oh, of all the times to cause a disturbance,' the Earth Elemental grumbled.

'Guard the Earth Prince!' someone yelled as the ground shook and rumbled some more. A group of Ling dressed in identical yellow robes corralled everyone together and directed them to the corners of the chamber for safety, while others formed a ring around the Earth Elemental, poised for combat.

The Earth Elemental only chuckled. 'I appreciate the intention, folks. But this is not a cause for alarm.'

'The army is crude, their paltry army easily defeatable, Your Highness,' the Priestess scoffed.

'Thank you, Priestess. I'll take care of this. Please watch out for the more vulnerable ones among us.' The Earth Elemental closed his eyes and raised his hands above him as though he was holding up the ceiling. Then, with a wave of his arms, he parted the earth.

The earth groaned again as the ceiling yawned open. Rocks and soil cascaded from high above, pelting them relentlessly. Meng threw himself against the wall with Yan and Yujin, close to where the Ling huddled by the corners they had been directed to. Wei reached for Desert Rose's hand just before she lost her footing, and they sprawled on the ground together. Only the Earth Elemental and the Priestess remained upright, calm and unfazed.

Sunlight streamed in through a hole the size of his room at the inn where Windshadow found him, and what seemed like hundreds of soldiers tumbled through it, screaming as they plunged through the air. Their screams died as soon as they landed with bone-shaking thuds. Meng flinched and turned away.

The Earth Elemental flicked a hand, and the ground did his bidding once again, coming to life and burying all the soldiers in packed soil at terrifying speed. Those who had miraculously survived the fall would now be buried alive.

Shouts aboveground echoed down the chamber. There were more of them out there.

When the Earth Elemental turned back to Meng and the Black Lotus Sect members, there was no trace of mirth left in his eyes.

'You dare lure the Imperial Army to our territory?' His voice was quiet with cold fury.

Yan and Yujin threw themselves into a deep bow, their hands clasped before them. 'We did nothing of the sort, Your Highness. We would never—'

'Evacuate everyone immediately,' the Earth Elemental ordered. The yellow-robed Ling leapt to action, directing the young and elderly to safety first.

Windshadow shifted back into her human form and stood by Desert Rose, watching the Earth Prince order the Ling to leave the chamber and the Priestess help them down the passageway towards safety. The process was fairly efficient, and all of the Ling made it out of the chamber just before a deluge of water poured into the chamber through the hole in the ceiling.

But it didn't end just there. The ceiling shook and rumbled once more, and the hole gave way further, growing even larger as more earth collapsed inwards.

Before the Earth Elemental could seal up the hole, he let out a cry as water droplets pelted him, then more water soaked him from head to toe.

Desert Rose crumbled to the ground, grimacing in pain as she and Windshadow too were both drenched.

'Ticha,' Windshadow rasped, letting out a few curses.

Meng rushed over to them. Wei was shielding Desert Rose with his body as he tried to get them to a drier spot.

The herb could not only negate magic, when used raw it could also cause unimaginable pain to magical beings. Meng had seen it being used as an instrument of torture in the imperial prison multiple times, most recently last spring when Han locked Windshadow up and force-fed her ticha.

Only the imperial family had the ability to use ticha so liberally, thanks to the plot of land behind the palace they had dedicated to growing the plant. If the Imperial Army was here with bucket-loads of ticha-infused water, that meant Han knew what he was dealing with here.

The Earth Elemental was shaking violently as he crawled to a corner. On top of the lacerations Windshadow had given him earlier, the ticha attack seemed to be the last straw for him. Desert Rose and Windshadow huddled by the side, where Wei and Meng tried to block them from the water as much as they could.

A ferocious blaze swept through the chamber with a deafening roar, knocking Meng off his feet.

Windshadow let out another string of curses. 'Lazar,' she croaked. Meng had learned from her how the Fire Elemental had split his loyalties between the Black Lotus Sect and Han, but it was clear now that his loyalties lay firmly with Han.

The tunnel where the rest of the Ling and the Black Lotus Sect members had escaped was now obstructed by debris and earth. The Priestess had just returned for the Earth Elemental after sending off the last Ling when the ceiling of the passageway collapsed, so she too was trapped here with them. Given the Earth Prince's current state, it was unlikely that he would be able to clear the path either. Almost all the lanterns in the chamber had been extinguished by now; the only speck of illumination came from the sunlight streaming in from the gaping hole above.

Wei yelled across the chamber from where he crouched with Desert Rose. 'Is there another way out of here? *Is there?*' he demanded when the Earth Elemental made no reply.

The Earth Elemental let out a moan, then raised a shaky finger and pointed to a dim spot of lamp light at a far corner about twenty feet away, possibly leading to another passageway out of this chamber. As far as Meng could see, all the other doorways and entrances were blocked from collapsed walls and ceilings, but if light could get through that opening, then that was a sliver of hope.

'P-Priestess,' the Earth Prince rasped.

The Priestess hurried back to his side and nodded, understanding his meaning implicitly. 'Follow me,' she instructed the rest before picking up the Earth Elemental and towing him towards the light. The Fire Elemental continued sweeping the chamber with his blast of flames. Heat seared dangerously close to them, baking the ground and the walls. If that exit plan failed, they could well be cooked alive in this earthen pot.

Wei swept Desert Rose up in his arms and trudged through the mud as steadily as he could behind the Priestess. He glanced at Meng, urging him to follow suit with his gaze. Meng reached for Windshadow, then tucked her arm around his neck and helped her up.

Voices rang out above them in a muffled echo. Meng kept as close to the walls as he could, trying to blend into the shadows. The spot of light in the distance grew larger until they arrived before it. Up close, the hole was large enough to only fit their head through. It would take ages of shovelling to enlarge it enough for several grown people to pass through.

Meng stared at the Earth Elemental, hoping he had some energy left in him to work his magic. The latter raised a trembling arm and, in several feeble motions, tore down the earth chunk by chunk to widen the gap.

The heat grew unbearable. Meng was starting to feel the world spin when, with a final burst of what energy he had left, the Earth Elemental ripped out the last chunk of earth and rock, creating a passageway large enough for them to step through. After the last of them had filed through, he sealed up the passageway again and proceeded to faint against the Priestess.

The cacophony of crumbling earth and rocks and the roar of fire outside died away as they ventured down the passageway, giving way to sweet merciful silence and cool, damp air. At last, Meng felt himself give in to the darkness as well.

Fourteen

Desert Rose

Pain seared through her. The familiar anguish of ticha made her knees buckle, even though Wei had attempted to shield her from the deluge as much as he could.

As they filed through the exit and the tunnel that led them out of the Grand Chamber, she felt close to passing out from the pain and heat like Meng and the Earth Elemental, but she held on to her consciousness as hard as she could. Only after peeling off the first layer of her clothes did she feel marginally better and was able to walk on her own. She watched the Priestess tow the Earth Elemental and Windshadow drag Meng along ahead of them, keeping her gaze fixed on their shadowy forms.

The air grew cooler the farther along they trudged. Was Lazar still out there with the Imperial Army? Had they given up? She couldn't hear any sign of a further attack—perhaps they assumed they had done enough damage, not knowing that everyone managed to escape. Yet, the question remained: how did they manage to find them? Had the Black Lotus Sect indeed led them here?

The Priestess's voice cut through the gloom, echoing in the tunnel. 'The Black Lotus Sect came to our aid,' she said, as though she had heard Desert Rose's thoughts. 'They killed every remaining one of them from the Imperial Army.'

'Even the Fire Elemental?' Desert Rose asked.

'His whereabouts are murky to my Eye. I can't trace him anywhere.'

Desert Rose shared a look with Wei. They had witnessed what Lazar could do. Even if he was outnumbered by the Black Lotus Sect, he could easily have incinerated all of them and retreated with the remaining Imperial Army. Could there be more to this ambush? Lazar's loyalties always left them guessing.

Desert Rose had no idea how far from the Grand Chamber they had gone. At last they arrived before a paved walkway that led to an arched entrance at the end. The doors were elaborately carved and slid apart to reveal a rather grand bedchamber fit for a prince, so this had to be the private quarters, the deepest part of this realm.

The Priestess set the Earth Elemental down on the bed and busied herself with towels, a basin of water, and a fresh set of clothes. She gestured for the others to follow suit.

The chamber they were in was large enough to fit all of them and possibly even all of the Damohai. The furnishings were designed with care, with rosewood chairs and bed frames, and the interiors were intact. It seemed the damage was only limited to the main chamber where they had gathered earlier, and the other parts of this labyrinthian quarters had been spared.

'They might have destroyed the rest of this city had the Black Lotus Sect not arrived in time to handle the Imperial Army,' the Priestess said, in response to her thoughts again—something she was starting to find annoying, although she appreciated the answers.

Wei watched as Desert Rose wiped herself clean of ticha water with a fresh towel, his brows pulled together in worry though he said nothing. After she had changed into the clean robes the Priestess provided, he handed her a cup of water in silence. With the Earth Elemental taken care of, the Priestess next attempted to tend to Meng with her limited but passable expertise and managed to make him rouse.

Windshadow sat alone in a corner, tending to her own wounds. She looked more battered than Desert Rose had ever seen her, but refused any help or concern from anyone. She seemed more annoyed at the fact that the Fire Elemental had one-upped her than anything else, and kept her thoughts to herself, but Desert Rose could tell she had a plan brewing in her head.

She went over to the other desert girl, who glanced up when she approached. 'How are you doing?'

'Still kicking,' Windshadow replied, rather brusquely, but did not protest when Desert Rose planted herself down next to her.

'Glad to see that.'

Windshadow shot her a look. 'You don't mean that. I left you to deal with those imperial scouts yourself back at the inn.'

'I don't blame you,' Desert Rose said, and she realized she meant it, even though Windshadow was right.

Windshadow snorted. 'Sure you don't.'

'It's what anyone would have done.' Windshadow's look deepened. 'Okay, it's what *you* would have done. And it's what you would continue to do. It's your nature to survive, whatever the cost.'

Windshadow's gaze drifted away as she mulled over her words. 'Whatever the cost.' She looked back up at her. 'And you don't resent that?'

'You saved my life back at Danxi Plains, and perhaps a few more times before and after.'

'I also betrayed you before,' Windshadow pointed out.

'You did. But if there's one other Elemental I'd be with at the end, I'd rather it be you than anyone else.'

Surprise flashed across Windshadow's face. Her gaze softened for a moment, but she only nodded. 'I suppose you're not terrible company, too.'

Rivals or not, Desert Rose was relieved that their previous encounter hadn't been their final one. *The end will come, whether you like it or not,* a little voice said in her head. She pushed it aside. Until they had both arrived at that decisive moment between the two of them, she would trust the sliver of goodness she had seen in Windshadow.

The Earth Elemental roused at last. Sitting up in his bed, he seemed shaken but for the most part recovered from the ticha attack. There was no trace of his earlier good-naturedness or smugness in his face anymore, only a stony expression as he stared into space.

Desert Rose couldn't tell how much time had passed before they gathered themselves and a messenger scurried into the chamber to convey that the rest of the Ling were safe and had dispersed into their homes. Only then did the Earth Elemental let out a sigh of relief, although his gaze remained sombre.

'Bring the Black Lotus Sect members to me.' His voice was brittle with cold fury. The Priestess nodded and disappeared down the entrance from which they came. The chamber was steeped in frosty silence until the Black Lotus Sect members were brought in.

How many casualties were there today? How much else had Han and the Fire Elemental destroyed? This was once a home for all these people, who had lived in hiding for good reason. The Ling were still too weak to go against the imperial family like they intended to— today's ambush demonstrated that clearly. As long as Han had the Fire Elemental and an endless supply of ticha, he had the upper hand.

The Black Lotus Sect members—who introduced themselves as Yan and Yujin—came in pleading for mercy right away.

The Earth Elemental's quiet voice cut them off. 'I'd like an explanation.'

'It's not their fault,' Windshadow snapped. 'It's the Fire Elemental. Notorious turncoat, just so you know. Loyal to Han one moment, joining the Black Lotus Sect the next, and now he's back with Han.'

He shot her an irritated glance. 'So the Black Lotus Sect let him go back to the emperor, and now he's tailed you all here with the Imperial Army in tow?'

'I believe he was here to kill *us*, not the Ling.' Windshadow's tone was terse. Desert Rose could tell she was mad at herself for letting her guard down against Lazar.

'Do you realize how much danger the Black Lotus Sect has put everyone in today?' the Earth Elemental roared at Yan and Yujin, breaking his demeanour at last. 'Our location—the White Ling Sect's territory—has been compromised. All the Ling in the chamber today could have died. The entire White Ling Sect could have been extinguished. All because the Black Lotus Sect let that Elemental go to the enemy! All our efforts in rebuilding the sect—no, our whole people—would have gone to waste if we hadn't responded quickly enough today.'

'Never mind all that now,' Windshadow said testily before Yan and Yujin could say anything. 'What are we going to do next? I'm not sitting here waiting for another attack.'

'*We?*' the Earth Elemental repeated.

'I wasn't asking *you*,' Windshadow snapped. She turned to Desert Rose. 'That turncoat lied *again*. He was here on Han's orders, otherwise he wouldn't have had the Imperial Army with him.'

'I'm certain he's not dead. The Black Lotus Sect couldn't have defeated him, even if they've killed the imperial soldiers.'

Windshadow nodded. 'And knowing him, he wouldn't assume that *we*'—she gestured at herself and Desert Rose, and shot a look at the Earth Elemental—'are dead until he's seen it with his own eyes. He will strike again if he can. I'll sneak into the palace and gather some intel, find out what he's really up to. Would be a good opportunity to destroy their ticha stores as well.'

'You're going back to the palace? That would be suicide,' Desert Rose said. 'Han would certainly have placed extra security around the palace, especially against Elementals. You would get caught as soon as you came near it.'

'Do you want him to catch us all off guard again like he did today? One of us has to stay within the enemy camp, so unless any of you here is able to travel as fast as the wind or become invisible as air, I'm the one who has to do this.'

None of them could refute that.

'Han will most certainly strike again, and we have no idea how quickly he can operate or how many spies he has everywhere,' Windshadow went on. 'Thanks to Lazar, he managed to tail us to the Ling's hideout within a day or two and ambush us there. Who knows how soon he will launch his next attack?'

'We'll come with you,' Yan and Yujin said. 'You can't do everything on your own.'

Windshadow nodded. She seemed to trust them implicitly despite only having joined them for a short period of time. This was the first time Desert Rose had ever seen Windshadow cooperate with others. The Wind Elemental had always operated on her own, not trusting anyone else to have her back. Desert Rose caught her eye, and for a moment she thought she caught a glimpse of what looked like joy in the other girl's eyes, unlike her usual manic excitement at causing chaos or her conspiratorial glee at destroying the system from within. Just joy and belonging, like how Desert Rose felt being among her tribe members.

When the Earth Elemental turned to Desert Rose this time, he no longer wore the levity he had earlier during the ceremony in the Grand Chamber. His expression was grim, even weary. 'Too many Elementals in the palace is a risk. You and I need to focus our energies on other things here.'

Desert Rose glanced at Wei. He hadn't said a word since they entered this chamber, but she knew he loathed the idea of the 'union', whatever that meant. He had his fists clenched by his side, but he made no protest this time. She longed to reach for his hand, but what would be the point of that if she was going to go ahead with the Earth Elemental's plan?

'I'm sure you see now why this union is important,' the Earth Elemental went on. 'Why it is the only solution to defeat the enemy. I cannot risk my people's lives simply because I am too weak to protect them. We are all we have left. If we want any chance at all to restore our kingdom, we cannot afford to lose even one Ling.'

Desert Rose stared at him. 'And you think *marriage* can solve this problem?'

'If it means that much to you, we can marry our powers together first with the Priestess's help. A natural union between man and woman might certainly help to amplify and speed up the process, but it's evident you're saving yourself for someone else.'

Desert Rose felt the heat rush up to her face.

His gaze shuffled between Wei and Meng. 'So, which one of you will take the throne? I was prepared to back you, Third Prince, until your brother showed up with his . . . proposition.'

Desert Rose shared a look with Wei, thinking about all the losses he had suffered that drove him to now fight for the throne. But Wei had never wanted it. All he wanted was revenge against Han and the Empress Dowager. Between them, they had orchestrated the murder of his brother, his mother, and Matron, all of whom Wei regarded as his closest family in the world. The only reason he wanted the throne was to protect the people he cared about, but those people were no longer around.

Unlike Wei, Meng truly wanted to rule. He had even gone to extreme measures just to crawl up the throne. Despite being guilt-ridden about the things he had done to get there, he had a clear vision for the kingdom and his people. He had told Desert Rose all the problems plaguing the kingdom and his solutions for them before, during those nights they had spent at the library, and Desert Rose had even, at one point, almost been convinced to help him overthrow his father.

Meng, having composed himself, now spoke up for the first time since the ambush. 'Han may have all the military strength and resources he needs to fight wars and ambush Elementals, but we all know that he who controls the magic in the land controls the land,' he said, pulling something out of his robes. Desert Rose recognized the battered scroll bound in a frayed hemp rope. 'And he cannot have full control without this.' He unfurled the scroll.

'You've . . . decoded it?' Desert Rose asked.

Meng sent her a wry smile. 'I have you to thank for this, actually. I wouldn't have had the first clue what to do with it, or even thought to approach the Ling.'

So much had happened since she and Windshadow retrieved the scroll from the bottom of the well in the White Crypt during the Trials, but Desert Rose recalled the contents of the scroll like she had read it yesterday. '*Duru-shel Minta.*'

The Earth Elemental's head snapped towards her. 'Not only will it unlock the magic in this kingdom, it will also reveal the position of the Immortal Spring and awaken it. This is the key back to the Old Kingdom. To Hesui.' He fell silent and shared a look with the Priestess, who gave an almost imperceptible nod. His gaze rested on the scroll as he sank into deep thought.

Hesui was a fabled kingdom to Desert Rose. She might have learned about it from her tribe—and in classes at the House of Night, where a different version was being taught—but she had never felt any affinity for the land that her ancestors, the Damohai, ruled. The Earth Elemental seemed to feel that bond more keenly than her.

At last, he looked up at Meng. 'We have a deal, Fourth Prince.'

* * *

The 'union', according to the Priestess, required Desert Rose and the Earth Elemental to go through a whole week of qi cultivation in isolation.

Neither Desert Rose nor Wei was thrilled about the idea, but the Earth Elemental seemed entirely too excited at the prospect of spending a whole week cooped up in a meditation chamber where he would have to cultivate his qi with Desert Rose.

They sat face-to-face now before each other, cross-legged. The chamber was cool and dark with arched ceilings, large enough to fit just both of them but cavernous enough for their voices to echo as though they were in the Grand Chamber. She shifted her position on the cushion beneath her, trying to refocus. The thought of staying in here for a whole week made her want to flee immediately. She longed for the open desert, the unfettered wind that gusted across the sands, the vast plains that she used to race across on horseback with her tribe members. As she closed her eyes, that was what she imagined. The wild abandon she felt back in the desert with her tribe.

She could hear the muffled sounds of the Priestess speaking outside with the head sorcerer of the White Ling Sect who would help to facilitate the process, but she blocked out the noise and focused on her happy place.

A gong rang from outside, rocking the walls of the chamber, and the sorcerer began chanting. Another voice spoke in the background, deep and familiar. Wei. Desert Rose opened her eyes and glanced at the entrance. Was he going to stay out there with the Priestess and sorcerer too?

'Concentrate, now,' the Earth Elemental murmured, his eyes closed and hands placed in his lap. 'This is a crucial process.'

'You really think this will work? You think defying the prophecy won't anger the gods or hurt our chances of staying alive?'

'I would rather try to create a different destiny if it means I can help my people. Wouldn't you?'

She could not argue with that. She would do the same for her tribe if there was a way for her to improve her chances of winning this fight. Her father had languished in Ghost City for long enough, and half her tribe was still adrift, waiting for their chieftain. If combining her qi with another Elemental could help her get closer to the end and defeat the others, then all this would be worth it. She held on to that end goal in mind.

'Besides, you and I know that on our own, we are no match for the Fire and Air Elementals. It would take both our powers combined to defeat them. So even if the White Ling Sect chooses not to back the Third Prince, this union is important if we want to survive long enough to see through what we came to do.'

In the quiet of the chamber, his low mellifluous voice began to quell all her doubts and soothe her frayed nerves. Regardless of which brother contested for the throne, which brother received the support of the Ling, the prophecy of the Elementals would play out anyway and affect them all. This cultivation process would benefit her as much as Wei or Meng in their bid for the throne.

'This concerns more than just us, you understand,' the Earth Elemental said. 'Whether you like it or not, our destiny is our responsibility to bear. If we fail, other lives are at stake.'

She nodded, subdued. Whatever argument she had prepared sounded trite against this. 'I understand.'

The Earth Elemental adjusted his position, stretching his waist. 'If we make it out of here alive, I promise I'll get the best chiropractor in our sect to tend to you. And perhaps we'll actually get to exchange our names, Water Elemental.'

Desert Rose let out a reluctant chuckle, grateful for the momentary distraction from her apprehension about this process. 'Call me Rose,' she said.

Fifteen

Windshadow

The House of Night contained several secret passageways, three of which were guarded. The fourth was unknown by many, even Shimu.

Windshadow had discovered it during one of her nightly patrols. It could have been an unintentional entry point not meant for or created by the House of Night, but it served as a very convenient way in for those in the know. It involved a tunnel leading all the way into the Red Circle from a nondescript herb shop in Ruxi Market, circumventing the layers of security around and within the palace.

It took the Black Lotus Sect members five days to arrive at the Capital (it was better for them to split up so that Windshadow could conserve her energy for the mission), by which time Windshadow had already infiltrated the palace on her own and spent a couple of nights scouting the grounds and figuring out the changes that had been implemented—from guard shifts to secret hiding spots for a certain Fire Elemental.

The air in the palace was somehow different now—a climate of fear seemed to have taken over now that Meng was no longer ruling. Particularly in the nooks and crannies of the palaces, the silence felt more sinister, as though something—or someone—was always lurking, always watching.

The last time Windshadow was in the palace, she had been cornered by Han and Lazar during her attempt to assassinate Han in his sleep, then thrown into prison where she was tortured with ticha. The humiliation of the memory still burned in her gut, spurring her on to seek out the exact places where the ticha was being grown and stored (indeed in the imperial garden and the shed behind it, as Lazar said).

On her fifth evening in the palace, Yan and Yujin arrived through the secret entrance. The House of Night was deserted—everyone was out on patrol or mission—so Windshadow met them at the secret door behind the armoury obscured by overgrown weeds.

'I can't believe the passageway worked,' Yujin muttered, adjusting his bag of equipment on his shoulder. 'I was expecting something to go wrong the whole time.'

Yan looked at Windshadow, her eyes gleaming with anticipation. 'What next?'

'Head straight, then turn left after the first pond you see. Keep going until you see a pavilion, then turn right. There's a gate by the side that might creak a little, so be careful with that. The plantation is right behind that gate.'

The first step was to destroy all the ticha. Windshadow would rejoice the moment Han—and the imperial family—could no longer use that wretched herb to torture them. The siblings had come prepared with the explosives Huzun had acquired for them in the market. She could sense their eagerness to cause some mayhem in the palace, and could only hope that they would also succeed in finding the escape route she had plotted out for them once their job here was done.

'Are you sure you'll have enough time? What if the guards find you before the entire ticha plantation is destroyed?' Yan asked.

'The plantation is about three to five *mu* large, not terribly big. It won't take long to burn. But with the guards stationed everywhere here, I might not have enough time to find the Fire Elemental.'

'We'll create a diversion,' Yan proposed at once.

'No,' Windshadow said. 'You're both compromised enough in a place you're not familiar with. If you linger any longer, it'll hurt your chances of escaping.'

'What's the point of us escaping if you're not going to achieve what you came here to do?' Yujin quipped. 'Go, we'll take care of ourselves.'

The siblings slipped away into the darkness before Windshadow could protest further. In the silence that followed, Windshadow got the sense that she was being watched. The air was as still as a bated breath. Someone was around, and they were close by. Very close by.

A willowy figure in a black tunic—the House of Night tunic—swooped down from the roof and landed soundlessly in front of her, knife brandished. Windshadow lunged at the assassin before the latter could attack, spinning low on the ground in a feigned attempt to trip her before ducking behind her and wrapping an arm around her throat at the speed of wind.

The assassin dropped her knife as Windshadow tightened her chokehold on her.

'You need to work on your reflexes there . . .' Windshadow pulled down the assassin's face mask. 'Xiyue.'

Xiyue's eyes widened when she glanced up at her. 'Windsha—'

Windshadow placed a finger on her lips, waiting for Xiyue to acquiesce before loosening her grip.

Xiyue spun around, massaging her throat. 'It *is* you. We thought . . . we thought you were dead.'

Windshadow smirked. 'Such little faith you all have in me.'

'Where have you been all these months? What happened? The emperor—'

'I don't have time to regale you with my adventures.' She started heading towards the armoury. 'I need you to walk away and not tell anyone you saw me.'

'But—'

'And not ask any more questions. It's safer for you not to know,' she muttered the last part as she walked away.

'Are you going to hurt the emperor?' Xiyue called after her.

Windshadow paused and turned back to look at her. The Capital girl watched her with her wide, curious eyes. She had always been the most trusting of the three Capital girls in the House of Night, sometimes to her detriment. But Windshadow knew better than to let her guard down against her—Xiyue might have been her ex-Housemate, but her duty as an imperial assassin meant that she could and would kill

Windshadow if she had the chance to, in the name of protecting the imperial family.

'That would be a stupid thing to do now, wouldn't it?' Windshadow kept her tone as neutral as possible, giving nothing away.

'It would,' Xiyue said, her gaze wide and earnest, as though sending her a message—or a warning.

Windshadow turned and walked away. *Don't let Xiyue get away*, a voice in her head nagged at her. She had to cover all her tracks. If Xiyue reported to Shimu and word got out that Windshadow was here in the palace, she would have come all this way for nothing.

By the time she turned back, however, Xiyue was gone. Only the inky darkness lay before her.

She hurried along, shifting partially so that the wind carried her towards Han's private quarters. Once she arrived, she shifted entirely to evade the guards and slipped in through the window before turning back into her corporeal form.

The room was steeped in darkness, and only a distant lantern from outside offered a scant bit of light for Windshadow to locate Han's sleeping form in his bed. It was tempting to kill him on the spot—after all, her mark was lying right before her, and she had waited a long time to exact her revenge. But she wasn't here for Han tonight; killing the Oasis Emperor now would ruin their plans in the future. She had to look at the big picture—what they wanted was to overthrow him, not get herself and the Black Lotus Sect implicated in a regicide.

A heavyset hand grabbed her neck from behind. Before she could react, she felt an unbearable burn around her neck as a rope was looped around it, burning where it came into contact with her skin. A sharp tug sent her reeling backwards, colliding into the hard chest of a tall burly man. The ticha-soaked rope seared her neck, the pain making her too weak and dizzy to struggle or fight back.

Han's voice curled around her ear, making the hair on the back of her neck stand. She quelled a shudder. 'Should I call you foolish or brave to come back here thinking I wouldn't have defences built up specially for you? I had my servant lie in for me as soon as I was notified about an intruder in the House of Night.'

Xiyue. She must have raised the alert for an intruder. She had likely even let Windshadow escape just now to lower her guard. *It is you*, she had said, which meant she had been informed it would be.

You should have killed her when you had the chance, Windshadow chided herself. She should have learned by now that sentimentality could kill.

The servant boy rose from the bed and bowed. Han nodded at him, a dismissal, and he retreated from the bedchamber, shutting the door behind him.

Her efforts to break free from the ticha-laced noose were futile. There was no way for her to shift as long as her skin was in contact with ticha, and Han had a physical advantage over her with his hulking build and tremendous strength. She clawed at him, kicking and squirming as hard as she could, but he only tightened the rope around her neck. Every fibre in her screamed in anguish.

Her throat began to close in as her vision started to blacken at the edges. *Fight, Windshadow!* she urged herself. *You are not going down without taking him with you.* This could not be how her story ended—not at the hands of this man.

Han let out a muffled grunt. She was dimly aware of him staggering backwards and dragging her along with him, until his grip on the noose loosened. She pulled free, whipping around just in time to see him crumple to the ground.

Yan and Yujin stood just behind him, holding their handkerchiefs soaked in the potent concoction they had created themselves. It had a deceptively cloying scent that masked the fact that it could knock their targets out for days. Windshadow had been so confident she could handle Han with her own abilities that she had rejected the siblings' weapon.

'Told you this would come in handy,' Yujin said, stuffing the handkerchief back into his tunic.

Windshadow massaged her neck, willing her body to recover quicker from the ticha attack. 'How did you find me here?'

'The ticha burned faster than we expected,' Yan said. 'We got away sooner to look for you.'

'That wasn't part of the plan,' Windshadow said. 'You're supposed to leave right after destroying the ticha.'

Yujin shrugged. 'Plans can be changed. You didn't think we'd leave you here to get choked to death by this scum, did you?'

Voices rang from outside Han's bedchamber, followed by the shuffling of feet.

'The guards are coming,' Windshadow said. 'Run. I'll catch up with you two after I nab the Fire Elemental.'

The siblings didn't need to be told twice. Windshadow watched them slip out through the back door before shifting into her element and racing out of the Red Circle.

The ticha plantation was ablaze when she passed by it on the way to the private bathhouse near the Seven Star Pond. Distant shouts cut through the night ('The ticha's on fire!') and the flames illuminated the sky, turning it a fresh shade of crimson. The Imperial Palace was in an uproar, and a part of her relished the chaos. Good riddance to ticha too.

She hurried along towards the bathhouse, leaving the sound and fury behind her.

The imperial bathhouse was strictly reserved for the royal family, but Han had given Lazar special access to it on account of the latter's need to stay alive. Windshadow had observed how Lazar would visit the bathhouse for hours each night to cool off his steaming body, then sneak off before anyone could spot him. At the rate Han was expending Lazar, the latter would burn out even before any of the Elementals could get to him. The stunt Lazar had pulled at Yeli Mountain must have taken a toll on his body—there was a limit to how much an Elemental could use their power in their lifetime, she had learned. Use it too much too quickly, and their bodies would wear out faster.

Lazar had finished his soak for the night when Windshadow arrived, oblivious to the commotion in the other part of the palace grounds. She slipped on her gloves, tightened her mask, and pulled out the sachet of ground ticha leaves tucked in her tunic. She couldn't hear the commotion from here, but if everything went well, it would be safe to launch her attack on Lazar this instant. Yan and Yujin should also have reached the secret escape route by now.

The Fire Elemental stepped out of the bathhouse, humming a little tune. Windshadow smirked, then flung the sachet of ticha powder at him from behind. She wrapped a gloved hand covered in more ticha powder around his mouth before he could scream out, then dragged him towards the pond. His resistance was feeble, half-hearted, as though he had already given up the fight.

'That was quite an ambush you and Han pulled off at Yeli Mountain,' she said into his ear. 'How do you like the taste of your own medicine?'

The Fire Elemental only spasmed in pain, unable to speak.

'Don't worry, I'm not killing you just yet, little turncoat,' she said, binding his wrists behind his back with ticha-soaked ropes. It burned a little through her glove, and she made quick work of the capture. 'I still have use for you.'

She shot him a warning look, daring him to make a sound, then towed him towards the shortest of the five escape routes in the palace. It took her to a trapdoor obscured by a peony bush near the Hall of Tranquillity, not thirty feet away from the ticha plantation, but with the diversion created by Yan and Yujin, no one would think to look in this direction. At least, that was the plan.

The escape route was a narrow tunnel that would lead them into a forest a few li away from the palace. Behind her, she caught the hint of the blaze in the distance. The ticha stores were still burning well and good. Voices broke through the night, amid the satisfying snap and crackle of flames lapping up the blasted herb. The fire would keep everyone busy for a good while.

She nudged Lazar through the trapdoor and escape route, not stopping until they came to the end of the cold dark tunnel and ended up at the foot of an oak tree in the middle of the forest. She was familiar with this place, having tailed Han here once to witness him murdering Meng's informants after he took the throne. Tonight, the forest was just as desolate, and the slightest stir made her neck prickle.

They were alone, as far as she could tell, but just to be sure, she made a quick check after sitting Lazar against the tree. Once she had confirmed that no one else had tailed them here, she untied Lazar and handed him a waterskin wordlessly.

He scrambled to scrub the ticha off his hands and face with his sleeves, then took a swig of water from the waterskin. 'And you say I'm dramatic,' he rasped. 'How long did it take for you to plan this kidnapping? Did you also get your Black Lotus Sect friends to help you out?'

She shrugged. 'Thanks to you, I managed to kill two birds with one stone—destroy ticha and steal you away—all without getting myself killed. Guess your attempt to lure me back to the palace didn't quite work.'

He chortled. 'How certain you are.'

She paused. 'Whatever plans you have cooked up to kill me will have to wait. You won't be able to survive in the end if you succeed in eliminating me now.'

He eyed her over the waterskin. 'Explain.'

'You left a rather strong impression on the Earth Elemental with your little stunt. He decided the best way to fight you would be to join forces with the Water Elemental. So now they are combining their powers as we speak. You and I alone won't be enough to defeat them once they're through.'

He wiped his mouth with the back of his hand after taking another swig. 'I just tried to burn you all alive and you're back here trying to partner up with me? You either trust me too much or are trying to make me walk into a trap, and I know for a fact that you trust no one but yourself.'

She snatched the waterskin back. 'I just thought you might still be interested in staying in the running, but it's perfectly fine if you aren't.'

He narrowed his eyes at her. 'What do you propose?'

'They have two more days to complete the process. If we make it back by then and put a stop to it, we might have a chance.' She raised her brows. 'Your choice.'

Lazar watched her for the longest time, but Windshadow had learned to never back down from anyone's silence or stare. 'I suppose it's time to finish the job,' he said at last, his eyes gleaming with wild excitement.

Sixteen

Wei

It had been three days since Desert Rose entered the chamber. Wei had only been able to snatch brief moments with her when she emerged for dinner. She would come out each evening looking physically drained yet energized in spirit. There would be an unearthly gleam in her eyes, but the cultivation process would render her less inclined to chat much, if at all.

'You don't have to wait out here for all seven days,' said the Priestess when she found him standing guard outside the chamber. 'I'm sure you have more pressing things to do, Third Prince.'

'No offence, but I'm sure you already know that I don't trust your Earth Prince one bit,' Wei replied. 'I'm staying here until it's over and I know Rose is fine.'

'Suit yourself, then.' She tossed him a lofty glance. 'Your attachment to the Water Elemental will only become a hindrance to you in the future. Instead of pining for her here, there's a lot more you can do to dethrone your brother in the meantime.'

He shot her a withering look. 'I am *not* pining.'

She smirked. 'You may not care for the throne, but vengeance and power are just two sides of the same coin. Zhao Han's rule is weakening, thanks to the battle with Lettoria and the Wall coming down. The Fourth Prince has also negotiated a cessation in trade with the kingdom's allies, promising a compensation once he comes back into power. He also has the scroll that can give him control of the kingdom's magic. What hope do you—a rogue prince who turned his back on his kingdom years ago—have in the face of all that?'

Wei felt the cruel sting of her words. It was one thing to doubt himself, but to have all his doubts thrown in his face by a mind reader felt all the more humiliating. What purpose did he have in Oasis Kingdom, now that he no longer had a family, and the only person he wanted to protect no longer seemed to need his help? He had let his mother down, as well as Yong and Matron, failing to be there for them when they needed him, and he would live with this guilt for the rest of his life. If he were honest with himself, dethroning Han was not merely a way to exact revenge, but to atone for his absence, his failure as a brother and son. Yet, even his revenge mission seemed laughable now.

'You want to matter. You want purpose,' the Priestess went on, watching him. 'But becoming emperor will not fill that hole inside your heart, and you know it.'

'I'd appreciate it if you would stop reaching inside my mind, thank you,' he said, irritated.

'You and the Water Elemental are ill-destined. And the White Ling Sect will need a leader after the Earth Prince fulfils the prophecy.'

He narrowed his eyes at her. 'What are you getting at?'

'I'm saying that after the contest among the Elementals ends, the sect will no longer have a leader. We will need a new one who won't be busy on the throne.'

He looked at her askance. 'And you think a mortal like me can do the job?'

'You are no mere mortal. You are the Third Prince, with connections to the imperial family.'

'I see. Political leverage is what the White Ling Sect is after then.'

The Priestess pursed her lips at Wei's conclusion. She tried a different tactic. 'What happens if the Water Elemental wins or loses the race? All that's left of her will be her soul, not her earthly body.' Her gaze was meaningful. 'The White Ling Sect comprises the highest-level shamans and sorcerers who can communicate with other realms. Realms far beyond this mortal one. Realms where she might reside in the future.'

The thought weighed on him the next evening he spent with Desert Rose. She ate less and less with each passing day, claiming she had no need for sustenance since the cultivation process started. Wei observed her sunken cheeks and gleaming eyes as she shared with him the day's progress in qi combination, trying to ignore the thought that she was turning into someone more and more unfamiliar by the day.

'Rong has been teaching me how to use my power without using too much of my qi,' she was saying. 'It's been—'

'Rong?'

'The Earth Elemental. His adoptive mother gave him the name because she saw him as her pride and joy.'

'I know what *rong* means.' He poked at his bowl of rice, suddenly losing his appetite.

She frowned. 'I know you don't trust him, but he's helped me so much in improving my control over my powers. It's less taxing for me to wield it now, and I recover faster after using it. With some practice, we might even be able to take on the Fire Elemental as soon as Windshadow brings him to us.'

He hated the use of the word *we*, but kept that thought to himself. 'Did *Rong* also tell you that you don't need human food?'

'I told you, I don't feel hunger anymore. It seems inconsequential to talk about food when there's still so much to do in the time that we have left.'

Again with the *we*.

He picked up a piece of fish and set it on her bowl of rice. 'You're still human, or at least possess a mortal body. Even if you believe you're immortal now after combining your qi with another Elemental, you need to build up your strength.'

She stared down at her untouched bowl of food. 'What matters now is to unify our people and prepare them for the rebellion.'

'Our people? You mean the Dugur tribe, right? Scarbrow, Qara, and the rest of them who are still waiting for you to return to them?'

She nodded. 'Of course. They're part of the Hesui Kingdom too.'

Wei set down his chopsticks. 'So we're classifying people into Hesui Kingdom citizens now? Does *Rong* also plan to rebuild the Old Kingdom and have all the desert tribes live in harmony with the Ling as one big family?'

A frown crossed her face. 'Don't be patronizing, Wei. Don't you understand? There is no physical boundary that can separate us. We're all one people, descendants of the Hesui Kingdom. That includes the Damohai, the Ling, the desert tribes and . . . us. All of us.'

'You're right. I don't understand. As far as I know, only the Oasis Kingdom exists now. The Hesui Kingdom is just a dream that hasn't been realized. Meanwhile, Meng and I are trying to fix what's in front of us because this is the reality we're living in, a kingdom run by our power-hungry brother with a powerful Elemental sidekick.'

'Well, my reality is one where I have limited time to reunite my people and establish a new ruler so that we no longer need to live in hiding, persecuted for practising magic. I don't know how much more time I have, when the next Elemental is coming for me, or when my magic will consume me.'

Neither of them had finished their meal that evening. Desert Rose even retired early to her chamber to avoid speaking with him further.

On the fifth day, he overheard news regarding a disturbance that involved the shouren. A White Ling Sect messenger boy rushed up to the Priestess just as she was asking Wei about his decision to join the sect.

'The Imperial Army ambush that day has made many of the sects antsy,' the messenger reported. 'Some of them are starting to fight over territory and resources. The Night Beast Sect is being especially belligerent against the Storm River Sect.'

'The Night Beast Sect?' Wei echoed.

The messenger nodded. 'The shouren. There are casualties on both sides.'

'While we typically help to resolve such altercations among the sects, the Earth Prince is preoccupied at the moment and cannot tend to such business,' the Priestess said. 'We can only wait until His Highness has completed the cultivation process to step in.'

Was Qiu caught in the clash as well? His sister had a particularly foolhardy brother-in-law who was not only prone to antagonization, but also implicating his brother and Qiu. If anyone was going to be part of a confrontation, Wei was almost certain it would be Zhong.

He had to make sure Qiu was safe.

Yet, he found himself reluctant to leave the White Ling territory, to leave Desert Rose alone with *Rong*. Besides, they had come this far without any incident or hiccups in the cultivation process. What if that changed as soon as he left?

'If you're worried about your sister, you should go and check on her,' the Priestess said. 'Nothing here is going to change for the next couple of days.'

Wei remained where he was, torn.

'There's nothing more you can do here anyway,' the Priestess added.

She was right. With Desert Rose in cultivation with the Earth Elemental, he felt redundant here. He still had a mission to accomplish, a brother to overthrow, and he couldn't do so hanging around here.

'I'll be back as soon as I can,' he said. With that, he left without a chance to inform Desert Rose.

It took him half a day to head up the mountain towards the shouren's territory. The beast-people were in shambles when Wei arrived, with several of them injured from the clash with the Storm River Sect, which consisted of shamans that drew upon the river's energy to sustain itself. Due to the Yarshe River being poisoned prior to the battle at Danxi Plains, its tributaries, including the Storm River, had been affected, cutting off their supply of food. The shouren— part of the Night Beast Sect, Wei learned only now—still shaken by the Black Lotus Sect's attack, had encroached upon the Storm River Sect's territory and stolen what little food supply they had, leading to the skirmish with them.

At Qiu's home, Wei found her tending to Zhong's shoulder wound while her husband Heyang was deep in conversation with an older man on the couch. Qiu paused in tending to Zhong when she spotted Wei, who hurried over to his sister.

'You're alive,' Qiu said, throwing her arms around Wei. 'We were so worried when you went after Desert Rose. Is she safe too?'

Wei wasn't quite sure how to respond. He gave a half-nod that could also be interpreted as a shrug. 'Are you hurt?' he asked, scanning her from head to toe.

She shook her head and nodded at her brother-in-law. 'Zhong is, though.'

Wei snorted. 'No one is surprised, I'm sure.' Zhong glared at him.

'Something is brewing among the sects,' Heyang said as he and the elder shouren joined them at the dining table. 'They're preparing for something. We fear this clash might just be a smokescreen. The White Ling Sect has been gathering its forces lately. The higher-level sects have been cannibalizing the weaker sects to grow in strength and numbers, and weaker ones like us have been forced to scrounge for scraps or worse, flee for our lives.'

'If we're of little use to the rebellion, the stronger sects won't think twice to steal our qi as nourishment,' Zhong ranted. 'I'm sick of being kicked around by them.'

'It's not just sect-level, these disturbances,' Wei said. 'The White Ling Sect is planning to overthrow Han, but they will only back Meng if he agrees to their terms. I think the White Ling Sect may not be interested in simply overthrowing the Oasis Emperor. Its leader, the Earth Elemental, is attempting to get stronger by combining his powers with Desert Rose's and the White Ling Sect is reshuffling the sect order. There's a high possibility that they're aiming to accomplish something far bigger than just overthrowing the current Oasis Emperor.'

Qiu's eyes widened. 'You mean they're not just attempting a rebellion . . . but a revolution?'

Wei nodded. 'Instead of installing a puppet emperor, they end the Zhao dynasty and establish their own, bringing back the glory days of the Hesui Kingdom.'

Wei watched as the shouren considered that possibility, their expressions turning conflicted.

If the White Ling Sect, led by the Earth Elemental, ruled over all the sects—all the Ling—and if the Black Ling sects were also conspiring with them, then that would essentially make the Earth Elemental the ruler of the new kingdom if the Ling managed to end the Zhao dynasty. Combining his powers with Desert Rose's would also give him the strength to eliminate the other Elementals . . . and eventually even Desert Rose too, with the help of all the Ling shamans and sorcerers under him. Which meant everything he was doing now was in fact to put himself in a position of ultimate power.

The elder shouren spoke, interrupting Wei's thoughts. 'The shouren should remain scattered for now. It would be easier for the other sects to attack if we all gather in one place. We don't know which other sect is eyeing us now.'

'With all due respect, Mo, I disagree,' Heyang said. 'We can only rely on strength in numbers now.'

'Or we could join hands with another sect.' Zhong's remark earned him a warning look from his brother.

'Some of us don't want a revolution, and we don't want to be sacrificed for this cause. We just want to live in peace,' Heyang said.

'Don't you get it, brother? Living in peace is no longer an option,' Zhong snapped. 'We're sitting ducks here if we don't fight back.'

'Zhong's right,' Wei said, surprising himself as much as Qiu and Heyang. For once, he agreed with the impulsive shouren. 'You don't have to be sitting ducks. You can fight back, form alliances with the other sects. The White Ling Sect needs the support of the sects, and if there's chaos among the sects, they will have their hands full enough to abandon—or at least, delay—their plans for a revolution.'

Zhong narrowed his eyes at Wei. 'Or maybe you just want to keep your family in power.'

'I just don't trust the White Ling Sect—especially its leader.'

If the Earth Elemental's ultimate aim was to start a Ling revolution, then him agreeing to help Wei or Meng ascend the throne was merely to manipulate them into doing what he needed them to do—for Meng to hand over the scroll needed, for Desert Rose to agree to the cultivation process, for Wei to stay out of their way while he combined forces with Desert Rose (if that was what they were even doing). Perhaps even this issue with the shouren was merely a distraction to send him away from the chamber . . .

'I have to go,' he said, ready to charge out of the cave.

Qiu stared at him, flummoxed. 'What? Where . . .?'

'I don't have time to explain,' he said over his shoulder, 'but I'll bring news from the White Ling Sect. Don't do anything rash,' he added as an afterthought to Zhong. And then he dashed out of the cave, ignoring the looks from the other injured shouren along the way. If he ran all the way, he might make it back to the chamber just in time before the cultivation process was complete.

The night thickened as he hurried through the encroaching cold. Thoughts of Desert Rose alone in that chamber with the Earth Elemental quickened his footsteps, along with the howl of wolves in the distance. But it wasn't the elements or wild creatures in the dark that worried him. In his time in the Snow Wolf Sect up in the Palamir Mountains, Wei had learned that it wasn't beasts that they should fear; it was the ambition of men who had nothing to lose. Men who were desperate to claim victory when their time was running out.

The Earth Elemental might be half-immortal, but he was just like Han when it came to his ambitions. And Wei would do anything to make sure he and Desert Rose would not be caught in the crossfire again.

Seventeen

Desert Rose

'I do hope you did not fall out with the Third Prince over me,' the Earth Elemental said the next morning when they entered the chamber again. 'It seems unnecessary to argue over what is simply a difference in opinions.'

She hadn't seen Wei ever since they parted at dinner the previous evening. Usually, he would be at the chamber at the same time as her and Rong, but there was no sign of him that morning. Had last night's conversation truly driven a wedge between them?

'We didn't . . .' Her denial died in her throat.

They *had* fallen out. For the first time ever, they had had a heated argument that revealed just how different they were. Before, they had always been on the same page about nearly everything, from fighting for the people they loved to power struggles to family and kinship. Even if they had their differences, they had always tried to look at things from each other's point of view. But this time, neither of them was willing to budge from their stance.

'He just doesn't understand where I'm coming from,' she admitted, letting a hint of frustration slip. 'He's so focused on overthrowing his brother that he can't see the bigger picture.'

'He cannot understand us, nor does he view the world from our perspective,' said the Earth Elemental. 'He may be mortal, but his time on earth is still longer than ours. We can only do what we can while we are still here. He has time to build his kingdom, or even his empire, if he so chooses.'

They had known that they would walk different paths in the end, that they were destined for different things. But never had Desert Rose felt their distance so keenly before. It hurt knowing that the person she had come to trust and rely on, the one person who knew her best, was now fast becoming a stranger to her.

They were halfway through the cultivation process now, and she could feel herself growing stronger by the day. She felt a strange pull towards Rong, a time-worn familiarity, as though they had grown up together and shared memories as vivid as those she shared with Qara, Bataar, and the rest of the Dugur tribe.

Rong was right. They were Elementals. It made no sense that they should be fighting against each other just because some stupid prophecy said so. They should be working together for the greater good, not to ascend to the heavens or to be the mightiest of all, but to rebuild a kingdom and restore peace and the balance of magic between heaven and earth. This was a sacred task, a divine mission, and she had the ability now to serve the greater good and save her tribe. Why couldn't Wei see that she was just trying her best?

That evening, when she returned to her chamber, Wei was still nowhere to be seen. The doubt in Desert Rose's heart grew heavier. Had he truly given up on them? The passageways were quiet, deserted in this part of the subterranean realm, the Earth Prince's abode. Not even a servant was in sight.

'He's gone to look for his sister,' the Priestess said, appearing behind her.

'Qiu? Did something happen to her?'

The Priestess offered neither affirmation nor denial. 'It's best that you stay focused on the cultivation process. This is important to His Highness, and we cannot afford to have you distracted. The Third Prince will return as soon as everything is settled with the shouren.'

Her dreams grew more intense each night. Sometimes, she would see her tribe—her father, Anar Zel, and Qara—their souls lingering among those trapped in Ghost City. Sometimes, she saw Wei on the battlefield, falling from the watchtower as she raced towards him as fast as she could. Each time, she would jerk awake in a cold sweat, her heart pounding and her hands shaking. Her dreams were haunted by her memories and her fears, and she no longer had Wei to talk to like she used to. She missed his familiar warmth and presence, the soothing timbre of his voice assuring her that she was strong enough to save them all.

Instead, she heard Rong's voice now.

On one of those nights, she saw the Elementals. Three of them—Windshadow, Lazar, and Ruslan—stood before her in a row, Rong by her side. She could feel the weight of their murderous gazes on her, especially Windshadow's. There was no kindness or solidarity in her eyes anymore, only enmity.

The three Elementals raised their hands in unison, each unleashing the height of their powers on her and Rong—flames that singed her skin, a piercing gust of wind that tore at her, a blade that pierced right through her chest.

'Destroy them all, Rose,' Rong said next to her. 'You have to do it, for the good of our people.'

She threw out her hands and felt the magic stream from her fingertips with a force that terrified her. There was a newfound dimension to her power that was boundless and depthless, infinite enough to consume her. She could feel her lungs filling up with water, making each breath more laboured than the last. She wasn't sure if she was still asleep anymore; the sensation felt surreal enough, as though she was awake.

She sat up in bed, drenched in perspiration, her chest heaving as she drank in the cool night air. When she stared down at her hands, they were cupped around a shimmering water orb, brighter than anything she had ever conjured before.

* * *

The final day of cultivation could not come sooner.

She towed her jittery body out of bed that morning. Days of troubled sleep and little food had left her feeling as though the wind could take her any moment, but she felt a consistent buzzing in her body, as though her blood was humming with anticipation.

The Earth Elemental was waiting for her at the chamber, deep in conversation with the head sorcerer when she arrived. She was eager to get through this final day of cultivation, eager to see the results of their work this whole week. Would they be strong enough to eliminate the Fire Elemental? Would they be able to defeat the Imperial Army and overthrow Han?

'Today's process will be a little more taxing than before. But please ensure that you endure it,' said the head sorcerer. Desert Rose nodded.

'You've done a marvellous job so far, Rose,' Rong said, gesturing for her to enter the chamber. 'You ought to be proud of yourself.'

The final step in the cultivation process made the humming in her blood intensify the moment she sat down. Her power roiled and churned inside her like a wave, and she let it wash her away into another realm, one that only she and Rong populated.

This is the right thing to do, she thought. *We are stronger with our powers combined. This is how we can help our people.*

Yet, something continued to niggle at her. She took a deep breath and tried to calm her pounding heart. Her magic swelled in her, threatening to spill out.

Voices from outside made her pause. A shout, then what sounded like a cry of pain. Desert Rose opened her eyes. Rong was still in a meditative state, his eyes closed and his hands entwined with hers, seeming oblivious to what was happening outside.

'Something's going on outside,' Desert Rose said.

The Earth Elemental's response was sharp. 'Ignore it. Focus. We are almost there.'

An unearthly heat settled upon the chamber, baking the walls and ground. Desert Rose squeezed her eyes shut and tried to concentrate, but something felt amiss. The energy flow had stopped, along with the head sorcerer's chanting outside. Everything felt as though it had come to a standstill. While the sorcerer's voice had filled the chamber before, now there was only a chilling silence, loud enough for the slightest sound to be caught.

The heat grew unbearable, pressing close like a steel blanket. Soon the ground was scalding her skin, and sweat was pouring down her face. Her breathing grew laboured, and the chamber seemed to spin. She leapt up at last, abandoning the ritual. The Earth Prince's calls trailed after her, but she ignored them as she coated herself with a sheen of cool water and stepped out.

Lazar stood three feet away with his hands outstretched, palms facing the chamber. By his feet, the head sorcerer lay unconscious on the ground. His robes were shredded and his skin lacerated. Desert Rose had seen the way Windshadow ripped someone apart with her power, and this corpse reminded her of the soldiers Windshadow had killed in the battle at Danxi Plains.

Windshadow was nowhere to be seen, but Desert Rose was certain she was here, in her elemental form. The Priestess was absent as well, and thankfully so was Wei. Where had he gone?

Lazar launched a ball of fire at her, pulling her back to the present. She ducked to the ground, thickening the coat of water around her.

'Surprise,' he said, retracting his flame when she straightened.

The Earth Elemental stepped out from the chamber, dripping in perspiration and almost tripping over her at the entrance. He took in the situation before him and looked up at Lazar. 'You must be our Fire brother,' he said, as pleasantly as though he were inviting a friend to his home.

The ground rumbled and shook, like a dormant beast coming to life. With surprising speed, it threw the Fire Elemental off his feet and sent him sprawling. Before Lazar could pick himself back up, the ground lapped him up again, soft and undulating like sand dunes that swallowed lost travellers. A burst of flames broke through the ground and made it peel back from him, as though the earth were recoiling.

Desert Rose gathered all the moisture she could find and directed it towards Lazar's nose and mouth, filling his lungs. The magic surged out of her and struck Lazar all at once. He fell to his knees, choking. Almost instantly, the ground folded over him like a blanket, squeezing tight enough to crush him.

A whip of wind lashed at Desert Rose, cutting through her sleeve and drawing blood. She dropped her arm and spun around to find Windshadow materializing before her. Whose side was she on here?

She was supposed to lure the Fire Elemental here so that they could all ambush him. Why was she attacking her?

'Follow my lead,' Windshadow hissed next to her ear. 'Trust me.'

The Earth Elemental grabbed her hand before she could respond to Windshadow and pulled her towards him. They stood side by side, unleashing a relentless stream of magic at the Fire Elemental. She could feel the magnitude of her power coursing through her body right down to her fingertips, amplified by the Earth Elemental's magic. They were stronger together now, even if the cultivation process had been interrupted, strong enough to destroy what was arguably the strongest Elemental among them all.

Lazar let out a roar, then transformed himself into a ball of flames that rolled out from the folds of the ground. Rong recoiled, as though physically hurt by Lazar. That moment was all Lazar needed to escape from Rong's control and launch himself at Desert Rose.

She tumbled to the ground, screaming as Lazar crashed into her and started burning up her robes. Her breath escaped her as soon as she hit the floor, and she struggled to shove Lazar off her, but he barely budged. She squeezed her eyes shut, trying to block out the pain from her flaming robes, and imagined a coat of icy cold water protecting her.

A merciful coolness drenched her from head to toe, bringing sweet reprieve from the heat. When she opened her eyes again, she found herself covered in a shimmering sheen of water that made Lazar leap away.

Windshadow materialized by her side and picked her up as soon as the water shield dissipated. 'I'll hold him. You two attack.'

Desert Rose nodded. Windshadow dove behind Lazar and shoved him towards Desert Rose and Rong, who both gathered their qi to direct it at him.

But before their energy could strike him, Lazar spun around so that Windshadow was caught between him and Rong. Then he threw out a stream of flames that struck her from behind.

'Windshadow!' Desert Rose screamed.

But it was too late. The other desert girl was caught in between the clash of their energies, Desert Rose's combined with Rong's, and Lazar's. She tried to pull back her power, but found it bound to the Earth Elemental's. He would not relent, no matter how she wrestled for control over her energy.

'Rong, stop!' she cried.

But the Earth Elemental continued aiming their collective qi at Windshadow, just as Lazar persisted in burning her alive. Her face contorted in pain, but she made no sound. Even at this moment, she held on to her stubborn pride. Her gaze settled on Desert Rose. There was a resignation in her eyes, as though the light had gone out, but Desert Rose could read everything the other girl wanted to say to her. Her mind drifted back to the conversation she had with Windshadow in Lettoria, after they found themselves on the same side.

'If it came down to you and me in the end . . . would you do it?' Desert Rose had asked her.

'Yes,' Windshadow had replied after a moment's consideration. 'I would.'

Yet, Windshadow had protected her time and again, coming to her aid and having her back in duels. She had dragged her out of the battlefield at Danxi Plains when the Ghost King and his army were tearing it apart. She had fought against a magical dragon alongside her in the White Crypt. She had been her only ally from the desert when they both trained at the House of Night, and she had taught her how to survive in the palace.

And this time was no different. She had risked her life to lure Lazar here so that they could all finish him off.

Windshadow might have been neither friend nor foe at the beginning, someone Desert Rose didn't know whether to trust. She might have once betrayed her and abandoned her, demonstrating that her loyalties only lay with herself. But she had also saved her life multiple times when she had no reason to.

And after everything they had gone through together, Desert Rose felt no hatred or resentment towards her. The other desert girl was a survivor who did anything and everything she could to stay alive, and she showed no remorse for the things she did. The way her tribe had treated her had shaped her into the person she was; she didn't have the love and protection of her tribe members like Desert Rose did growing up. She had had to fight her way to the end, saddled with the burden of her destiny. Like her, Windshadow had only done the best she could with the fate that had been thrust upon her.

'See you on the other side, azzi,' Windshadow said with the ghost of a smile. She closed her eyes and her body fell limp.

As soon as Windshadow was no longer a threat, Rong and Lazar directed their power away from her and took aim at each other. Desert Rose scrambled over to Windshadow just as her body collapsed to the ground, catching her before she hit the floor.

Even in death, Windshadow looked just like she did the day Desert Rose first met her at the House of Night—proud, defiant, wilful, but underneath it all, loyal. It seemed absurd to call her that, but Windshadow was the only person who had stuck by Meng when no one else did—not even Desert Rose—when he was overthrown, abandoned, and betrayed by the imperial court. And she was the person who had repeatedly come back for her and fought alongside her, even when Desert Rose hadn't counted on her to.

She tucked a stray tuft of Windshadow's hair behind her ear and carried her inside the chamber, where she laid her gently on the ground.

As soon as she stepped out, she flung out her hands, channelling all her rage in the qi she directed at Lazar.

Her magic surged through her like a tidal wave. She felt the boundless power of her qi combined with the Earth Elemental's and she leaned into it, drawing upon it and feeding it, becoming both the source and the vessel.

The world spun around her, reeling from the collision of energies. She swayed on her feet, struggling to keep her eyes open. Every inch of her body screamed in protest. But while a part of her felt as though she might collapse from exhaustion, another part was invigorated by her power. She forced herself to hold fast against Lazar's magic.

At last, an ear-splitting scream cut through the air, and she felt the force of Lazar's energy die down. She opened her eyes and found him on the ground, his body contorted and immobile, as though an invisible force had broken it from within.

The air rang in the aftermath of the fight, crackling as though a wildfire had blazed through the chamber. Desert Rose stared at Lazar's body, then up at Rong, who shot her a triumphant grin.

They had done it. Both Air and Fire Elementals were dead. That left her and the Earth Elemental in the final race to fulfil the prophecy. But she only felt a hollowness in her gut, as though someone had carved her empty. Her power continued pulsing through her, so strong it made her almost lose her footing and pant as though she had just run several li.

Rong beamed at her, though he looked spent himself. 'Good work, Rose. You and I make a fantastic team.'

That was the last thing she remembered before her knees buckled and darkness consumed her.

Eighteen

Meng

'You want to become emperor again.'

It was a statement, not a question. The Priestess could read his mind, so Meng saw no point in denying his ambitions.

He sat opposite her in a low-ceiling chamber adorned with red lanterns and drapes. A pungent, heady scent wafted from an incense pot in the corner, making him drowsy. The Priestess's private quarters were surprisingly elaborate in furnishings, and isolated from the rest of what appeared to be a palace. The longer he stayed in this underground realm, the more areas Meng discovered, and it seemed as though the White Ling Sect's territory had no bounds.

'We need that scroll if we are to help you take back your power. Only by unlocking the magic in the kingdom will we have a chance of seeing this rebellion through.'

The scroll was the only secret weapon he had left against Han. If he lost possession of it, he had nothing left to fight his brother. Yet, without having someone unlock the magic, the scroll was as good as a stack of dry wood to him.

But giving the Ling the key to the magic within the kingdom was giving them the key to the kingdom, the means to establish a new dynasty.

'Rebellion or revolution?' Meng asked quietly.

'Your brother is building his secret army as we speak. The Wind Elemental may have destroyed his stash of ticha, but he has other stores of it. We can now only take advantage of the tumult caused by the Wall being taken down, but our window of opportunity is closing. If we delay this further, the Oasis Emperor will attack before we have completely restored our magic.' She observed his expression, noted the hesitation in his face. 'Our goals are the same, Fourth Prince.'

'Until they are not . . .'

The Priestess tilted her head. The incense smoke grew thicker in the chamber, curling around him like an encroaching vine. 'You may not trust us, but it is an irrevocable fact that you have no one else to entrust this task to. You need our help, as much as we need that scroll. We are simply wasting time haggling over the details of what happens after that.'

Meng fell silent.

'Remember the betrayal, Fourth Prince. Remember how your brother took everything from you as soon as he returned to the kingdom, and how your mother sat by and watched.'

Meng needed no reminder. The memory of that day remained fresh in his mind, and not one day passed where he didn't dream of taking it all back from Han. He had worked his way up to that moment—all for the sense of duty he felt to his family, for the vision he had for the kingdom—only to have it stolen by his elder brother who had spent the last few years in exile and contributing nothing to the family or the country.

He pulled out the scroll from his robes. 'I trust that we are people of our word.'

'Our goals are one and the same, Fourth Prince. It will not benefit me or my people to double-cross you now.'

Meng nodded.

The Priestess glanced over his shoulder and nodded. Five sorcerers, whom Meng hadn't noticed standing by the entrance, stepped forward. How long had they been waiting there? They took the scroll from him, then gestured for him to stay back. A part of him wanted to snatch the scroll back. He had kept it close to him for months; to hand it over now felt like losing a safety net, his final leverage in this power struggle.

Yet, he also knew that nothing would move forward if he did not unlock the magic in this land. The scroll was just a key. He had to let it go in order to access the greater treasure of this kingdom.

'You may watch, if you'd like,' the Priestess said. 'But we ask that you do not interfere at any point no matter what happens.'

Meng had had enough experience with magical objects to understand the importance of not getting involved. He could still hear the screams of the dying Lettorian guards who got crushed in the cave where they found the Immortal Spring.

He hung back as requested and watched as the sorcerers sat in a circle on the ground around the scroll. They closed their eyes and held out their hands before them, palms down. In unison, they began chanting in the Old Kingdom language, the one that *Duru-shel Minta* was written in. Meng had no idea what they were saying, but their voices rose and dipped like waves, strangely hypnotic. Coupled with the musky incense, it started to lull Meng into a deep slumber . . .

He was vaguely aware of the ground falling away beneath him, of himself reeling as the air in the chamber closed in on him, its weight almost unbearable. With his eyes shut, all he saw were spots of light in the unending darkness. Everything blended into one—the drone of the sorcerers' collective voices, his laboured breaths, the suffocating darkness that was eventually replaced by the shimmering lights—until he felt like he was one with the earth and the air, as though he were somehow connected to everything around him, no longer an independent entity . . .

A ripple ran through the ground, pulling him back to the present. He continued to keep his eyes closed, feeling the energy of the earth right down to his bones. There was no way to tell how much time had passed, or how much longer the ritual would take. But he knew that things in the Oasis Kingdom were changing with each passing moment. He might not have supernatural abilities or senses, but he could feel the energies shift and morph, as though the very earth had been rocked to its core.

The chanting reached a deafening crescendo, then died down almost abruptly. The wave of energy subsided, and the rocking inside Meng ceased.

When he cracked his eyes open, everything seemed to be the same. The ground was still. Everything was intact in the chamber, yet something felt irrevocably different. The air felt as though it now wore a brand-new skin, thick and heavy as in a prelude to a thunderstorm. Something pulsed through the ground, beating new life into it.

The Priestess stood by the circle, her eyes still closed. A silvery light rose from the ground and flowed up towards her, silhouetting her stately figure. When at last the light dimmed and died out, the Priestess opened her eyes. Something in her had changed; there was now a quiet potency that rippled through her.

'It is done,' she said in a faint voice, as though the ritual had sapped her of her life force. But she was shaking with unbridled energy, as were the other sorcerers. One of them raised a hand and directed it at an empty earthen pot across the room. A warm glow illuminated the pot before shattering it.

A couple of the other sorcerers were tearing up as they tested out their newly reinstated powers. 'Our magic has been fully restored,' one of them declared in a voice shaking with emotions.

'For so long, the seal that the old sorcerers had put on this land had bound up a good part of our magic,' another said with a glimmer of excitement in his eyes. 'It's all coming back now.'

The Priestess turned to Meng, the harshness in her face now softening in gratitude. 'You have aided us in reclaiming our stolen powers. The Ling will not forget this, Fourth Prince.'

Meng nodded, a little breathless in the aftermath of the ritual even though he had not actively participated in it. He had done it. After years of seeking ways to unlock the magic in the land, Meng had finally done what his forefathers had never dared to do, what his mother had forbidden him from doing, if only to keep him in line.

After centuries since the Great Purge, he had brought magic back to Oasis Kingdom. All this latent magic that had been locked up in the land by the first sorcerers, that the kingdom had denied since its inception—he had restored what belonged to this kingdom, undid what his ancestors had done to the indigenous people of the Hesui empire. Perhaps now, they would no longer need to live in fear and resistance against magic, but would learn to embrace it as part of the natural order and live in harmony with it. It was a step, a first step but a crucial one nonetheless.

As he trailed after the Priestess along the labyrinthian hallways of the White Ling Sect's realm, still reeling from the gravity of what he had done, news of the death of two Elementals spread like wildfire.

'It seems that the cultivation process has worked. The Earth Prince and the Water Elemental have jointly eliminated the Fire and Air

Elemental,' the Priestess informed him as they made their way towards the Earth Elemental's chamber.

Windshadow was dead.

The news hit Meng like a cart of bricks. He tried to wrap his head around it, but failed to imagine Windshadow being slain. The desert girl had always seemed so resilient and undefeatable, ever since he had first met her in the imperial prison, where he had caught her trying to escape using her powers. It seemed impossible that someone like her—who had become so good at surviving, regardless of what it took—could die. If anyone was to survive the Elementals' prophecy, Meng had expected it to be her.

He had grown so accustomed to having her on his side that he had never considered the possibility of her no longer being here. They were a team; they had been so ever since they had come to that agreement in the imperial prison, where she would help him get on the throne and he would free her tribe from the territorial wars in the Khuzar Desert.

And now he was truly on his own, without his only ally, the only one he had come to trust.

The Earth Elemental was sitting cross-legged in the middle of his chamber when Meng arrived, eyes closed and body still as though he was meditating.

'Your Highness,' the Priestess greeted with a deep bow. 'The magic in the kingdom has been unlocked, with the Fourth Prince's help.'

'I thank you on behalf of the White Ling Sect and all the Ling, Fourth Prince. As promised, you have our support in overthrowing your brother,' the Earth Elemental said, his eyes still closed.

Meng nodded. 'I heard the Wind Elemental is dead.'

The Earth Elemental opened his eyes at last, barely bothering to hide his gleeful smile. 'Indeed. It was a tough fight, a very close call, but the Fire Elemental switched his strategy at the last moment, and we eliminated the Wind Elemental jointly—and rather efficiently, might I add. He would have made a good partner, but too bad he's not a team player. So, of course I had to seize the opportunity to kill him as well.' His tone was light, almost flippant, but Meng could detect a hint of malice in it.

'The Wind Elemental could have been a good ally,' Meng said. 'She has been instrumental in getting me this far, at least.'

'But she was also powerful and ruthless. Surely you don't expect me to keep this threat alive. As I said to Desert Rose, it was the right decision to combine our powers. Without that, we might not have been able to eliminate both the Air and Fire Elementals, both of whom are stronger than us. This clears our path significantly.'

A part of Meng wanted to tear that cold, uncaring look off the Earth Elemental's face. There was something about him that was unnerving—it was not simply his smugness, but the quiet danger that lurked underneath that mask of civility. Now that he was done with the Fire and Air Elementals, would he go after Desert Rose next with the same methodical ruthlessness? Meng felt his fists clench by his side.

The Priestess shot him a warning stare, daring him to act on his impulses. Meng remained where he was and suppressed all his rage to gather his thoughts.

Now that the Earth Elemental had combined his powers with Desert Rose and there were no other Elementals in the running, he was unobstructed in leading the Ling towards the new future he had envisioned for his people. He might have promised to help Meng overthrow Han, but as soon as that was achieved, Meng might not be able to hold him back from his ambitions.

One problem at a time, he thought.

'I need an army as soon as possible,' he said.

He had bided his time for long enough. Without his Fire Elemental, without magic on his side, Han was at his most vulnerable. Meng had to strike now, even if it meant teaming up with the Earth Elemental.

'Take your pick, Fourth Prince. The Ling Army is at your service,' the Earth Elemental said. 'The throne will soon be yours again.'

Meng had to admit, he rather liked the sound of that.

Nineteen

Wei

Something was amiss.

As Wei neared the tree leading to the White Ling Sect's subterranean realm, a strange sense of foreboding settled in him. Something felt different about the mountain, the air, the very ground he trod on.

The sect quarters were abuzz when Wei returned—not only from an overpowering qi that pervaded the air, an energy that seemed to hum through the chambers and hallways that Wei wound through in search of Desert Rose, but also from the news of the Elementals' deadly fight.

Wei only heard snatches of conversation, but he gathered enough to understand that in the time he was gone, everything had changed. Two Elementals were dead, and Meng had handed over the scroll to unlock the magic in the kingdom. That would explain the strange, palpable energy in the air.

His footsteps quickened. If two Elementals were dead from the duel, how did Desert Rose fare?

The chamber was empty when he arrived. It seemed that the cultivation process was over—had they gone through with it?

'It is done,' someone said from behind him. Wei whipped around to find the Earth Elemental looking somehow more resplendent than ever before.

There was something different about him now, as though he was radiating more energy and it was spilling out of him. While Desert Rose had grown more worn over the week, he seemed completely unscathed from the cultivation process or the fight with the other Elementals.

What exactly had the cultivation process entailed? How was it that a process that was meant to amplify both Elementals' energies had left such an imbalance in qi between them?

'We have decided to lend our support to the Fourth Prince in the end.' The Earth Elemental turned around with a flourish of his sleeve. 'I understand that you might feel slighted by us switching alliances from you to the Fourth Prince, but he did offer a stronger proposition than you. Consider us betting on the stronger horse.'

'Never mind that,' Wei snapped. 'Where's Rose? What exactly happened here?'

'Fret not, she's just a little drained after that fight among us Elementals, but we've sorted things out nicely.' His insouciance made Wei's fists clench, but he kept them by his side. 'Now, we have more pressing issues at hand. The Fourth Prince has helped us to unlock the magic in this kingdom and we will be launching our first attack on the Imperial Army on the night of the harvest moon.' His face twisted into a gleeful smile. 'It's quite poetic, I'd say—the Children of the Moon staging our rebellion on the solstice moon.'

'I'm thrilled,' Wei said dryly.

'You should be,' the Earth Elemental replied, not missing a beat, 'since you will be leading the Ling Army into the palace. The Priestess tells me you've been waiting for the moment you meet your brother again, so I shall not deny you the pleasure of that.'

'You mean send your pawns to the frontline while you stay safely in your little tunnel,' Wei sneered. Yet, he could not deny that the Priestess was right. Han had not only executed Matron, but he had also ordered imperial scouts to track them down and kill them. The sight of his mother's body after the explosion they set off in Ghost City would forever be branded in his mind. It had spurred him on every single day since then, to arrive at the moment where he would avenge his mother and Matron's deaths.

The Earth Elemental was watching him intently. 'I will most certainly be there to ensure the Ling army succeeds. It would be sweet justice to see the downfall of the Oasis Emperor, especially since our victory is certain. Not only is every soldier in the Ling army handpicked, the best of each sect—'

As a result of all the infighting and aggressive competition, Wei thought. This was how they were building the Ling army, by sacrificing the weaker sects to beef up the stronger ones.

'—the enemy that we are up against has been made for us to defeat. So don't worry, I am not sending you all to your deaths.' He turned to leave before Wei could ask any more questions. 'Rose should have recovered by the harvest moon, so there's plenty of time for you two to get ready.'

Despite himself, Wei asked, 'You're letting her go?'

He spread out his arms. 'She's not a captive here, nor are you. She's resting in her bedchamber as we speak, but give her some time to recuperate and she will be as good as new.'

When Wei sprinted over to Desert Rose's bedchamber, he found her lying awake in bed, her brows pulled together as she stared at the ceiling. She sat up when she spotted Wei, only to be overcome by a dizzy spell. Wei hurried over and propped her up against the bed frame.

'You came back,' she rasped, barely able to hold up her head. 'I thought you . . .'

Wei peered at her ashen face as she leaned against him. She looked completely drained, and her face bore a couple scratches while her hands were singed. He brushed a gentle finger against her cheek. 'Of course I came back. What happened here?'

'Windshadow and Lazar are dead,' Desert Rose said, her voice shaking. 'Windshadow died trying to save me . . .'

Wei laid his hand gently on her cold ones and rubbed them in slow, calming strokes. Despite the other desert girl having once betrayed her, they had shared a kinship from having similar backgrounds and being bound to a prophecy and destiny larger than them. He might not be able to forgive Windshadow for her betrayal and for murdering his brother, but Desert Rose was a lot more magnanimous than him and had regarded Windshadow as a friend.

At length, she raised her head from Wei's. 'You weren't here on the last few days of cultivation. What happened?'

Wei narrated in detail the trouble the shouren had gotten into, along with how the Ling army was recruiting Ling from various sects. His misgivings about the altercation between the Night Beast Sect and the Storm River Sect grew the more he spoke about it. It wasn't just a case of two displaced sects competing for resources; there was clearly a deeper reason why the larger sects were cannibalizing the smaller ones now, just as the White Ling Sect was preparing to storm the imperial palace. They were picking the best to go up against the special army Han was assembling.

'And now that Meng has handed over the scroll and let the White Ling Sect unlock the magic in the kingdom, the Ling have recovered their full magical abilities. It's only a matter of time before the Earth Elemental attempts to revolt—not just against Han, but the entire imperial family,' he finished.

Desert Rose frowned, taking a moment to absorb everything he had said. He tucked a stray tuft of hair behind her ears.

'That seems rather far-fetched,' she said at last. 'Rong said he has promised to overthrow Han so that Meng can ascend the throne. He mentioned nothing about ending the Zhao dynasty.'

He sighed. They pulled apart and sat next to each other on the bed, but Wei was aware of the distance between them now. 'Is it so hard for you to believe that his ambitions are much larger than that? He didn't persuade you to do the cultivation process out of the kindness of his heart, you know. He's clearly benefited from it by having his powers doubled. There can only be one Elemental remaining, and he's clearly planning to be it.'

'His goal is to unite his people. Our people. The Damohai.'

'If his intentions are truly that pure, why are the sects in a tumult right now? Why are the shouren being targeted by the larger sects? Don't you remember how the Black Lotus Sect attacked them?' He gestured at her. 'And look at you. Did the cultivation process benefit you at all? I don't see the Earth Elemental being as weak in bed as you are. In fact, he's off with Meng to plan their attack on Han.'

She stared at him for the longest time. He wanted to kiss her right then, if only to chase away the disappointment in her eyes, but also because this might be one of the last few opportunities he could do so. The end felt as though it was looming closer with each passing day, with each Elemental being eliminated.

Finally, she dropped her gaze. Her smile was sad, with a trace of bitterness. 'Windshadow used to say I trust people too easily.'

Wei wrapped her hand in his. 'Do you trust me?'

She looked up at him. 'Of course I do.'

'More than you trust the Earth Elemental?'

She straightened and looked him in the eye. 'You know I do.'

'He has already killed two Elementals. You can be sure he'll come for you next. We need to get you out of here. Every moment you remain in his territory is another moment you're at risk.'

She shook her head. 'No, I'm not going to run.'

'At least until the rebellion is over,' he pleaded.

'I'm not going to run and hide,' she insisted. 'I have as much of a chance to kill him as he does me. And if I manage to kill him before the rebellion takes shape, you won't have to worry about the Ling becoming too powerful and destabilizing the kingdom.'

'It's too dangerous—'

'Wei.' She stared him dead in the eye. 'I'm an Elemental, and I can fight just as well as you. What are you so worried about?'

He didn't give voice to what he truly feared—that they were dangerously close to the end, with only two Elementals left—and he was clutching on to the only way he knew to keep her safe. But he had realized by now that there was no stopping destiny; it came for them when it chose, and they could only fall in line and let their stories play out.

'They're expecting me to support the rebellion, help Meng where I'm needed,' he replied instead. 'The Earth Elemental will likely make his move on you while everyone is distracted.'

But how could they outsmart the most powerful sect among the Ling, one that consisted of soothsayers and mind readers? How could they stay one step ahead of them so that Desert Rose could kill him?

Desert Rose gave his hand a squeeze. 'You do what you need to. This fight is between us Elementals—I can handle Rong on my own.'

He nodded. 'If you find yourself in danger, look for the shouren. Look for Qiu. The sects are regrouping, you can rally their support.'

'I will.'

They held each other in their eyes, neither of them saying anything more. Nothing else needed to be said. They had come all this way from their first meeting in the desert, as unlikely acquaintances who doubted each other's intentions, to crossing paths again in the palace, to becoming allies, then friends, and finally doomed lovers.

Wei knew with all his heart and soul that he would trust this girl sitting before him with his life, and he would lay down his life for her if he had to. But fate had different plans for them. And if this was the last time they would be in such proximity to each other, then he was thankful that he at least got to have this moment with her.

He pulled out the coin that the Ghost King had given him and tucked it into her palm. It was an ancient token, a currency used among desert merchants centuries ago that no longer held any significance—except now, dug up from a tomb in the Darklands, it was the one thing that bore any remnant ties Wei had with Ghost City, the only item that he could use to reach out to the Ghost King and his army of trapped souls.

'The Ghost Army is behind you,' he said. 'They're still waiting to be freed.'

Desert Rose scrutinized the coin in her palm. 'What's this?'

'A way for you to summon the Ghost King. The Wall might be down, but he might not have access to where you are, should you need help. He proposed using a token from one of the tombs in the Darklands you can use to reach out. I got it before Zeyan and the Dugur tribe shamans reunited my soul with my body.' He nodded at it. 'You'll need a medium's help with that, I suppose. But if you ever find yourself in need of some aid, remember you're not alone.'

She closed her hand around the token and looked up at him. They reached for each other at the same time, wrapping their arms tightly around each other.

'Thank you.' Her voice was muffled against his shoulder, but Wei heard everything else she didn't say loud and clear. It sounded exactly like what he wanted to say to her.

The best way to destroy the enemy is first by being his friend.
—*The War Handbook,* Lu Cao

Twenty

Desert Rose

With the Ling army, Wei, and Meng gone, the White Ling Sect quarters seemed all the more ominous, with its cavernous chambers and long, winding tunnels.

Desert Rose had found a spot not too far from the shouren's lair to scatter Windshadow's ashes. As soon as she recovered, the first thing she did was return to the chamber where she had left Windshadow's body, burn it, and bundle up the ashes.

The morning was cool and dry. It was a near perfect autumn day to trek up Yeli Mountain, as though she were taking a quiet walk with her desert friend. It felt right to set her free rather than bury her in the ground; Windshadow would hate being stuck in one place for eternity.

She arrived at the clearing that led to a cliff overlooking an expanse of forest. Its vibrant foliage of scarlet and gold lay at her feet like a painting, and a cold gust of wind snapped at her, almost as if Windshadow had come to say one last goodbye.

She unhitched the bundle and cradled it in her arm as she unwrapped it. 'Goodbye, azzi,' she whispered.

A rustle behind her made her whip around. Desert Rose recognized the pair of Black Lotus Sect members who had interrupted the White Ling Sect ceremony more than a week ago. They appeared to be siblings, well trained in combat. After all, they were from the Black Lotus Sect. Desert Rose assumed a fight stance, ready to attack or flee any moment.

But the girl only said, 'We're not here to hurt you. I'm Yan, and this is my brother, Yujin.' She turned her sombre gaze to the bundle of ashes. 'It's Windshadow, isn't it?'

Desert Rose nodded. 'She died trying to save me.'

Windshadow had never asked for forgiveness for her betrayal during the Spring Ceremony, where she had framed Desert Rose for murdering the Oasis Emperor, nor had she expressed remorse for what she had done. But somehow, everything the other girl had done since then had atoned for her betrayal—from dragging her out of the battlefield to fending off that attack from Lazar.

'She talked about you a lot,' said the boy. 'I think she saw you as her only friend.'

Desert Rose swallowed the lump in her throat and got down on a knee. She unwrapped the bundle and grabbed a handful of Windshadow's ashes, then turned around to look at the siblings, inviting them to join her. A cool breeze swirled from the north, and they each released a handful. In silence, they released Windshadow into the air until there was none of her left.

At last, Desert Rose folded up the cloth bag and turned to the siblings. Like Yan said, they didn't appear to have intentions of hurting or capturing her. In fact, there was a mutinous spark in their eyes, as though they had been betrayed in some way.

'Windshadow was lured to the palace by the Fire Elemental,' Yan said. 'She told us that he revealed the location of the ticha stores to her, and that was where we were ambushed. We would have been captured if it weren't for her.'

'I don't understand,' Desert Rose said. 'Why are you telling me all this?'

'What would you do if you found out that your tribe has been lying to you for a while now?' Yujin asked quietly. 'That they have been secretly building an army for the emperor.'

Desert Rose nearly dropped the cloth bag in shock. 'The Black Lotus Sect has been helping Han build his special army? But . . . why would they?'

'Because the best way to ensure their victory is by building a fake army that they can defeat. Or rather, the White Ling Army can defeat.' Yan shot her a meaningful look. 'What the emperor doesn't know is that the Black and White Ling have united to overthrow him. He only knows that the Black Lotus Sect is helping him build his magic army, not knowing that the White Ling Sect has been gathering its forces to invade the palace and destroy both his special army and the Imperial Army.'

Desert Rose had to admit she was impressed. Windshadow would be too. The Ling—especially the Black Lotus Sect—were masters at this game of subterfuge.

Desert Rose frowned. 'And the ambush that the Fire Elemental led that day . . .'

Yujin rolled his eyes. 'How do you think the Imperial Army managed to ambush the White Ling Sect that day? Lazar tipped off the emperor because we let him go. Our sect leader *let* him go.'

'So the ambush was . . . planned? But why would the Black Lotus Sect do that?'

The twins shared a look. 'Why wouldn't they, is the better question,' Yan said.

'What's a little sacrifice if it means they can gain the trust of the emperor? The best way to destroy the enemy is first by being his friend,' Yujin added. 'Better yet if that ambush could get rid of a few White Ling—a sneaky win for the Black Ling. Perhaps the Earth Prince himself knew about the attack. Who can be certain anymore?'

Was that possible? Would he really sacrifice his people just to keep up the charade and lower Han's guard?

'The Black Lotus sect is split right now,' Yan went on. 'Some want to join in the rebellion, others want to be independent.' She shared a look with her brother. 'Like us.'

'Half the sect has joined the Ling army and will storm the palace to fight the emperor's special army,' Yujin said.

'But it's a guaranteed victory for the Ling. So what's the problem?' Desert Rose asked.

Yujin let out a dry chuckle. 'The problem is, the Fire Elemental knows about the army that the Black Lotus Sect helped to build. In fact, he was involved in the task, sent by the emperor to monitor the sect. So who's to say the emperor doesn't know about the sects' plans, that he isn't lying in wait for the Ling army to march up to his doorstep so he can wipe them out in one clean sweep?'

'Even with the White Ling Sect's soothsayers, the emperor's army has shamans that can block their Eye and prevent them from seeing through the emperor's plans, so we don't know how much he knows,' Yan added.

'Also, the larger sects have been cannibalizing the smaller ones to beef up the Ling army. All this conflict among the sects was caused by the White Ling Sect building and mobilizing the Ling army for the rebellion. As much as we would love to overthrow the Oasis Emperor, we're not interested in being pawns in a rebellion led by a sect that would sacrifice its own people to gain power,' Yujin finished.

Desert Rose took a deep breath. Then another. This stream of revelations was making her dizzy. Everything Wei had told her was true.

Despite all that he had said about uniting the Ling, the Earth Elemental had chosen to sacrifice the smaller, weaker sects in order to build his army—all for a rebellion that he believed could succeed.

Something struck her then. The memory of what had happened that day outside the chamber, when Lazar and Windshadow had interrupted the cultivation process.

The Earth Elemental and Lazar had worked in tandem to kill Windshadow. They had joined hands in attacking Desert Rose, and then Windshadow when she came to Desert Rose's defence, and they had been relentless in attacking Windshadow until she breathed her last.

Lazar had known Windshadow would bring him back to the White Ling Sect territory; he had known they were planning to kill him off there. And he had turned the tide against them instead. Perhaps he and Rong had been conspiring to eliminate her and Windshadow that day at the chamber.

'But he killed Lazar too. I witnessed it myself,' Desert Rose said.

'Every Elemental for himself, I suppose,' Yan said quietly, watching her face as she arrived at the answers.

It wasn't just about overthrowing Han anymore; everything the Earth Elemental had planned so far was to set the stage for his ascension to power.

The Earth Elemental, who had proposed an alliance with her, who had even persuaded her to combine their powers, had been serving only himself this whole time. To think she had believed his intentions to rebuild the Ling and the Damohai were true.

The Earth Elemental's ambitions were far bigger than just a rebellion. Not only was he planning to overthrow Han and end the Zhao dynasty, he also intended to eliminate her and become the last surviving Elemental so that he could revive the Old Kingdom and rule over it.

He had never been interested in backing Wei or Meng, only agreeing to that so that she would consent to the cultivation process, where he could amplify his powers by combining it with hers.

Windshadow was right—she was too trusting, and that was her biggest weakness.

The Earth Elemental had planned every step of this rebellion—building his own army, working with the Black Lotus Sect to build a fake army in order to ensure a guaranteed victory, recruiting Meng's help to unlock the magic in the kingdom, and persuading her to go through the cultivation process. He had laid out all the chess pieces, and she was just one of them. So were Wei and Meng.

Desert Rose's gaze snapped up as a jolt of panic seized her. 'Wei. Wei and Meng are leading the Ling troops into the palace as we speak.'

'That's why we're here,' Yan said. 'Princess Qiu said that her brother told her to look for you in case you needed some help against the Earth Prince.' She jabbed a finger over her shoulder and gestured for her to follow. Yujin was already leading the way.

They came to the outcrop where Qiu lived with her husband and brother-in-law. This time, instead of a cave full of shouren, there was a motley mix of various unfamiliar faces in distinctly different clothing. Some of the shouren were gathered here—including Heyang, Qiu, and Zhong—but they stood among an assortment of sect members dressed in their sect colours, the Storm River Sect in their grey-green robes and jade talismans, and the Black Lotus Sect in their black tunics and onyx tokens. Qiu had taught her to recognize each sect that way the last time they had met, and Desert Rose was glad that knowledge was coming in useful now.

Upon a cursory glance, there were possibly two hundred people in the cave, and the ones not from the Night Beast Sect looked incredibly out of place here.

'Welcome to the Night Lotus Sect,' Yujin said with a flourish. 'We came up with that name just today,' he added with a wink.

'Rose!' Qiu emerged from the crowd, hurrying over to her and pulling her into a tight hug. Relief washed over Desert Rose at the sight of Qiu's familiar face. 'Thank heavens you're alive. Wei came looking for us before setting off with the Ling army and told us you might need our help against the Earth Elemental.' She glanced at Heyang, who stepped forward with a grim smile.

'We are not interested in being part of the rebellion,' said the fox-man. 'But the Black Lotus Sect members here told us what the White Ling Sect has been doing to strengthen the Ling army and secure their victory with the throne.' He shook his head. 'It's time we band together to fight against the other sects—'

'Finally,' Zhong piped up from a corner. Desert Rose remembered how the belligerent shouren was always ready to take action, even if it meant leaping into a coup at the imperial palace. 'Why should we stay loyal to the White Ling Sect when they're trying to tear our sects apart and cause conflict among the Ling?'

It seemed, therefore, that the sects gathered here—Night Beast, Storm River, and Black Lotus—had been torn apart due to a difference in beliefs, not unlike how her tribe had split. Desert Rose felt a pang in her heart at the thought of her tribespeople, now displaced because of this unresolved conflict. They weren't quite so different after all, and now she was in a position to help them. This was her fight as much as it was theirs.

'The Earth Elemental has already killed the Fire and Air Elementals,' she said. 'I'm the only other Elemental remaining. So if we want to fight for our survival, we will need to band together—against the White Ling Sect and against the Earth Prince.'

'You're the Water Elemental, aren't you?' one of them asked. She was an elderly woman from the Storm River Sect, as indicated by the telltale talisman hanging on her waist belt. Clearly, despite this brand-new alliance, word spread quickly among them. She hobbled to the front of the crowd and stared at Desert Rose, then placed a hand over her heart and sank into a deep bow to her. 'It is an honour to be in the presence of an Elemental.'

Desert Rose hurriedly gestured for her to be at ease, but more of them—mostly from the Storm River Sect—began to follow suit, placing their hands over their hearts and bowing to her. She stared around at them, at a loss for how to respond.

'The Storm River Sect has always had an affinity with water, the giver of all life on earth,' said the Storm River Sect elder, her eyes shining with tears as she stared up at Desert Rose. 'I have never dared to dream of meeting the Water Elemental in my lifetime.'

A young Black Lotus Sect boy spoke up from the back of the cave, making no disguise of his scepticism. 'Are you strong enough to fight against the Earth Prince though? He's not only powerful, he's ambitious too.'

'So I've discovered,' Desert Rose replied. 'With all his soothsayers and mind readers around him, it will be hard to catch him off guard, what more kill him. But now that our powers are merged, I have a keener sense of his energies and can try to deplete his qi.' In fact, she was now fairly certain that was what the Earth Elemental had done after the cultivation process, leading to the imbalance in qi between the two of them.

'The cultivation process does indeed bind you to him, and him to you,' the Storm River Sect elder said. 'So every time your qi is depleted, his will compensate for it. In other words, you being weaker makes him stronger. The reverse is true. So we need to make sure you don't expend your qi until you come face-to-face with him, and even when you are duelling with him.'

'Whatever you need, Water Elemental,' said a young Storm River Sect man with a steely gaze, 'the Storm River Sect is ready to be of service.'

'And if you need something that can quickly—but temporarily—deplete his qi, I can always brew up something,' Qiu said, gesturing to the door leading to the herb storage room.

Desert Rose reached into her pocket, where the nondescript old coin that Wei had acquired for her sat. Her mind was racing, already concocting a plan. All she needed was for a diversion to buy her the time she needed to attack the Earth Elemental, someone to block the Priestess's Eye while she slipped him Qiu's brew. And then she would be free to lead the Ghost Army to Wei's aid at the imperial palace . . .

'Sounds risky . . .' Yan said when Desert Rose detailed her plan out loud.

Yujin nodded. 'But no success comes without some risk. So count me in.'

'And me,' Yan said, taking a step closer to her.

Desert Rose nodded at the twins, grateful for their solidarity. If Windshadow, the least trusting person she knew, had once trusted them, then perhaps they truly were people of their word. She pulled out the coin and held it out in her palm, wishing fervently that this would work. The Ghost King was not someone to be summoned, especially high up in the mountains here. But this was her last chance to help Wei, and to destroy the last remaining Elemental. It was worth a serious shot.

'I need a medium for this,' she said.

'Is that . . . a spirit token?' A Black Lotus Sect member—a medium, judging by his robes—edged towards her for a closer look.

Desert Rose nodded as he surveyed the coin in her palm. 'You are familiar with these things?'

'This is ancient—more powerful than what I'm used to summoning—but I will try.'

The medium held out his hands over the coin, palms down, and closed his eyes. A hush fell over the cave as his lone voice murmured a string of incantations. A long moment passed where it seemed like nothing was happening. Someone in a corner coughed, another shushed her restless child. Desert Rose narrowed her focus on the coin in her palm, which seemed to be growing heavier over time. Her hand began to tremble with the effort of holding out the coin.

Just as she was about to drop it, the Ghost King's telltale pearlescent glow lit up the centre of the cave, much fainter than it had been in Ghost City. The medium gasped softly next to her as the Ghost King took shape, starting from his crown all the way down to the hem of his long undulating robes.

'Who dares summon me?' His sonorous voice rumbled through the cave, but save for the mediums in the crowd and Desert Rose, no one else seemed to be able to hear or see him.

Desert Rose bowed. 'Greetings, Your Highness.' Next to her, the medium was quaking as he stared up at the Ghost King's foreboding figure, not realizing he had helped to summon a spirit this ancient and powerful. 'It's the Elemental who struck a deal with you. My father is still in your custody, and I haven't forgotten my promise to free you all. But now, I need your help to finish off the last Elemental.'

Qiu glanced around the cave. 'Who . . . who are you speaking with?' she asked in a small voice.

'You push your luck, Elemental,' said the Ghost King. 'I have involved myself enough in your worldly affairs after the last battle.'

'And you will not have to again after this,' Desert Rose assured him. 'The Earth Elemental is after the throne at the expense of his own people while also trying to kill me. If I can finish him off before the Ling army reaches the imperial palace, I can stop this fatal mission *and* fulfil the prophecy.' The Ghost King remained unmoved. 'It is down to me and him now, and our chance to strike is now. Please. We had a deal.'

'Our scouts tell us he's on his way to the imperial palace now,' one of the Black Lotus Sect members interrupted. 'We still have time to waylay him.'

Desert Rose nodded and turned back to the Ghost King. 'I know these matters are of no concern to you anymore, and all you want is for the prophecy to be fulfilled—'

'The fate of this bastard kingdom concerns me not in the least.'

'But without an army like yours, our victory is uncertain,' she went on. '*My* victory is uncertain against the Earth Elemental. What happens at the Imperial Palace will determine who survives the prophecy. Please,' she said again. 'Help us just this once more, and you and your Ghost Army and my father can all be freed at last.'

She didn't care that she was begging now. She, along with the Night Lotus Sect, was not strong enough to stop the Ling army from potentially walking into a trap, and the Earth Elemental was a formidable rival. Without the help of the Ghost Army, their chances of victory were slim.

The Ghost King spoke at last, his grave voice ominous as a warning. 'Our freedom hinges on your victory. Do not let us down.'

Twenty-One

Meng

The harvest moon hung overhead, swollen and bright, illuminating their path through the Capital. The familiar roads and landmarks sent a pang through Meng's heart. This was the longest he had ever been away from home, and coming back made him remember all that he had left behind and his reason for leaving.

The last time he had been through these streets was with Windshadow, after he had broken her out of prison and she had taken the both of them out of the kingdom and towards Lettoria. He had been a bundle of guilt, shame, and heartbreak back then, and coming back now brought on a wave of equally mixed feelings.

Next to him, Wei appeared stoic, indifferent. The Capital had never been home for him the way it had been for Meng. Wei's childhood had been different from Meng's, so it was no wonder that he had been desperate to leave this kingdom and seek a home elsewhere.

They had travelled all the way here barely speaking to each other except for practical and logistical matters. Meng was still surprised that Wei had agreed to lead the Ling into the palace and help him return to power, given the things Meng had done to secure his power the first time round. There was no way for Meng to ever compensate Wei for what he had taken from him, and perhaps Wei would never forgive him for plotting to eliminate Yong. And while he knew Wei hadn't come here for his sake, Meng was still grateful that his half-brother was willing to lend him his support to overthrow Han together.

'We split up here,' Wei said, pulling Meng out of his thoughts. He drew his horse to a stop and nodded at Meng.

They had arrived at the forest with the secret entrance leading into the palace, where Wei would lead the Ling in and attack at night while Meng distracted Han by showing up in his chamber. As soon as the Ling army defeated Han's army, Meng could successfully—and legitimately—overthrow Han.

Being flanked by a large group of White Ling Sect members—a handful of whom would accompany him on his mission—did little to soothe Meng's nerves. He felt even antsier now than on the day of his coronation or Han's homecoming. They were adequately veiled, hiding under the cover of night with the added invisibility from the shamans' magic, but in the middle of the pitch-black forest, he couldn't help but feel as guilty as a felon. They had managed to evade the imperial scouts and patrols all this way thanks to the disorientation spells the shamans had cast, and a small part of Meng worried that this infiltration mission had been a little too smooth so far.

Wei gestured at the team of Ling who were to enter via the secret passage with him, and they headed towards the specific tree where the entrance lay. Meng watched until they had all disappeared into the passageway before signalling to the three Ling who were to follow him down the open road towards the palace. Unlike Wei and his team, they were not here undercover. In fact, the more notice he drew from the public—the more of Han's attention he occupied—the better.

After emerging from the forest, they rode unhindered down the streets of Dongmu Market. This deep in the night, where the silence was as thick as the darkness, all the shops were closed and the lamps in the streets and in homes were out. Only the inns were lit, but just barely, with a pair or two of lanterns hung on the front offering a scant bit of light.

Yet, even with the Capital in a heavy slumber, a strange tension lingered in the air. Meng wondered how much had changed since he had last been here. Word of the battle with Lettoria and the Wall being destroyed had to have spread across the kingdom by now. A palpable cloud of fear seemed to hang over the Capital, haunting it like a sleepless ghost.

They released their horses and made the rest of the way to the palace swiftly. After the Ling shamans put the guards at the door to sleep, Meng hurried through gate after gate, door after door. Maids and servants stared, but thanks to the shamans' enchantments, no one waylaid them.

At last, he entered the Red Circle, where the imperial family's private quarters sat heavily guarded. Yet, there was no guard or servant in sight when he approached Han's chamber, only a chilling silence that swept through the grounds. The warm glow of lamps inside was the sole indication that Han was there.

Meng strode up the stairs towards the chamber, half-expecting a House of Night guard to swoop out of nowhere to stop him. But no one did. He pushed the doors open to find Han lounging by the tea table with a jar of wine.

Han seemed unsurprised at Meng's intrusion. He merely poured himself some wine and raised the goblet at Meng. 'This is top-grade wine imported from Hobeska,' he drawled. 'Care to join me, brother?'

Meng inched farther into the room, ready for an attack. Guards to pin him down like the last time, perhaps. But it was just him and Han in the chamber.

'Shut the door. You're bringing the wind in.' Han eyed him askance while he downed his wine, as though waiting for a reaction from him.

Meng offered none, keeping his face as passive as he could. Did he know about Windshadow? Was he expecting him tonight? He pushed the door to close but left it ajar.

'I must say I'm rather impressed you managed to stay alive,' said Han.

'I had to stay alive so that I could one day take back what you stole from me,' Meng said, not bothering to disguise his caginess. Everything felt like a test, and he would not give anything away.

'A lofty aim. How bold, how unlike you.' He eyed Meng over the rim of his wine goblet. 'I suppose you've come prepared with backup.'

The three Ling who had followed him to the chamber were on the roof now, ready to swoop in if anything went awry here. The sudden shuffling of footsteps and low voices made Meng pause—that did not sound like the Ling.

'The palace is under attack! Protect the emperor!'

Guards. They made no disguise of their presence. A few moments later, they had all taken their posts outside Han's chamber, weapons drawn.

Han was unperturbed by the commotion. He chuckled. 'How dramatic. You'll have to excuse my personal army—the Night Wolves are busy taking down the ragtag bunch of people Wei brought in.'

Han knew. He *had* been expecting them. That was why he was so unruffled by Meng's intrusion and the commotion outside, why Meng's entry into the palace was so smooth. Han had known Wei was leading the Ling army to attack the Imperial Army, and that Meng was here to dethrone him.

'You knew we were back in the kingdom,' Meng said. 'You let us back in and then had us tailed.'

Han smirked. 'Would your journey back home be so unobstructed if I hadn't granted you entry?' He took a sip of his wine and chuckled. 'Funny, isn't it? You thought you'd come here and distract me and Wei thought he'd ambush my army in the middle of the night, both of you brimming with bravado, thinking you've got the Ling on your side when I've already got them building my army for me. It's useful having an Elemental by your side, I must say, especially when they're cooperative. I'm sure you agree.'

'Building your army?'

'The Black Lotus Sect has been extremely helpful in developing my Night Wolves.' Han watched in amusement as Meng struggled to keep the consternation out of his face. 'Did you think you were the only one who would seek out the Ling? I am not our father, fearful of magic and magical folk. Instead of forcing them into the mountains, I find it more practical to put them to good use, particularly to remove pesky brothers coming after me and the throne.' He shot him a smirk. 'And of course, I took some more precautions. After your Elemental partner broke into the palace the last time and destroyed my ticha stores—a trap that we laid for her, by the way, for we had extra stores of it stashed elsewhere—I knew it was only a matter of time before you and Wei made your move.'

Meng felt his fists clench by his side. It was becoming a struggle to maintain his demeanour. He hated that Han was always two steps ahead of him. He had done everything he could to pave the way to this moment—negotiated with the Monan and Mobei desert lords, acquired the scroll and had the magic in the kingdom unlocked, allied with the White Ling Sect—only to have Han sit here drinking his wine, ready for his attack.

Han took another sip from the goblet. 'The Wall is down, magic is in the kingdom once more, I'm on the throne, and both my brothers have come to meet their end. What a time to be alive.' The manic gleam in his eyes reminded Meng of his brother's unfettered ambition, his insatiable hunger for power that would have him tear down everything that this kingdom was built upon just to remake it in his image.

'That's *if* you're alive,' Meng spat.

Han's smirk deepened. 'Don't you worry, little brother. I will be here to witness your second downfall. In fact, we will have plenty of time to capture you once the Imperial Army and my Night Wolves defeat the Ling army. I'm sure Mother would be pleased to see you again. She talks about you from time to time.'

Rage shot to his head. Before Meng realized what he was doing, he had lunged forward and knocked the wine goblet out of his brother's hand. He grabbed him by the neck. 'Do not speak about Mother with me.'

The guards outside made to enter the chamber, ready to drag him away, but Han only stilled them with a glance through the ajar door. He watched Meng's uncharacteristic outburst with undisguised scorn, barely putting up a struggle. Up till now, Han did not believe that Meng was capable of true rage or savagery, the kind that could consume a man and drive him to kill his own brother. But perhaps it resided deep inside him all along, amassed from years of buried resentment.

Meng had done everything asked of him, everything he could to be the perfect son. Yet, in the end he was still second to his brother in everything. His brother, who had done nothing but cause trouble in the family, who had been exiled by their father, and then came back and caused mayhem in the palace, starting with overthrowing Meng. It seemed like nothing Meng ever did was enough. All that assurance from High Advisor Mian that he was born under a lucky star had merely been a ploy between him and his mother to groom him into the seat warmer for Han.

Han's lips spread into a wide smile now, looking almost feral in the sliver of moonlight that slanted into the chamber through the crack in the door. 'All that rage with nowhere to go. You don't even have the guts to kill me yourself, brother?' he taunted.

Meng faltered. His Ling entourage should have been here by now to ambush Han after getting rid of the guards outside. He had stalled for long enough, buying enough time for them to jump in now. What was the delay?

Outside, the clamour intensified. Voices, footsteps, distant shouts, and the ghost of a scream. Meng peered through the door he had left ajar. More guards were hurrying in the direction of the parade square, the barracks where the Imperial Army was stationed.

Meng had half a mind to rush out to Wei's aid, but what help would he be? He was not trained for combat, and he alone was a pitiable addition against the Imperial Army.

He remained where he was, torn between wanting to help Wei and warn the others, and having to wait for the Ling. If Han knew about this coup, then there was no way the guards outside were the only protection he had set up for himself; he had to have planned an escape route too. Perhaps the Ling had been taken down by his guards. Perhaps he was all alone and would have to fend for himself now. If that were the case, he had two options: nab Han on his own or leave to help Wei.

This moment of hesitation, was all Han needed to gain the upper hand. He kneed Meng hard in the gut and broke free of his grasp. The pain made Meng gasp and stumble backwards. He barely had time to react before his brother reached for his dagger stashed under the table, and then lunged at him.

'Parting tip,' Han snarled, after crashing into him and pinning him to the ground. 'Never hesitate when you have the chance to kill your opponent.' He raised his dagger.

Meng grabbed his brother's wrists, throwing all his might into keeping the tip of the blade away from his throat. Rage burned in his gut, fuelling him with all the strength he needed. He could not relent. He could not lose to his older brother, not now. This was not how his story would end, not at the hands of Han.

A thud came from outside, stealing both their attention. The guards outside collapsed one by one. In unison, the Ling leapt down from the roof, their silhouettes flitting across the windows.

The doors swung open, revealing at last two of the three Ling who had accompanied Meng to the chamber. The last one slipped in through the window at the back of the room without a sound.

Han whipped around, loosening his grasp on Meng, just in time to dodge an attack from the Ling's outstretched hand. Meng rolled out of the way, dodging the Ling's burst of energy that sent the nearby wooden tea table exploding to pieces.

The other two Ling came to Meng's side and helped him up. 'We got waylaid. There are more guards on the way as we speak. We need to leave now.'

The third Ling was still focused on Han, intent on capturing him. He threw out his hands repeatedly, sending furniture flying across the room and shattering upon impact. Han ducked left and right, dagger still clutched uselessly in his hand. He eventually leapt to his feet, but he knew the futility of a mortal weapon against a Ling's magical one.

He reached for a lever with a carved lion head by the bed frame, then pulled it down fully. A trap door at the foot of the bed fell open, just wide enough to fit one person at a time. In one practised move, he slipped down the trap door before any of them could reach him.

The two Ling urged Meng to leave. 'Hurry, Ganshou will take care of it,' they said. Indeed, Ganshou was already hurrying down the trap door in pursuit of Han.

The hallways appeared to be free of guards for now—if he wanted to make a break for it, it would be now. If more guards came, they would come with ticha and capture all of them present. He had to think about the bigger plan.

Meng dashed out of the chamber towards the courtyard together with the two Ling. They still had a fighting chance—as long as Wei and the Ling army hadn't come head-to-head with the Imperial Army, they could still retreat.

His feet pounded across the ground, but a part of him already knew it was too late. The battle was about to begin, if it hadn't already.

But Meng refused to give up hope. This night would turn out the way he envisioned, with Han overthrown and Wei leading the Ling army to victory. Meng would make sure of it. He would do whatever he could, even if he had to fight shoulder to shoulder with Wei.

He hurtled towards the fray, praying for one last shot at victory.

Twenty-Two

Wei

The Ling army was nowhere near the size of the Imperial Army, but it consisted of useful figures from various sects.

The sorcerers from the Yellow Star Sect could help them infiltrate the palace by breaking through all the physical defences along the way. The Poison Peony Sect could weaken the troops with their assortment of potions and spells before the battle, while the Blue Mountain Sect could obfuscate them during battle.

But Wei knew better than to let his guard down. Han would have extra protection around the palace after the last security breach by Windshadow. Having lost his Fire Elemental, he had one less powerful weapon that could guard him. This meant that he would fortify his other defences by way of his special army, which would be equipped to counter the Ling army.

The secret passageway into the palace was long and narrow, and the autumn chill had seeped in. Wei had only used the imperial palace's secret entrances twice in his life, once when he had left the kingdom at age sixteen, when he hadn't put on the extra bulk he had now, and another when he had fled the kingdom with his mother, Desert Rose, and Qara last winter, following the Spring Ceremony coup.

Behind him, the Ling offered some light, illuminating the way. When at last they emerged through the secret door obscured by a stone lion near the Hall of Tranquillity, the Ling put out the light. Wei led the way towards the parade square, where the Imperial Army would be finishing up their duties for the day and retiring to their quarters, and the guards would be changing shifts.

The parade square was empty, without a single guard or sentry in sight. Moonlight fell upon it as though setting up a stage for them, and lanterns lit up the corridors around the square, revealing them to be equally deserted.

Out of nowhere came the faint whistle of a weapon.

'Watch out,' one of the Poison Peony Sect members hissed, shoving Wei out of the way and ducking aside herself as an arrow soared through the air towards them. It landed on the spot where Wei had been standing just a moment earlier.

More arrows rained down on them, arcing through the night and narrowly missing them. Wei unsheathed his sword as the Ling began to mutter incantations to build a defensive dome around them.

But before the magical barrier could be erected, several arrows struck two of them, one in the chest and another in the arm. The one who was struck in the arm let out a cry and began to convulse in pain. He raised a shaky hand to continue drawing up a defensive dome, but his magic no longer seemed to work. Wei yanked out the arrow from his arm and got a whiff of its steel tip.

Ticha. Despite Windshadow's attempt to destroy them, there was still a secret supply of it in the palace.

This was a trap. The Imperial Army had known they would be coming; they had been lying in wait to ambush them. That meant Han was expecting them, which meant the army was specially prepared to kill the Ling.

'Run,' Wei ordered.

They scattered across the parade square, ducking in the shadowy recesses of its borders, out of shooting range. The attack was coming from the watchtower, which meant that the troops would be assembled in the barracks behind it, waiting for them.

There were only fifty Ling that the White Ling Sect had assembled for this mission, thinking that they could count on the element of surprise to ambush the Imperial Army. But now that the Imperial Army had been prepared for the attack, they were close to being outnumbered.

But there was still a chance they might turn the tide in this battle. As Wei cut through the troops, the Ling threw out spells that would impede or disorient the soldiers, while the more powerful ones cleaved through hordes of soldiers, wounding them with sharp bursts of energy. But he was just one person against hundreds of thousands in the Imperial Army, and the Ling's qi would be depleted too. What then?

'Seize the rebels!' the general roared from the watchtower, his face illuminated by the torch next to him. It was no longer General Yue leading the army. General Yue, who had been loyal for decades to the imperial family, had been replaced by a foreign-looking man who appeared to be from the north, possibly Hobeska.

In fact, the row of soldiers positioned atop the watchtower did not appear to be of Oasis breed at all. They all looked Hobeskan, with their uniform strapping build and cold eyes. Despite their heavy armour, they carried no weapons, relying only on their raised hands to attack.

This had to be Han's special army, the one that was built specially for this war. Wei had seen what a manufactured army looked like, after last summer at Lettoria where he had met the Ferros, King Falco's iron army. This army consisted of regular men who didn't seem to bear any Elemental-forged weapons, but Wei knew better than to underestimate them.

First, cut off the head, his Snow Wolf Sect master urged him in his mind.

Wei grabbed a bow and arrow off the body of a slain soldier and took aim. Behind him, a Ling cast a protective dome around him, offering some reprieve from the onslaught of attacks as he scanned the watchtower for the general.

The shot struck a soldier square in the neck, and another in the shoulder. The others came to their aid, firing a series of crackling energy orbs at Wei. He ducked aside as a couple of White Ling leapt to his defence, fending off the orbs and launching them right back at the soldiers.

Meanwhile, the general dipped in and out of the shadows, staying out of the reach of Wei's arrows. Wei kept his eyes on him even while he fought off imperial soldier after imperial soldier on the ground, waiting for the opportune moment to strike.

'We need more backup,' a Ling next to him cried to another as he staggered under the waning strength of his own force field. He was a young Yellow Star Sect sorcerer who had been brimming with confidence over an easy victory. 'We can't fight both the Imperial Army with ticha and the special army with their magic.'

'Don't worry, His Highness will send more people to assist us,' the other Ling replied with absolute conviction as he launched an energy orb into a throng of imperial soldiers pressing closer to him.

In the distance, a familiar figure came dashing towards the courtyard, trailed by three Ling who cast a protective silhouette around him as they leapt from rooftop to rooftop. When they arrived at the courtyard, Meng headed straight towards Wei while the Ling leapt to the ground and threw out a collective wave of energy that blasted several soldiers across the courtyard, killing them on the spot.

'Meng,' Wei said as his brother picked up a sword lying next to a slain soldier. 'What are you doing here? This was not part of the plan.'

'This was a setup,' Meng said, joining him.

Wei slashed an imperial soldier in the torso just as the latter charged towards him, aiming for the chest, then went back to tracking the general on the watchtower. 'Yes, I figured as much. But what are you doing here?'

Meng's blade clashed against a soldier's dao, and Wei kicked the soldier in the chest before slicing his torso.

'The Ling is planning a concerted attack on the Night Wolves on the watchtower,' Meng said once the soldier had fallen dead at their feet. 'We just need to hold off the Imperial Army long enough.'

Wei nodded, then signalled to the Ling hiding behind the pillars. The four sorcerers shared a glance with one another and began to chant in unison, their hands raised. Their voices rose louder than humanly possible, echoing through the courtyard, filling the night.

Wei had never witnessed the full extent of the Ling's magic before. And now with magic restored in Oasis Kingdom, their abilities were a sight to behold. A shimmering energy wall rose from the ground, illuminating the watchtower as it reached towards the sky.

Then came a deafening crack, followed by a thunderous boom. The watchtower began to shake and crumble, collapsing at immense speed. Soldiers came plunging off it, their screams dying as they hit the ground. Some were struck by the Ling army amid the chaos, while others scrambled to find solid footing. Wei squinted for a glimpse of the general, but he seemed to have disappeared from the watchtower.

'Look out,' Meng yelled, pulling Wei back to his immediate surroundings. Wei spun around just in time to see Meng throw off an attack from an incoming soldier. Wei jumped into action, slashing the soldier in the gut as Meng held the soldier in place from behind.

As the soldier crumpled to the floor, Wei stared at Meng, who looked visibly shaken by the blood that had splattered onto him. 'Seriously, Meng, what are *you* doing here?'

Meng could not look more out of place here if he tried. Wei had never seen his brother pick up a sword since he was fifteen and they were made to train together under General Yue. Meng had always hated violence and bloodshed. He belonged in the library, not here in the battlefield, wielding a weapon intended to kill and maim.

'Something I've wanted to do for a while,' Meng replied. He gripped his sword tighter and looked Wei in the eye, steeling himself. 'Stand on the right side.'

It felt almost surreal that Meng was the one fighting alongside him now. This person standing back-to-back with him now was nearly unrecognizable. Wei had never imagined the two of them—born under the same star but having such different fates—would one day stand on the same side fighting the same enemy. So much had happened between them over the years—from Wei's jealousy and resentment since they were children to Meng arranging for Yong's homicide—that it seemed unlikely they would ever become true brothers in arms. But for the first time ever, Wei let himself wonder about the possibility.

Something seemed different about Meng now. A resolute glint in his eyes that Wei had never seen before. An unflinching resolution that made Wei envision him as an emperor in his own right, no longer manipulated by anyone.

'We will stick to the plan until victory is ours,' Meng said.

Wei nodded. 'I'm with you on that.' Then he leaned against his brother's back and fought on.

Twenty-Three

Desert Rose

The battle was raging when Desert Rose arrived with the Night Lotus rebels.

Almost all the palace guards at the front were asleep at their posts—every gate and door leading to the parade square. Upon closer inspection, Yan and Yujin confirmed that it was the Ling who had cast their spells on the guards. That cleared the path for them.

Yet, as they sprinted towards the clamour, where the distant ringing of steel blades could be heard, it seemed that the Ling's advantage had run aground. They were clearly outnumbered, with the Ling taken down faster than they could make a dent in the Imperial Army. The watchtower was now a mere pile of rubble; only half its edifice remained upright, and soldiers lay dead at its feet. Yet, more of them kept coming, not just regular soldiers but ones with magic that could launch energy orbs back at the Ling army.

'Isn't the Ling army supposed to be able to defeat the special army?' Desert Rose asked, watching the rapid-fire attacks launched all around the courtyard.

'They're outnumbered,' Yan said, tracking the attacks from both sides. 'The emperor is well prepared for this attack, both in size and might.'

In the middle of the courtyard, Wei was back-to-back with Meng, surrounded by imperial soldiers closing in around them. A shimmering orb sat over them, offering some protection against incoming attacks. From within, Wei fired arrow after arrow at the soldiers while Meng fended off those closer to them. But they were two against a relentless, encroaching throng.

The dome vanished suddenly, throwing Wei and Meng into temporary shadow. Desert Rose scanned the surroundings to find the Ling who had been conjuring the protective dome tackled by Xiyue and a Black Crane assassin.

As soon as the dome disappeared, an arrow soared towards Wei from his left.

'Wei, look out!' Desert Rose yelled. He leapt out of harm's way just as she threw out her hands, unleashing a wave of water large enough to knock a horde of soldiers back several feet and sweep more of them further away from Wei.

Someone crashed into her and tackled her to the ground, where they rolled for a few paces before Desert Rose pulled away and leapt to her feet. Her attacker flipped upright, crouching low with her dagger drawn.

Liqin scowled. 'What is it with you desert girls always causing mayhem in the palace?' She charged at Desert Rose again, this time dodging cleanly as Desert Rose sent a spray of water her way. The House of Night girls had been trained to fight Elementals now.

Liqin swerved low as Desert Rose lobbed a water orb at her. It careened off into the distance, knocking a soldier off his feet. Another orb made Liqin stagger backwards as she dodged, giving Desert Rose the opportunity to whip out her double knives and lunge at her. But Liqin was ready for her, throwing her to the ground and pressing her dagger dangerously close to her neck. Desert Rose gripped Liqin's wrists, pushing back as hard as she could.

'Aren't you a piece of work, Desert Rose,' Liqin sneered. 'Shimu should never have taken you and Windshadow in. Both of you are traitors and murderers. You killed Shuang, and now you're here to assassin the emperor and destroy the Imperial Army with those two rebel princes.'

In a burst of strength, Desert Rose rolled over and tackled Liqin to the ground. 'I know you still blame me for Shuang's death, and I know whatever I do can't bring her back. But I'm not here for your forgiveness today.'

As they split apart, Liqin flung her dagger at Desert Rose in a last-ditch attempt to defend herself. The blade wedged itself into

Desert Rose's calf. A shot of pain pinned her to the ground as the familiar burn of ticha spread through her leg, making her knees buckle. She forced herself to yank out the offending blade and toss it aside, swearing mentally. It would take a while for her body to expel the ticha, so she was unable to use her magic for now.

Just as Liqin went to retrieve her weapon, a tiger shouren pounced out of nowhere and swiped at her with a hefty paw, sending her dagger clattering a good distance away from her. A pair of leopards came to its aid as the Black Crane assassin joined Liqin.

Desert Rose winced as she tried to staunch the blood flow. The wound wasn't deep, but the ticha stayed stubbornly in contact with her skin. The corners of her vision began to blacken when someone caught her in a firm grip from behind, leaning her against him before she could sink to the ground.

Wei's breath was warm against her ear. 'I've got you.'

'Coin . . . medium . . .' she rasped. Wei understood her at once, reaching into her pocket where she directed him and pulling out the spirit token.

Around them, the battle continued at full steam, imperial soldiers clashing with the Ling's magic. What the Ling army lacked in size, they made up for it in magical might. But with the Imperial Army's arsenal of ticha-coated weapons, it was only a matter of time before the Ling's powers were neutralized and they were defeated by Han's special army.

Desert Rose scanned the fray for the Night Lotus medium. Finally, she spotted him behind a pillar several feet away and gestured to him. A protective dome went back up around them, and Desert Rose glanced around to see another Ling casting it while Yan and Yujin fought off a pair of imperial soldiers.

It was hard to tell which side was winning. Energy orbs hurtled around the courtyard, striking soldiers left and right, though more of them kept coming. The clang of blades rang out in the courtyard, but upon closer look it was the imperial soldiers fighting each other, likely thanks to the disorientation spells cast by the Ling. Meanwhile, ticha-covered blades were maiming and killing the Ling, driving the remaining few into the periphery, where it was harder to cast protective spells over Wei and Desert Rose.

The medium hurried over to them, flinching at the onslaught of attacks despite the protective spell his fellow Ling had cast around him. He held out his hands, palms down, over the spirit token in Wei's hand, and began an urgent chanting.

No sooner had he completed the first round of incantation did the earth start to groan.

An ear-splitting crack ripped across the courtyard amid the tumult, making the soldiers waver and pause mid-action. The ground trembled and split apart right down the middle of the courtyard like a gash. A moment later, the Ghost Army rose from the ground like a mirage, their unearthly glow throwing the entire parade square into stark relief.

The Ghost King turned to Desert Rose, who was starting to feel the effects of the ticha wear off slightly. She nodded at him, then struggled to her feet with Wei's help.

The Ghost Army stormed across the courtyard, mowing down everything in its path. Desert Rose had witnessed its fury before during the battle at Danxi Plains, when they had showed up at the last moment to assist her.

This time, their might was just as fearsome. They swept through the mob of clashing soldiers, near invincible with their otherworldly weapons and armour. Earthly magic and energy orbs hardly fazed them, doing no damage, and mortal weapons made no dent on them.

Desert Rose nudged Wei. 'Run.'

He glanced at her, then back at the Ghost Army. 'Are you sure—'

'They will take care of this. *Run.*'

Wei wrapped Desert Rose's arm around his neck and held her by the waist. Together, they stumbled out of the fray, ducking from the attacks launched left, right, and centre.

The Earth Elemental appeared before them seemingly out of nowhere. Calm and collected in his sky-blue robes, he stood amid the chaos of the battle, gaze pinned on Desert Rose. There was none of the cordiality he had possessed when she had first met him in Yeli Mountain, none of the comradeship he had displayed when he had implored her to combine their powers. Now, there was only wild hunger in his eyes, an almost manic determination that transformed him into another person.

In that instant, she knew why he was here.

She pulled out the vial Qiu had given her and flung it to the ground. Qiu's noxious brew filled the air as soon as the vial shattered, releasing a dense midnight-black cloud that rose to obscure her and Wei. She picked up Liqin's dagger lying a few paces away from her and they took off in the direction of the secret passageway.

Her calf was still bleeding, leaving a trail of blood behind her, but she forced herself to push through the pain. Wounded, her qi was definitely weaker than the Earth Elemental's, which would give him an advantage in dominating their shared power. Furthermore, being stabbed by Liqin's ticha-covered dagger meant that she was unable to use her magic and be a proper match for the Earth Elemental until she could purge the ticha out of her body.

They left the fray behind in the courtyard and took the shortcut towards the Seven Star Pond, after which they arrived at the deserted imperial garden.

But the Earth Elemental was dogged in his pursuit of her.

'You can't run from me, Rose,' he said as he stalked towards them. He waved a hand casually, making the ground crack and uprooting a pear tree just three paces behind them. 'I came all this way for you.'

Desert Rose buckled at last from the pain in her calf. Wei scooped her up and ran despite her protests, but the Earth Elemental sent a branch from the uprooted pear tree slamming into his back, sending both of them sprawling to the ground.

The Earth Elemental loomed closer. 'It's down to the two of us now. You can't run from this. It's time to fight, Rose. Fight!' he roared.

Another emphatic wave of the arm sent the earth exploding where she lay, but she rolled away in the nick of time, catching some of the debris on her back.

'All that noble talk about fighting for our people. Was that all a lie?' she demanded. 'The Ling were just pawns in your bid to seize power, to kill me and overthrow the imperial family?'

He launched a relentless series of exploding earth at her, forcing her to retaliate. She dodged out of the way just barely each time, ignoring the scream of her calf wound as dirt scraped against it.

'I have done whatever I could to help them. This battle between the White and Black Ling is out of my hands. Now it's just you and me, and we both know who the stronger, more deserving Elemental is. I have bided my time for long enough!' he screamed.

A violent sweep of his arm tore another tree apart right down the middle. Wei grabbed her arm and dragged her out of the way just before the tree toppled to the ground with a groan. Desert Rose ducked, feeling Wei throw his arms around her to shield her.

'I'll hold him, you attack,' he whispered in her ear.

Then he was on his feet before she could respond. Desert Rose threw out her hands, feinting an attack at the Earth Elemental. All she had to do was to grab his attention for the split moment Wei needed. She aimed a jet of water squarely at his chest, an obvious attack that he would be well-prepared for. As expected, he fended off her attack with a wall of earth.

But before he could launch the wall of rock and soil at her, Wei had crept up behind him and seized him. Wei kneed him in the back before locking his arms behind him. 'Rose, now!' he yelled, fighting against the struggling captive.

Desert Rose whipped out Liqin's dagger. The distance between her and Rong was too wide for her to lunge forward without him potentially attacking her first even with his arms bound. She flung out the dagger and released a jet of water at it, driving the blade deep into the Earth Elemental's heart in the speed of a breath. The Earth Elemental stared at her, his face frozen in shock and disbelief as he let out a choked gasp.

It took only three heartbeats for the ticha on Liqin's blade to take effect. By the time Desert Rose pulled out the dagger, dodging the spray of blood from his chest, the Earth Elemental was dead.

Wei let go of him, letting his lifeless body slink to the ground before meeting Desert Rose's gaze. A look of disbelief passed between them. Relief swept down to her feet. All she heard was the rhythm of her racing pulse and their ragged breaths in the silence that followed.

She had done it. She had eliminated the last Elemental. It was over.

A cold wind seeped through her, sudden and unnatural, though the trees around her were still. A chill skittered across her skin like a warning ripple. She shivered, dropping the dagger as a strange weightlessness overcame her.

Wei's gaze was transfixed on her. 'Rose . . .' He gestured at her body.

She glanced down to see her body dissipating, illuminated by the golden glow of a breaking dawn. The distant roar of the battle faded into a muted hum; all that remained was the sound of gently flowing water, as though she were dissolving into a river that was carrying her off to the sea. She did feel light enough to float away . . .

No!

Her gaze found him again, this time not budging. She wanted to memorize his face, hold on to this final moment where she could still look at him. She held out a hand, reaching for him, but her fingers were dissolving too. Wei took a step towards her, reaching for her hands, but he only managed to grasp air.

There was still so much she wanted to do—see her father again, reunite with her tribe, explore the world with Wei. Her story could not end here. She had to fight this!

But even as she struggled to hold on to what she could—the sound of bird calls, the scent of pear trees—she felt her grasp weakening, her connection to this world fading. Soon, the world disappeared in a shard of light that blocked out everything.

There was no fighting the fate that the gods had long ago laid out for her.

It was time for her to go.

Twenty-Four

Wei

Wei watched her dissipate inch by inch, as though she was nothing but air. As though she wasn't made of flesh and bone and blood, warm to the touch; of thoughts and feelings and wit and laughter that made Wei drunk on the sound of it. As though she would dissolve in his grasp rather than slip her hand into his.

He wanted to reach out to grab her hand, pull her close to him and never let go. He wanted to take her and run as far away from here as possible.

But there was no outrunning their destiny, and Desert Rose had met hers now. He could try and hold on to her all he wanted, but deep down he had known that this moment would come, that there was no use trying to run from it or change it. At least she hadn't been killed in battle like the others. At least she was the last Elemental standing, and could, as the prophecy went, ascend to the heavens.

She was beautiful, even in this final moment. In fact, Wei had never seen her looking this heavenly. Her hair, free from its messy braid, now floated around her as though she were drifting in a lake, and she rose a couple feet above the ground like she was weightless.

Inch by inch, she disappeared into the air, merging into the morning light, until at last there was nothing left of her. The sun shone through the canopy of a tree, illuminating the spot where she had last stood, now unbearably empty, as though she had never existed.

The loss felt like a gut punch.

Grief carved out a giant hole in him with its serrated teeth, sharp enough to saw through bone and large enough to consume him whole.

He remained rooted to where he was for the longest time, even after
a distant horn declared the battle over, after Han's army was declared
defeated, after maids, servants, messengers, and court officials began
scurrying about to survey and clean up the wreckage, casting him wary
glances as they passed.

He stayed at the very same spot, hoping against all hopes that she
would reappear. That somehow the prophecy would have a different
ending, that she would *create* a different ending.

But she never came back. Fate had gotten the final say ultimately.
He was well and truly alone now, and he felt the loss of Desert Rose
like the loss of a piece of his soul.

Twenty-Five

Meng

The Council was atypically subdued the next morning when Meng called for a meeting. The ministers shuffled nervously among themselves, exchanging glances with one another as though seeking a clue on what was to happen next.

Meng stared at the empty throne at the end of the Hall of Justice. He was so close to returning to that seat. If everything went well during this session, he would be the one sitting there again soon. He turned to his mother sitting next to it. She was staring imperiously ahead, a hint of impatience in her face as she avoided his gaze. Meng no longer felt the need to catch her attention, nor did he yearn for an approving nod from her.

The doors swung open. General Yue entered, then stepped aside to reveal Han flanked by a pair of imperial soldiers pinning his arms behind his back. The Empress Dowager straightened in her seat, her neck stiffening, and the Council ministers let out a collective gasp at the state of their emperor. Han looked worse for wear, the change noticeable in the short period of time since the Ling had caught him attempting to flee after the battle.

Meng spoke with more authority than he felt standing among the Council again. But he would not quail before them; this time, he was here with ample charges and evidence, and he would stand firm on his ground.

'Thank you all for your time and attention today. I appreciate the Council's full attendance,' he began.

'We granted you our time and attention so make this quick,' the Empress Dowager said, her words sharp as icicles as she stared down at Meng. 'Perhaps you should start with explaining why you have the *emperor* held like a criminal.'

Meng ignored his mother and went on. 'I sought this session to raise two charges against Zhao Han. The first count is forming an alliance with the Lettorian king to destroy the Wall. And the second is smuggling illegal weapons of the magical sort into Oasis Kingdom. The Imperial Army—along with Zhao Han's special army, which he had built using black magic smuggled in from the desert—was sorely defeated last night.'

The ministers broke out into feverish whispers. On the podium, the Empress Dowager's lips thinned and her face turned mottled.

'General Yue has reviewed the evidence and testimonies I have,' Meng said over the din, 'and according to Oasis law, any ruler found guilty of treason is to be immediately stripped of his position and put on trial—a decree I'm certain Zhao Han is familiar with, given that it was what he charged me with last spring.'

The battle had ended at dawn just as the sun cast its first rays on the courtyard. The Ling Army, with the help of the Ghost Army, had destroyed not just the Night Wolves but also a good portion of the Imperial Army.

Meng had watched the Earth Elemental give chase after Desert Rose and Wei, but he had been unable to tear himself away from the battle to abet their escape.

With the appearance of the Ghost Army, invisible to the human eye until they chose to reveal themselves, the Night Wolves' defeat had been swift. Han's soldiers were slain before they could react, stabbed with invisible weapons that not only left no open wounds, but also drew out their souls. The Night Wolves were entirely wiped out as a result, and the White Ling Sect members had seized Han shortly after and forced him to surrender.

According to Desert Rose, the Ghost Army's weapons could only hurt the souls of corrupt men. Meng remembered every little detail she had shared with him—every piece of lore she had grown up hearing—in the nights they had spent in the imperial library.

'Lies.' Han's voice pulled Meng back to the present. His older brother struggled against the two imperial soldiers who held him in place. 'You have no evidence of treason against me,' he spat.

Meng turned to face the Council. 'I have witnesses by way of the desert lords of Mobei and Monan. Their testimonies can be found here, along with proof of said illegal trade.' He pulled out the scrolls that the desert lords had written months ago when he had paid them a visit, followed by the books that captured the transactions. 'Members of the Dugur tribe have also provided their accounts from Lettoria, where they found evidence of correspondence between Zhao Han and the Lettorian king, discussing ways to take down the Wall and stage a battle to eliminate the Third Prince Wei. We can, in due course, summon them for their testimonies, but rest assured that the evidence is sufficient to charge Zhao Han with both counts of treason and illegal trade.'

Meng had him cornered. There was no escaping this for Han.

'What about you colluding with the Ling to overthrow me, the *emperor*,' Han snarled. 'By that count, you should be charged for conspiring with rebels too!'

Meng remained unflappable—he had known this was a counterargument Han would raise. 'Firstly, what proof do you have that the Ling and I conspired? Second of all, had the White Ling Army not defeated the special army that you built, the kingdom would be under the leadership of an emperor who dabbles in black magic to augment his power.'

He turned back to the Council. 'Credit should be given to the Ling, not punishment. Furthermore—and more pertinently—the White Ling Sect are Oasis citizens who have been ostracized for far too long, under a punishing regime that persecutes them simply for existing as they are. The magic they practise is pure and natural. Thanks to the Wall being taken down—the Wall that Zhao Han conspired with our enemy to take down, might I remind the court—they have had a chance to emerge from the shadows of Yeli Mountain.

'On the contrary, Zhao Han colluded with the Black Lotus Sect, a deviant black magic–practising sect that has been found responsible for multiple homicides in the Yan County—to develop his abominable personal army. Thankfully, the White Ling Sect defeated them last night, under the leadership of Prince Wei. His valiant efforts to defend the court—and our kingdom—against Zhao Han's dastardly deeds should also not go unnoticed and ought to be lauded.'

The ministers had, by now, reviewed the documents Meng handed them. They murmured intently among themselves, wearing identical disapproving expressions.

Meng glanced at his mother. The Empress Dowager was shaking with unbridled fury, lost for words for once. Her face had turned as white as her knuckles as she gripped the armrest of her seat, but there was nothing she could say that would defend Han from Meng's charges against him and from all the evidence Meng had laid out.

'Regardless of whether the Wall exists,' said Minister Luo, 'magic—used in whatever capacity—is blasphemy. It goes against the very principle upon which Oasis Kingdom was established.'

'For centuries, we have feared magic,' Meng replied. 'But this fear has turned into prejudice and blind hatred over time. Magic, when used as a force for good, is not something to be feared or reviled. The White Ling were the only ones who could defeat Zhao Han's dark army, and I had to form an alliance with them to expose his crimes.'

Half the ministers nodded, while the others remained unconvinced. Nevertheless, they shared a unanimous vote that Minister Luo voiced on behalf of the Council.

'Based on such incriminating evidence, and given the special, unprecedented circumstances, Zhao Han's criminal activities are indeed irrefutable,' he declared. 'The Council concedes to reinstating Zhao Meng—previously the Fourth Prince and Sixteenth Oasis Emperor—as the new legitimate emperor of our kingdom.'

General Yue clasped his hands and got down on one knee. 'The Imperial Army, too, recognizes the Fourth Prince as the new Oasis Emperor.'

Zhao Han let out a roar that made even the Empress Dowager flinch. The soldiers struggled to tame him as he fought against them, until General Yue stood up and held him at sword-point.

Despite being shaken by Han's feral outburst, Meng nodded, a wave of relief washing over him at last. Unlike the sense of unease or doubt that had gnawed at him the first time he was declared emperor, this victory was hard-earned. He had fought hard for this position, not by unscrupulous means, but by rallying his own form of support and calculating the right moves. More importantly, this time, he had done it without unfair manoeuvring or the hollow backing of his mother and the High Advisor.

'For the severity of his crimes, Zhao Han will be immediately placed in the imperial prison under high security until trial,' Meng declared. 'High Advisor Mian will also be demoted from courtier to court scribe.' He nodded at General Yue. 'Take him away.'

Han put up one last struggle before he was towed away by the imperial soldiers, throwing Meng the filthiest look he had ever received. 'You will pay for this, Zhao Meng! I swear on my life you will—'

'Help! The Empress Dowager has fainted!' someone cried.

* * *

Meng's footsteps stalled as he neared the Hall of Tranquillity.

It had been months—an entire season—since he had taken back the throne and banished Han to the imperial prison, where he eventually went mad and took his own life; months since his mother had fallen sick from grief and had to be moved to the Hall of Tranquillity to recuperate in isolation. Meng had received regular reports of her condition, which was worsening by the day. She rejected food, and her sleep was troubled. The imperial physician had seen her multiple times, alongside a Ling medium to help her meditate, all to little effect.

Meng nodded to the messenger boy, who announced his arrival. The doors swung open.

Han's defeat and death had taken a massive toll on his mother. She appeared to have aged a decade since the last time Meng saw her. Her hair was grey at the roots, and her face was bare and ashen. Dressed in plain white robes, she appeared a far cry from the immaculately coiffed Empress Dowager she used to be.

Meng stepped in and poured her a cup of ginger tea. 'Greetings, Mother.'

Seated on a silk-draped lounge bed next to the tea table, his mother stared at him as though she could not recognize him, as though he were a mere stranger trespassing in her room. And perhaps he was. Perhaps she too had always been a stranger to him.

'My son . . .' Tears welled up in her eyes.

Meng felt a twinge of remorse that was soon taken over by a stoniness that straightened his back, one he had never felt when he was still duty-bound to her and doing everything she asked. He was no longer the Meng she knew, the Meng she could manipulate out of guilt and shame. He had fought for his own life without her help, survived till this moment without her support, and clawed his way back to the palace to stand before her now, having taken back all that he had lost while she sat by and watched.

How long had he yearned for her approval, her love, when he had carried out every task she had set him, even if he loathed doing them, even when he had had to cast aside his conscience.

'My son Han . . .' she rasped, snapping Meng back to reality. 'What have you done to him? *What have you done to him?*'

'I merely gave him the ending he deserved,' he said coolly. 'For his illicit activities, for treason, for organizing a coup and overthrowing me, for killing Matron and many other people who have been loyal to the imperial family for decades.'

'You killed him,' she spat. 'You're a murderer through and through—first Yong, then your father, and now Han.'

Meng didn't think it was possible to be hurt by someone he had turned his back on, but the wound cut just as deep. Han had always been her favourite, and Meng had accepted that. But everything she had done ever since Han was exiled—and perhaps even before that—had been to bring him back and bring him into power, even if it meant sacrificing Meng. Even now, all she could think about was her firstborn son. Nothing Meng did would ever amount to anything in her eyes, even if everything he had done under her orders had been for her approval.

'What he did was his own decision,' he said, hardening his tone. 'He chose to give up on his life.'

Her glare was venomous, but her voice cracked with misery. 'You are the most heartless person I know.' It seemed as though the irony— that she was the one who had taught Meng to harden his heart in order to attain power—was somehow lost on her. She turned away from him. 'Leave. I never want to see you again.'

Meng bowed. There was nothing more that needed to be said, nothing more he could do now to fix this relationship with his mother. He had done everything asked of him, everything within his capacity as a son. He no longer owed her anything, nor did she seem to want anything to do with him anymore. This piece of his heart had died, and perhaps it was best to let go of dead things.

'Take care, Mother. I will visit you another day,' he said. But as he left her chamber, he knew that his mother no longer regarded him as her son.

The throne was a lonely place to sit. Being emperor meant that he would no longer have true friends or confidantes, only allies who remained loyal for as long as it benefited them. Meng knew that early on, even back when he first decided to strive for that seat, but some days the loneliness struck him harder.

Some days, he would imagine Windshadow blustering into his study with her typical irreverence. *Sentimentality is for fools,* she would say, a refrain eerily similar to his mother's. Other days, he would sit in the imperial library with two cups of tea, thinking about the stories a girl from the desert had once told him, a girl he had been too scared to open his heart to.

And sometimes, he could almost believe that he wasn't alone.

Twenty-Six

Desert Rose

Blinding white light stabbed her eyes when she cracked them open. She was weightless. Beneath her, the ground appeared to have fallen away. The world seemed boundless, the light stretching on for as far as she could see.

The din of the battle had long died away, replaced only by a gentle silence. The light softened into a golden glow, and her eyes soon adjusted to the brightness. Her wounds had healed, and the pain had subsided. All she felt was a sense of calm. Yet, something continued to niggle at her, the sense that she had left something behind unfinished.

'We have waited a long time for you, my child,' said an ethereal voice, light as a feather but resounding all around her.

Desert Rose spun around to see a lady dressed in a resplendent white robe embroidered with gold, not unlike the warm rays of the sun against pillowy clouds. It was hard to tell her age—her features were as delicate and youthful as a young maiden's, but she carried the air of an ancient being.

'You have made a tremendous achievement, child,' she said. 'You have restored the balance between the two realms, a feat no one has achieved in ages.' Her smile was beatific, proud.

'Am I . . . am I dead?' Her voice was a hoarse whisper.

'Death is but another realm to step into. You may call yourself dead, but in a way, you are also reborn.'

Her answer was annoyingly cryptic, but Desert Rose did not dare to reveal her impatience. 'Who are you?' she ventured.

Her smile was rueful, revealing a glimpse of humanity behind her sentience. 'I'm the one who caused the Immortal Spring to be boarded up in the first place. So, in a way, I suppose you're undoing my mess.'

The Sky Princess. The fabled character out of myths and folktales she had heard from her tribespeople since she was a child. This was her in the flesh (*if* she was made of flesh, which Desert Rose doubted). She and the Earth Prince's forbidden romance and elopement had angered the gods of both the heavenly and earthly realms so much that the Immortal Spring where the lovers had their clandestine meetups was blocked up, effectively tearing them apart for eternity.

As the story went, blocking the Immortal Spring had led to the imbalance of magic flowing between the realms, causing magic to leak out across the earth and land into the hands of men, thus causing mortal strife and the power struggles between kingdoms that Desert Rose had been caught in—until now.

She was certain her jaw was hanging open as she stared at the Sky Princess. Technically, if Desert Rose was a Damohai, then that meant the Sky Princess was her ancestor. She was *family*. The thought almost made her laugh out loud. The realization that she was a descendant of immortals was just starting to hit her.

'The prophecy played out exactly like the gods intended it to,' the Sky Princess said, oblivious to Desert Rose's staring. 'The first Elemental died for freedom. The next died for glory. Another died for honour. And the last one died for love.'

Desert Rose thought back to all the Elementals she had crossed paths with. The Metal Elemental had died trying to be free of King Falco, to escape servitude and forge a new life with his mortal brother. Lazar had died for power, conspiring with a despotic emperor to secure his place ahead of the rest of them. And as much as she hated to think of Rong as remotely noble, he had died leading the Ling in the rebellion. His methods might have been misguided, but perhaps he had truly believed he was fighting for the liberation of the Ling.

And love?

'The Wind Elemental had died to save you,' the Sky Princess said, her gaze gentle and sad. 'Her death ended up being the purest of all.'

Desert Rose felt the familiar pang in her heart—she was starting to get used to carrying grief around. She broke the Sky Princess's gaze before her tears could get the better of her and glanced around. 'Is this it, then? This is the result of all that rivalry with the other Elementals?'

The Sky Princess spread her arms, gesturing at the nothingness around her. 'This is your reward for all that you have suffered on earth, child. You are in the heavenly realm now. Your next life begins here and now. For your accomplishment in restoring balance between the realms, you get to have anything you want—immortality, eternal contentment, freedom from death, sickness, and suffering . . .' She held out a hand. 'Come. Let's go home.'

'Home?' Home was not here; it was back with her tribe. The thought of calling a place without her family *home* made no sense to her.

The Sky Princess sensed her hesitation. 'You've already ascended. Your spirit was used to unblock the Immortal Spring and restore the balance. There is no need for you to struggle on earth as a mortal anymore. Your new home awaits.'

Desert Rose stared down at the Sky Princess's proffered hand, as fair as fresh snow tinged with sunlight. 'I . . . I don't want to be here, though,' she found herself saying.

The Sky Princess blinked, her hand still outstretched. 'I'm sorry?'

She looked back up at her. 'I'm just saying that if I'm to be rewarded for whatever I did, I would much rather be back with my tribe.'

The Sky Princess dropped her hand and cocked her head, her brows pulling together in confusion. 'You can have anything you want. Why would you choose mortality?'

'I never asked for this destiny. I never wanted to ascend to the heavens or whatever this is. My life was simple, and I loved it. I don't need immortality or eternal contentment. I belonged there with my tribe, with my father, with . . .'

The thought of Wei wrenched her heart. She had left him there at the imperial garden, in the palace—the one place that brought him the most painful memories—all alone. She had left without even saying goodbye. How long had she been here? What was he doing now?

'I didn't get to spend enough time with the people I love,' she said. 'This just feels more like a cruel punishment.'

The Sky Princess looked aghast that Desert Rose would regard immortality this way. 'You do realize that mortal lives are incredibly fleeting. You will only get to spend a few more decades on earth before you have to eventually part anyway. Why put yourself through that when you can live eternally in the heavenly realm, free from pain and suffering?'

'The heavenly realm that tore you and your love apart for all eternity, according to the story?' Desert Rose blurted.

The Sky Princess froze, staring at her. For a moment Desert Rose thought she might get in trouble for speaking this way to an immortal, not just a heavenly being but also her ancestor.

But then the Sky Princess's gaze fell. 'Our love was forbidden to begin with . . .'

Desert Rose observed her expression. 'But you don't regret it.'

Her smile was woeful. 'No one ever regrets a love that was pure and true.'

'So you can understand if I would rather pursue life with a love like that—however fleeting it may be—than an eternal one without it.'

The Sky Princess smiled, looking almost proud of her. 'Indeed I can. You are truly my descendant.' She nodded. 'You may return to earth and live out your mortal life.'

'I may?'

The princess nodded. 'What is a few decades compared to an eternity, after all? You will come to us soon enough anyway.' She took a step closer. 'Are you sure you would like to go back? There is no changing your mind after this.'

Laisha. That was where she wanted to go. *If you ever get lost, Rose, just go home. I will always be there,* her father had always told her. She missed him dearly, along with her tribe, her family.

And Wei. She ached to see him again. She wanted to visit the farthest corners of the world with him, keep exchanging stories and more with him in the days to come. Their story had only just begun.

'Yes,' she said, her heart swelling with anticipation. 'I would like to go home now.'

Twenty-Seven

Wei

Yeli Mountain in spring was a verdant sanctuary. The air, woven with birdsong, was cool and crisp with the scent of fresh pine, and the flowers were vibrant in bloom. Overhead, the azure sky sprawled for as far as the eye could see, interrupted only by the jagged snow-capped peaks of distant mountains.

Wei thought he might get accustomed to this beauty over time, reminding him how much there was left in this world to appreciate and enjoy. How, out of the ashes of everything he held dear destroyed, there were still embers of hope.

Yet, something always felt missing. A hole that could never be filled again.

It followed him wherever he went, an unshakeable companion that he had grown used to. Two seasons had passed since the battle at the palace, and the loss had only grown larger by the day.

In the immediate days after the battle, the absence of Desert Rose had been so unbearable that he had left the kingdom—missing Meng's second coronation ceremony—and joined his Snow Wolf Sect brothers, Zeyan and Beihe, in helping the Dugur tribe reunite. With the prophecy fulfilled, the spirits lingering in Ghost City had also been freed, including the Dugur tribe chieftain, Scarbrow. Bataar and the clan leaders who had overthrown Scarbrow had returned to the tribe, explaining how the coup had been their way to protect themselves against the warring kingdoms around them, only to find that protection did not come from those kingdoms or a magical spring; it could only come from staying united as a tribe and not choosing sides.

On the White Moon Festival, the darkest and longest night of winter, Wei had watched Zeyan and Beihe dance with Qara and the younger clan members from afar, wondering if there was a place in this vast world where he would ever feel like he belonged again. Desert Rose would have been dancing with them, if she were there. She would be dragging Wei closer to the bonfire and chatting with her tribespeople.

Without a word, Scarbrow had sat down next to him with two bowls of mulled wine while the rest of the tribe revelled around the bonfire.

'I would like to properly thank you for all that you have given my daughter,' said the chieftain. 'You were the first person she met after breaking away from the tribe.'

And the last person who was with her in her final moments. Wei kept that thought to himself. The image of her dissipating into the dawn light remained fresh in his mind.

'Her fate was determined the moment she was born. There was nothing any of us could have done to stop it or protect her from it.' He sounded as though he was saying that to himself as much as he was saying it to Wei.

Wei nodded, fighting down the lump in his throat. 'She was brave right down to the last moment. The bravest girl I ever knew.'

The chieftain's eyes were shining. He raised his bowl. 'Here's to her.'

Wei brought his bowl against Scarbrow's and downed the wine like he did. They sat in silence for a moment, watching the tribespeople in the midst of their merrymaking. Wei had never quite been a part of a tribe or sect this large, and he could see why Desert Rose had been so attached to hers. It was a shame she never got to see her tribe reunited and back under the leadership of Scarbrow, a shame she never got to see her father—and everyone else—again like she would have loved to.

'Will the tribe be okay?' Wei asked. 'Do you trust the clan leaders?'

'They had believed in creating change, even if it meant upsetting the order and getting involved with the warring kingdoms' politics; I preferred to play it safe and shield my daughter from her fate. But I choose to believe their intentions towards me and Rose have never been malicious.'

Wei thought back to all his encounters with Bataar. It had never seemed like his aim was to kill Desert Rose, only to persuade her to join them.

'In a way, this was all predestined,' Scarbrow continued. 'Had that coup not happened a year ago, Rose wouldn't have left the tribe, away from my overprotection, and the Elementals' paths wouldn't have crossed the way they have. The prophecy wouldn't have been set in motion. The gods had their plans for us, for her, and this was all meant to be'—he glanced at Wei—'just like you and her were meant to meet.'

For a vagabond like him, Wei didn't quite believe in the gods or predestined fates. But if that were the case, then he should thank the gods for letting him meet Desert Rose again last winter. It had changed his life. He would never be the same again after meeting her, and he was glad he had gotten the time he had with her, however brief it had been.

Scarbrow's voice broke into his thoughts. 'Will you return to your kingdom next?'

Wei shrugged. 'Perhaps. Or I might return to the Snow Wolf Sect. I haven't decided.'

'With time, rivers can carve their way through a valley. You too will carve out your own path. Just give yourself time.' He laid an assuring hand on Wei's shoulder. Wei nodded in response, thanking him, before he rejoined his tribe in their festivities.

It seemed like everything had fallen into its rightful place and the world had gone on in its inexorable rhythm, while he was left scrambling in its wake. Where would he go now with a heart that was adrift?

* * *

On his return to Yeli Mountain a week later, he carried the chieftain's words with him. He would let time show him where to go next, what he was meant to do.

Oasis Kingdom was flourishing under Meng's rule. Wei had to admit that out of all the brothers, he was the most fit to rule. He had maintained robust trade ties with the Mobei and Monan desert lords, and even negotiated a truce with Lettoria and Sorenstein. The damage wrought by the Wall being destroyed had been mitigated by the magic Meng had unlocked in the kingdom with the Ling's help. The Ling were now recognized as legitimate citizens of Oasis Kingdom, and a few of them were even engaged by the court as officials, according to Zeyan's letters. He and Beihe had joined the Imperial Army shortly after they left the desert with Wei, while Wei had taken a while longer before deciding to return to Oasis Kingdom.

It was too early to tell, but it almost seemed like peace was on the horizon, if it wasn't already here. At least in the idyllic Yeli Mountain, it was almost easy to believe that.

Wei continued his hike up the mountain with no destination in mind. It felt good to amble in this place of memories. The spot where they had run to after Desert Rose had rescued them all from a fire that his father had ordered to get rid of the shouren. The spot where he had once told her he had never seen her as an abomination. The clearing where he had found her fighting with the Ling snatchers after he had returned from the dead. In this sun-dappled corner of the world, it felt as though those memories could live on forever, and that brought him some comfort.

A rustle on his left caught his attention. A reddish-brown fox emerged from the undergrowth and dashed in front of him. It stared up at him with a sentient gaze, then scurried a few paces up the path ahead and turned around to glance at him.

Wei followed its lead, already guessing where it might lead.

The outcrop was overgrown with flowering shrubs that nearly obscured the cave entrance this time of the year. Wildflowers bloomed at his feet along the path leading towards the cave. This place seemed like a little piece of paradise that his sister had managed to carve out for herself and her beloved.

Heyang shifted back into his human form and gestured for him to enter. 'Look who I found, love,' he called as he and Wei stepped inside.

Qiu emerged from the kitchen, wiping her hands on her apron. 'Wei,' she cried, rushing towards him to give him a long, tight hug when she spotted him. When they pulled apart, her eyes were shining with tears. 'I heard about . . . her, what happened to her.' Her voice was quiet now.

Wei did not reply. Perhaps he would never find the words to describe this ache that he would carry for the rest of his life.

'How have you been? Where do you plan to go next?' Qiu asked.

He shrugged. Meng had told him he could return to lead the Imperial Army if he wanted to, and it was probably the option that made the most sense now. It was predictable and comfortable, but Wei had never cared for predictability or comfort. Returning to Yeli Mountain had been a spontaneous decision, one that he had made out of the blue after months of roaming the desert and helping displaced tribes relocate. He was still waiting for a sign on his next destination.

'Well, you can stay here for as long as you'd like,' Qiu said. She glanced at her husband. 'Right, Heyang?'

The fox-man nodded. 'Don't worry about it. Plenty of room here.'

That night, Wei fell asleep to the crackle of a steady fire in the hearth. Desert Rose came into his dreams unbidden again, along with Yong, his mother, and his Snow Wolf Sect brothers who had abetted him in entering the palace last winter and been put to death by his father. They were gathered around a fire, chatting and laughing like old friends. Wei approached that circle, waiting for one of them to notice him. But none of them did. He was right next to them, just three feet away, but the distance between them had never felt larger.

At last, Desert Rose spotted him over the fire from across the circle. Her gaze was steady and calm, but carried its usual twinkle. The distance between them seemed uncrossable, and she slowly faded into the shadows . . .

And then she was standing in front of him, laying a cool hand on his cheek. Flesh and bone, too real for a dream. His breath caught in his throat. He felt her name escape him in a breath.

When he opened his eyes again, the flame-lit night had given way to morning light slanting through the cave entrance.

The dream faded. Everyone else—his brothers and his mother—receded into the corners of his mind once again.

Yet, she was still there. Desert Rose, silhouetted by the dawn light, just like the last time he saw her. Only this time, she wasn't dissipating into the air. She sat firmly before him in a dark crimson robe, with that familiar sparkle in her eyes.

He sprung up in bed. 'Rose . . .' He hated the hope sprouting in his heart, the hope he had managed to beat down after all these months. He hated how quickly that flame could be reignited.

This had to be a dream.

She reached out and laid a hand against his cheek. Warm. Human. Alive. It felt all too real. 'It's been a while, Wei.' The familiar lilt of her voice broke him from inside.

This was not a dream. She was here, sitting before him.

'I don't understand . . . How did you . . .? Are you . . . are you human?'

She chuckled. 'As human as you are.' She raised a hand, as though about to summon her magic, but nothing happened. Her palms remained empty, emitting no water orb or stream. Nor was there the glow of ethereal light in her eyes whenever she used her powers. She was . . . mortal.

'That's not how the prophecy goes,' Wei said. 'I thought you're supposed to be rewarded for all your efforts in restoring the balance between the realms.'

'This *is* my reward,' she said. 'A life on earth with you and my tribe.'

'You gave up immortality for this?' He grasped her hand, a mix of emotions overtaking him. She could have taken her place amongst the gods; she was destined for a much bigger destiny, a grander ending than this mortal one, where she would go through pain, old age, sickness, and death. She had given up what the gods had intended for her to be back here without her powers or a special fate.

Her eyes shone, as though she could read all his thoughts. 'This is what I want. This is *all* I want. I don't care for immortality or ascending to the heavens—what am I even supposed to do there when the people I love are down here? I don't want a life dictated by the gods; I just want a mortal life that I get to carve out for myself, however fleeting it may be.'

She leaned closer and her lips found his instantly, as though she hadn't forgotten her way around them despite the time that had passed. He pulled her close, hardly daring to believe that this was all his again.

That he could once again hold her and taste the salt on her lips. That they were both now free to write their own story, to go wherever the wind took them, and find a corner of the world that belonged to them only.

When they pulled apart this time, Wei felt only a calmness that filled his heart as he looked into her eyes. Without the flare of her magic in them, they were a warm shade of dark brown in the sunlight, shining with tears.

'You came back,' he said, finally convinced that this was not just a dream.

'Infinitely worth it,' she whispered.

The Last Elemental

Exactly a decade has passed since the five Elementals fulfilled the prophecy laid out by the gods, a decade since the last Elemental ascended to the heavens and ultimately chose a mortal life to be with the ones she loves.

The effects of the Immortal Spring being unblocked—an unprecedented event known to mankind—can be felt kingdom-wide. While Oasis Kingdom is no longer protected by its magic-resistant Wall, with the flow of magic between heaven and earth now as steady and calm as the beating heart of a sleeping giant, the kingdom no longer sees the need to isolate itself from the rest of the world.

Does this mean that magic no longer exists in the tightest, darkest corners of the earth? Hardly. Magic remains here among us, in the trees, in the air, the rivers, and everywhere else. But no longer does it lie concentrated in the hands of a few men. It flows freely between the porous borders of kingdoms and nations, no longer hoarded by any individual.

The last surviving Elemental continued to roam the farthest corners of the earth together with the Third Prince, who was merited the highest honour of protecting the kingdom. On occasion, they have been spotted around the Capital and the imperial palace when they return to visit.

The story of the last Elemental and her intertwining fate with Oasis Kingdom has spread far and wide across the land, reaching the sand-swept edges of the Khuzar Desert and even beyond. In time to come, the tale of the five Elementals will become one for the books, one that will live on and be passed down for generations.

For now, we will sit in the brave new world fought for by the valiant tribes and sects that were once shunned and trampled upon. We will take comfort in the knowledge that light can triumph over darkness, that sinners can be redeemed, and that sometimes those who wield the coldest blades can have the warmest hearts. And we will turn the page on a new tale as we forge ahead in a world forgiven by the gods at last.

—Excerpt from *Journals from the New Kingdom:*
Magic and the New World Order
by the Eighteenth Oasis Emperor Zhao Meng

Acknowledgements

They say a book is a dream one holds in their hands, what more a series of them. Writing this trilogy—and seeing it published—has been nothing short of a dream come true. I first had the idea about a desert girl running for her life back in 2016, after a holiday in Beijing. What followed was years of holding on to that vision for that girl—the trials, tribulations, heartbreaks, and finally, her deserved ending—years of believing that there was space for her story in the world.

This series would not have been possible without the love and support of many people, and I can't thank the following ones enough:

The Penguin Random House SEA team—Nora for taking a chance on my books and giving them a home; Garima and Chai for your endless enthusiasm and passion (our video calls always leave me invigorated and excited knowing that my books are in good hands); Almira for your tireless efforts in ensuring that my books are well-stocked in all the best places; extraordinary editors Thatchaa and Surina for meticulously whipping this manuscript into shape and making it the absolute best it can be; and the rest of the team including Pallavi, Alkesh etc. for your dedication and support, for taking my suggestions into account, replying to my emails and texts even on weekends, and championing our work and taking it to other parts of the world.

Scribe sisters—Kayce Teo (Leslie W.), Catherine Dellosa, Eva Wong Nava, and Marga Ortigas—for always lending a listening ear, being the best hype-women, and for being the best author support system a girl can have. I am so thankful we found one another and clicked almost right away.

The Muses, Meredith Crosbie and Nicole Evans, for being an unwavering source of love, kindness, and support, ever since we found each other online in 2016. What are the odds that we would all cross paths that way! I adore you both and your writing, and absolutely cannot wait for the day I get to see your books on the shelves and shout about them from the rooftops!

Authors friends on social media—Amélie Wen Zhao, Tanvi Berwah, K.X. Song, Ann Liang, June CL Tan, and so many more—who constantly inspire me with your dedication to craft, impeccable storytelling, and sweeping, immersive stories that keep the flame in me alive. We may be miles apart but I'm always here rooting for you all!

Offline author friends—the Penguin authors fam, Vivian Teo, A.J. Low, Lauren Ho, and more—for your invaluable advice, feedback, and insights as we navigate the waters of publishing together. My publication journey since being published by Penguin has never been lonely because of you all.

Readers and bookstagrammers for doing what you do—shouting about your favourite books and authors, recommending our books, cheering us on, fangirling with me over books, drama series, and 'hot, tragic male leads'. Your enthusiasm has kept me going every time I considered giving up. I love hearing your thoughts about Desert Rose, Windshadow, etc. and how you identify with each of the characters. I love getting to know you all this way, and it moves me every time my stories and words connect with you all. Thank you for picking up this book (and the ones before it) and giving it a chance. My stories might come from me, but they all end with you. Thank you for giving life to them too.

Last but not least, my dad—even though you're not an avid fiction reader, you always make the effort to read and understand my books. Thank you for always being here. You are my rock.

Writing this trilogy has taught me so much—it's my first ever completed fantasy series and I've grown so attached to my characters. I'm so thankful I got to tell this story, and to have the complete series published. *The Children of the Desert* trilogy will always have a special place in my heart. Desert Rose, Wei, Meng, and Windshadow's stories might have come to an end, but they will forever live on in these pages. Thank you for accompanying them—and me—on this unforgettable journey.